THE OTHER SIDE

A CHRISTIAN COWBOY ROMANCE

WOLF CREEK RANCH
BOOK FIVE

MANDI BLAKE

Mandi Blake

The Other Side
Wolf Creek Ranch Book 5
By Mandi Blake

Published in the United States of America
Cover Designer: Amanda Walker PA & Design Serv
Editor: Editing Done Write

CONTENTS

CHAPTER 1
THEA

Crouching in the woods behind her mom's house wasn't Thea's idea of a fun Saturday night. Well, it had been her home too at one point in time, but to say she was unwelcome now was an understatement.

Shifting to stretch her leg out of a crouch, she brushed against a bush, sending a flurry of snow falling from its branches. She pulled the collar of her coat tighter around her neck. It had been years since she'd experienced a Wyoming winter, and she'd forgotten to bring a scarf.

Thea's gaze darted back and forth over her mom's backyard. Despite the darkness covering everything, the place seemed unchanged.

Five years could be a day or half a decade. For Thea, it had been a century.

Five years since she'd been in Wyoming. Five years since she'd seen her mom. Five years since she left without looking back.

Coming home was often romanticized. Reunions, kisses, hugs. Thea would get none of that tonight. She'd been hiding in the woods behind the house for half an hour, and this was hardly a welcome home party. If she was lucky, she could see her mom's face and kiss her.

Hopefully, it wouldn't be the last time.

The constant shivering tightened every muscle in her body. After half an hour in the cold woods, even her lungs burned with the frozen air. Her teeth chattered together, making her jaw ache. Emerson said the coast would be clear by six thirty, but Thea couldn't risk checking the time on her phone.

A bright light shone over the backyard, and the screech of the screen door cut through the quiet night. Just as she'd been warned, a towering man stomped out into the darkness.

Thea released a shaky breath only to regret it as the puff of her warm breath billowed in the cold. She rested a hand over her mouth and nose.

The last five years hadn't been good to her uncle. He still walked with the same unbalanced gait, and his bulging middle only served to make him look more off-kilter. The shadows blended with the night, making it hard to tell much else about him.

Her cousin, Emerson, had pretty much confirmed the dark family secret Thea had only guessed before–their Uncle Tommy had gotten everything he'd wanted all those years ago. Thea's dad was out of the way, allowing Uncle Tommy to sit high and mighty on the Howards' family throne. To top it off, he'd slithered his way into Thea's old home under the pretense of taking care of his brother's widowed wife.

What a joke. Sharon Howard knew how to stay out of trouble. Thea's mom just knew too many family secrets, and Uncle Tommy wanted to make sure she stayed quiet, right under his oppressive thumb.

Disgusting. As if they didn't have enough to worry about with the family rival, the Pattons. Uncle Tommy had done his own part in tearing the Howard family apart, starting with moving in with his brother's wife before Thea's dad was cold in the ground.

The injustice ignited a new spark of heat inside her, despite the dusting of snow that landed on her eyelashes. Did the man not care that he'd thrown fuel on the fire?

Then again, that's what she'd been accused of all those years ago.

It had been a long time since Thea had even dared to think about the family she left behind.

Distance and time had done at least a little to numb the painful memories.

Her dad's death had only been the beginning. At the time, she hadn't had a clue she'd end up losing everything before the month was out.

Everything. Absolutely everything.

Thea swallowed hard and kept her gaze locked on Uncle Tommy as he climbed into an old pickup truck and slammed the door. The tired engine roared to life and carried her uncle down the driveway. He turned left on the road and disappeared.

Finally, Thea could breathe. She stood slowly from her crouched position and groaned. She was barely twenty-three, but a pain shot through her knees and down her shins. She stretched her back to the right and left before taking the first step.

An ominous thought ghosted through her mind. Emerson had seemed sure that the coast would be clear this evening, but what if she was wrong?

Too late to turn back now. Thea had flown halfway across the continent to see her mom, and this was the best chance she'd get. Her uncle was the biggest threat, and he'd just left. It was go time, whether she was ready or not.

Thea snuck through the woods bordering her mom's backyard, stepping over the underbrush and winding her way around small trees. When she reached the dark road, she looked both ways.

The main road was anything but a prominent

street. She'd fallen into the habit of calling it the main road because that's what the men in her family had always called it. Several unmarked roads and trails led into the wooded area behind the property, and they all had code names. It was one of the many ways they protected the moonshine stills in the hollers.

A thin layer of white covered the blacktop, and Thea stopped to stare at her feet. Her boots sank two inches in the otherwise undisturbed snow. She'd have to be careful with her tracks. It was the whole reason she'd avoided just waltzing through the backyard and up to her mom's door. Tracks in the yard wouldn't go unnoticed.

The compressed tire tracks in the road were her best bet. Thea took a big step, trying her best to put her feet in the tracks. She looked over her shoulder and took a few steps to test for footprints. Nothing.

The hard part was over. Now to see her mom. Thea jogged up the road until a stinging ache settled in her chest. The cold air burned like fire in her lungs, but she couldn't stop for a break. She needed to get this over with and get out.

She was already dreading leaving. Her whole reason for coming was to see her mom, but would she be able to turn around and leave again? It had almost torn her apart the last time. She'd spent her first two years in the South depressed and lonely. Would she have to endure that again this time?

When she reached the driveway, Thea kept to the tire tracks, shuffling her feet when the snow hadn't been disturbed enough to hide her prints. She stopped twenty feet from the house and scanned the outside of her old home.

There were floodlights on both ends of the house. There wasn't a way around them, but if no one was here, who cared about the light? It was a risk, but did she really have a choice?

She could have stayed in Alabama, but could she live without ever hearing the voice of the woman who loved her so much?

No, she couldn't.

Thea would risk everything for her mom, and the woman needed to know. She slowed her pace and walked up to the house, ignoring the weight that settled on her shoulders the nearer she got to the door.

The house had been falling apart a decade ago, and time had worked its awful magic on the place. The gutters on one side of the door hung from the roof to the ground, overburdened by the weight of leaves and snow, a rusty truck sat up on cinder blocks in the side yard, and a metal barrel riddled with holes sat beside the door. When Thea got closer, she peeked inside. It was half filled with cigarette butts.

She stepped up onto the first of two cement steps and shook her hands out. She'd forgotten to bring gloves–another rookie mistake. One thing she'd loved about the South was the mild winters. She didn't need to be able to feel her face to meet her mom after all this time, but it would be nice.

Thea knocked on the door and let her hand fall. She pushed a few inches of snow off the sides of the steps. Back when Thea had lived here, the front door had been a forgotten part of the house. Her footprints near the back or side doors would have been noticed, but not at the front of the house. The front was useless. Too formal for use by the family, and too dangerous for door-to-door salesmen. The "No Trespassing" signs were the first line of defense, followed by "Enter at Your Own Risk" signs.

Laws were mere suggestions to the Howard family and rarely followed. They lived in an imaginary world above the law of the land. The Howards made their own laws based on blood and a warped sense of loyalty.

Funny, Thea had once thought the Howards provided her protection. She'd given up that perk when she left town. They'd disowned her when she passed over the Wyoming state line. Emerson had warned her about that little fact when she called with the news earlier this month.

"It's your mom. She's not gonna make it through this one."

Emerson's warning had been simple and clear. If

Thea wanted to see her mom again, she needed to act now.

Thea brushed the back of her cold hand over one eye, then the other. She'd cried over her mom on and off for years. It seemed the well never ran dry.

Her mom had been her rock–the one person in her life who loved her and would do anything for her.

A stray memory jolted through the sadness. There'd been a time when she'd thought there was one other person who loved her. Thoughts of the whirlwind summer with Brett Patton carried more pain than happiness.

Stop it. He didn't love you. He–

The thought came to a halt as someone shuffled behind the door.

"Who is it?" The soft voice shook with weakness and fear.

Thea pressed her palms against the door, desperate to be closer to the woman on the other side. "It's me. Thea."

"Thea?" Her mom's voice held more strength now, along with a higher pitch, and the lock clicked. Seconds later, the old wooden door creaked open a sliver. Her mother's soft-blue eye was framed in the small space.

"It's me," Thea said softly. The sight of her mom and the sound of the sweet voice that had once soothed her to sleep now wrapped around her throat like a noose, choking her with a mixture of joy and fear.

Her mom threw the door wide and opened her arms. Thea moved to the top step and fell into the embrace. Her mom's once strong frame was small and thin, but nothing could compare to this feeling. Holding her mom meant more than anything in this moment.

"Baby, what are you doing here?" her mom seethed in Thea's ear. "It's not safe. You have to go."

"I know, but I had to come. Emerson said–"

Her mom tugged Thea inside and looked both ways before closing the door. "Emerson shouldn't have told you. You shouldn't have come."

The sobs broke from Thea unannounced, and her mom gathered her back into the embrace. Her whole body shook as she buried her face in the crook of her mom's neck. "I had to. I missed you so much. I–"

"I missed you too, baby, but you know..." Her mother pulled away and let her gaze roam over Thea's face. "You've changed so much."

"Not really." Thea sniffed and wiped her eyes.

She took her own chance to study her mom. Sharon Howard's hair was a lighter shade of brown almost overtaken by gray. The lines around her mouth had deepened slightly, but her eyes had changed the most. They'd lost all traces of youthfulness.

Thea stared into those eyes that had once mirrored her own as something broke inside of her. She could practically hear the crack. The moment when her heart finally accepted that her mom–this beautiful woman–was slowly dying from a disease with no cure.

Cancer. The old nemesis had taken her grandmother too–another woman who could have been a light in the darkness had she not died before Thea knew how to walk.

Her mother's chin quivered as their stares locked. "I'm so sorry about what happened to you."

Thea shook her head. "I'm okay. Let's not talk about that."

Her mom's arms wrapped around her again. "I'm so proud of you. You did what I could never do, and I hope you never come back here."

Thea tightened her hold. "No, Mom. I can't leave you again."

Her mother's words were stronger this time. "You have to. Or else all of this will have been for nothing."

Thea shook her head, wiping her cold tears in her mother's hair. "I miss you so much."

The soft caress of her mother's hand trailed down Thea's hair. "I miss you too, but you have a chance to get away from all this. Take it. Use it. Have the life you couldn't have here."

"But it won't mean anything if you're not there,"

Thea cried. It was the horrible truth she'd been carrying for years. She'd escaped, just like her mom said. Why didn't she *feel* free?

Because her mom wouldn't be there to see any of it. A potentially full life with a husband, kids, and a successful career–it all fell flat when Thea remembered that the woman who'd loved and protected her wouldn't be there for any of it.

"It's not about me, baby. It's about you."

Thea pulled back, struck by a question she'd been dying to ask for years. "Why did you let him in? Why did you let that man into our home?"

Her mother sighed and shook her head. "No one *lets* Tommy do anything. I didn't have a choice, and I still don't. But you? You do. Get out of here."

Everything twisted in her gut. Fear, injustice, and heartache–it was all fresh and raw, boiling into the hatred she knew all too well.

Thea's jaw tightened. What she wouldn't give to see Tommy Howard get what he deserved.

"Don't let him have that power over you," her mother said. "It'll eat you alive if you let it."

"He ruined everything," Thea seethed through clenched teeth. "He took everything from us!"

"Keep your voice down," her mother said.

The tears stung behind her eyes. Thea's life had been one disappointment after another, but her mom had endured that sadness even longer. Maybe her mom's life had been decent before she met and married Thea's dad, but the years since had erased anything good there had ever been.

Her mother lifted a frail hand and brushed her fingertips over Thea's cheek. "Hating him doesn't help us."

A sharp huff spewed from Thea's chest. "It sure makes me feel better."

"Does it?" her mom asked.

Thea paused to think, but the moment only confused her more. Did it make her feel better to hate Tommy? "It might."

The hand on Thea's cheek dropped to her shoulder. "You shouldn't stay much longer. This is goodbye. I need you to promise that you won't come back."

The last shred of hope crumpled in her middle. "Mom, no. We can see each other. I can come back. We could find a way to talk on the phone."

"You know he watches everything I do. I won't risk your safety. You need to get out of here."

Anger boiled inside Thea again, bringing on a warmth that the cold couldn't touch. Why couldn't she have her mom? Why couldn't she be here for her mom when she needed help? "Will you tell Emerson about any updates?" Thea asked with a shaky voice.

"I will, but you have to promise you won't come back. Not even when I'm gone."

"But, Mom–"

"Promise," her mom snapped. "I love you, and I

know you love me too. That's all we need, no matter where we are."

Thea nodded, only half agreeing with her mother's wisdom. "Right."

Her mother peeked over Thea's shoulder out the small window. "You need to go. There's no telling when he'll be back."

Pulling her mom into another embrace, Thea let the last of the tears fall. She'd never see her mom again, and it didn't matter that they were both still living. A part of Thea's heart was gone. All that was left was dark and ugly–worn down and beaten up by loss after loss.

When her mother backed up, Thea held her ground. She couldn't leave yet. It couldn't be over, but her mom was opening the door, and she couldn't make herself walk through it.

Her mom took Thea's hand and tugged her toward the door. A simple push on her shoulder forced Thea outside. "I love you," she said through a closing throat.

"I love you too, baby. You'll do fine. You'll get past all this and be better for it."

Thea shook her head and turned, wiping the last of the icy tears from her cheeks.

The light disappeared from the yard as her mom closed the door. Just like that, all the goodness was gone.

Thea walked back down the driveway and

tucked her arms around her as she started on the road. It was over, and she couldn't bring herself to care about anything. The numbness from the cold had seeped into her heart and soul, leaving a hollowness that she'd have to carry from now on.

The low rumble of an engine grew behind her, but she kept walking. She tucked her chin to her chest and prayed as her pulse raced.

Lord, please let it be a stranger. Anyone but Tommy. Please. Please.

The headlights shone on the road ahead of her, casting her long shadow on the gray snow. The truck was slowing down, and every muscle in Thea's body tensed, ready to jump on cue.

The truck crept by her, and she kept her head down. She didn't dare look up even to see the color of the vehicle.

When it didn't stop, Thea released half a breath. The tree line was twenty feet away, and she could disappear into the maze until she found the path back to Emerson's house on the back side of the woods.

But the red brake lights steadied, and the truck stopped between Thea and her freedom. Adrenaline kicked into overdrive, sending her heart speeding.

Now. Now was the time to go.

Her feet were moving before she registered the need to run. Thea darted into the yard and cut a diagonal trail toward the woods. If she could get into the covered darkness, she might be able to lose them.

The truck doors opened, and she made the mistake of looking over her shoulder. Two men. There was no telling who they were, but everything inside of her swore they were her kin. Her cousins? Her uncles?

Her brothers? Would they run her down with the rest of them if given the chance?

The burn in her chest grew as she pumped her arms and gasped for breath, pushing her legs faster than she'd run in years. Would it be enough? Would she be fast enough to make it back to her car? If she could just beat them by a dozen feet, she could jump in and head straight out of town.

The darkness wrapped thicker around her as she darted into the woods. Underbrush and fallen trees left the ground uneven, slowing her down every few steps.

Coming here had been a risk, but even as her ankle twisted on a hidden rock, she couldn't bring herself to regret it. The only thing she had left was her life, and whoever was behind her might very well take it from her if they caught her.

Their shouts behind her grew louder, but Thea's energy renewed when she burst out of the thick trees into the narrow path. She changed direction and set her sights on the house at the end. She'd run around the right side of Emerson's house where her rental car waited on the other side.

A dark figure stepped into the path in front of her, stealing a gasp from her throat as she dug her heels into the snowy ground. The attempt to stop was too late, and the man's arm wrapped around her throat as she tried to scream.

CHAPTER 2
BRETT

Brett gave little Abby a thumbs-up as he strode toward the refreshments table. He'd already danced with the four-year-old, and she seemed happy to spin alone on the dance floor.

Colt and Remi's wedding wasn't a formal affair as weddings typically go, but he kept tugging at the collar of the shirt his sister had coerced him into wearing.

Colt and Blake stood next to the refreshments table, while Hudson, a young teen from the church, poured orange punch into squatty cups.

Brett stepped up beside his friends and slammed his flimsy punch cup on the table. "Make it a double."

"Easy, tiger. How many have you had?" Colt asked with a smirk. The only thing anyone would suffer from after the reception was a sugar crash.

Brett made a show of counting all of his fingers before pinching his brow. "I'm not sure. Are we counting these as one or a quarter?"

Blake chuckled. "Note to self, never spike the punch when Brett is around."

Brett leaned against the wall and watched the wedding guests laughing and dancing. Everyone looked happy, which was good because Colt and Remi deserved to be celebrated.

Colt had done the impossible and clawed his way out of the friend zone with Remi. Everyone in the room had been waiting for those two to get their heads on straight and tie the knot.

Hudson handed over the punch, and Brett tipped his imaginary hat at the kid. "It's a dessert. What's not to like?"

"I don't think it's meant to be a dessert," Blake said. "We might be running low on the only flavored drink if you keep up this rate."

Brett raised the foamy drink to his mouth and downed half the cup. "I asked Everly to make sure she had extra. I ate a light dinner so I could have more punch."

Blake laughed. "I saw your plate earlier. Six slices of pizza is not a light dinner."

"I normally eat a whole pizza on my own," Brett said. "Also, why isn't pizza served more at weddings? Genius and less cleanup."

Blake shook his head. "Everly would lose her

mind if brides started requesting pizza for their receptions."

Everly was an excellent wedding planner. So was her business partner, Linda. Brett had been to quite a few of the weddings they'd planned at the ranch over the last few years, and they'd all been on the fancy side. Four-tiered cakes and three-piece-suits kind of affairs. Colt and Remi's pizza party reception was more Brett's style.

Colt nudged Brett's elbow. "You found a dance partner?"

"I've been a stand-in for a few songs, but overall, I'm a loner in this one, gentlemen."

"I've heard weddings are a good place to meet women," Blake said. "At least that's what Everly said when you told her you weren't bringing a date tonight."

"Why..." Brett had almost asked why Everly cared if he had a date, but she was a hopeless romantic, and she'd tried to set him up with a handful of her friends. "It's no big deal. I'm meant to fly solo."

Blake and Colt shared a look that wasn't the least bit discreet. They were both newlyweds and eager to urge Brett to settle down and give the old married life a try.

Too bad. Brett didn't have any plans for marriage, and his reasons had nothing to do with wanting to play the field. He'd already found his one and only. Unfortunately, she hadn't cared enough to stick around.

Remi practically bounced up to Colt and launched herself into his arms. The white dress that billowed behind her contrasted against her auburn hair. She looked up at her husband with a bright smile. "Ready to dance again?"

"You bet I am," Colt said.

Brett remembered that look–the same one Thea used to give him.

Sometimes, he thought it had just been dumb, blind love. Other days, he remembered that what he'd had with Thea hadn't been just a fleeting thing. The memories still kicked him in the chest every time he thought about her, which was regularly, since he couldn't look at a woman without thinking of her.

No one had compared in the last five years, and he was pretty sure no one would. Their love didn't have borders. Unfortunately, that meant the heartache ran wild, burning away all the good memories.

"Where's your woman?" Brett asked his remaining friend.

Blake waved his hand toward the room. "Somewhere doing wedding things. I basically go to weddings solo because Everly has to supervise everything."

Brett caught sight of little Abby in the crowd as

her puffy dress fanned out around her. Weddings had to feel like a dream to a four-year-old. “Looks like Abby needs a partner.”

Blake pushed off the wall. “You know, that’s a good idea. I’ll catch up with you later.”

Brett raised his cup to his friend. “Happy to help.” When Blake faded into the crowd, Brett headed for his table. He’d officially danced with every woman who needed a dance, and his work here was done. Hanging around until it was time to clean up was his next order of business.

He’d barely sat down when Everly stepped up beside him. “Hey, can you help me get the gifts into Colt’s truck?”

Brett coughed on the sip of punch he’d just swallowed. “We were supposed to bring gifts?”

Everly chuckled and waved him to his feet. “Not really. Colt and Remi don’t need anything.”

“Whew.” Brett stood and tossed the rest of his punch down his throat. “Let’s do this.”

He followed Everly to one of the Sunday School classrooms where a table filled with wrapped gifts waited for them.

“Liar. I was supposed to bring a gift,” Brett said as he extended his arms for Everly to stack them.

“You know Colt and Remi. They’re not materialistic, and they’ve technically been married since September. They didn’t even have a registry. I bet half of these are really for the baby.”

Brett adjusted his hands around the bottom gift. “I’m still having trouble processing Colt and Remi having their first kid. I mean, they’ve had Abby and Ben for six months now, but a baby is different.”

Everly’s smile widened. “I know. They’re going to be awesome parents to this baby too, and Abby and Ben are excited about getting a sibling.”

When they’d gathered all the gifts they could hold, Brett followed Everly to the side door of the church. Colt’s truck was parked near the door, and Everly unlocked it.

“Biggest gifts in first,” she said as she placed the boxes in the backseat.

“You think we’ll need my truck too?” Brett asked.

“Probably not. I already moved the kids' seats over to Stella’s car. They’re staying with her tonight.”

Snow floated down in the darkness, and Brett closed the truck door as Everly shivered.

“Let me take the rest. You don’t need to be out here in a dress. It’s too cold.”

Everly wrapped her arms around her middle. “Thanks. I’m ready for spring.”

Headlights lit up the parking lot around them, and the roar of a truck engine jarred the otherwise silent night. They both turned as an older truck slid into the parking lot, sending puffy snow flying as the brakes locked. The passenger door opened before the truck rocked to a stop, and a limp woman fell out onto the thin layer of snow.

The force of the woman hitting the ground had Brett's shoulders tensing immediately. She hadn't even tried to break the fall.

Brett bolted into a run as he shouted over his shoulder. "Get Jameson!"

The truck peeled out of the parking lot and back out onto the road. Brett didn't even check to see which way it went. His attention was locked on the woman lying lifeless on the ground.

Brett slid to her side in the snow. Blood was tangled in her dark hair, and he pushed it aside to shout, "Ma'am. Ma'am!" Her silence heightened the sickness in his stomach as he slid his fingers into her matted hair. Gently, he turned her head toward him. Where was the blood coming from?

He pressed his fingertips to her neck and closed his eyes. He needed to settle the loud pounding of his own heart so he could feel for hers. Her skin was cold beneath his fingertips, and he prayed for a pulse. When he sensed the rhythm beneath his fingertips, he released a shaky breath. He leaned forward to listen for the woman's breath, but he couldn't hear anything. Were her breaths just light, or was she not breathing?

Giving up on the breath, he pushed the wet hair from her face, searching frantically for the source of the blood. Multiple quick footsteps behind him signaled help was coming.

Good, because helplessness was growing big enough to strangle him.

When his fingers brushed over her hair, revealing the face behind the fear, everything in Brett's world stopped. Everything around him disappeared, leaving only the familiar face in front of him. The bruised and cut features of the woman he'd been missing for years.

"Thea."

The word was small as he prayed the scene before him was all a twisted nightmare. Then, the tingling of adrenaline surged through his entire body, releasing a terrified scream. "Thea!"

Someone was beside him, pushing him out of the way, but he scrambled back to her side. "Thea!"

It was Jameson this time, shoving a hand against Brett's shoulder. "Give me some space."

"That's Thea! Help her!"

Someone else knelt on Thea's other side. Noah Harding. Of course. Noah was a paramedic too. Brett had forgotten he was at the wedding. Between Jameson and Noah, could they save her?

Please, God. Please help her.

Someone else was at their side–a woman carrying a bag. "The ambulance is on its way."

Brett barely heard the words as he watched Jameson and Noah assess Thea. The blood was everywhere. Brett's own blood roared in his ears, and every word that reached him was muffled as if he were listening from underwater.

"Steady pulse," someone said. "Gash on her left arm."

"Loss of consciousness," someone else said.

Brett pressed a hand over his mouth, fighting the sickness that threatened to climb up his throat.

"What's going on?" The familiar voice of Brett's sister filtered in and out of his thoughts, but he couldn't tear his gaze off Thea.

Jess gasped behind him. "Is that–"

"Thea," Brett said as he watched Jameson and Noah assess her vitals and body. There was too much blood and not enough movement from Thea.

"What is she doing here? I thought she left."

Wasn't that the question of the hour. Brett would give his left pinky finger to know why Thea was here and what happened to her, but it didn't look like she'd be answering those questions anytime soon.

The wails of the ambulance started low in the distance. How many minutes had it been? What was taking so long?

"Is she okay? Jameson? What's wrong with her?" Brett leaned closer to examine the bruises on her face–that face he'd been praying to see again for years.

"She's been beaten pretty bad," Jameson said.

"Calm down, man. We'll get her checked out at the hospital."

A concussion. Bruises. Cuts. Swollen face. In his dreams, she'd looked so different. In his memories, she was beautiful and happy, looking up at him with that heart-stopping smile he loved. Then, he'd remember to be mad that she left him without a backward glance. Even then, she was beautiful and flawless.

The ambulance slowly parked nearby, and two paramedics jumped out. Jameson and Noah briefed the men on Thea's condition, and they were preparing to move her to a stretcher within minutes.

Careful not to jostle her, the four of them lifted Thea from the snow. A low groan came from her throat, and Brett took a step toward her.

A hand wrapped around his upper arm, but he pulled away from it.

"Brett, give them space," Jess said.

When Thea was on the stretcher, some of the tension in Brett's shoulders eased. "Where are you taking her?"

One of the paramedics looked up at Brett. "Are you her spouse?"

"No." The truth came out quickly. Did this guy think Brett had beaten his wife or something? "I'm an old friend."

The man looked around. "Is anyone here related to her?"

"No," Jess said quickly.

Brett ignored the sharpness in his sister's tone. She'd lost all love for Thea years ago, and the fighting between their family and Thea's only managed to fuel that fire. "I'm the closest you're gonna get."

"We'll be taking her to Cody," the other paramedic said as they transferred the stretcher into the ambulance.

"Can I ride with her?" Brett asked.

"No," Jess said behind him.

He ignored her. He loved his sister, but if he could put his own anger aside given the situation, he didn't care one bit about what Jess thought about Thea right now.

The paramedic pointed to a seat on the right side in the ambulance. "You can sit there, but try to remain out of the way."

Jess grabbed his arm again. "Brett, let her go. Forget about her. She's not your problem."

Brett pulled his arm from his sister's grasp. "She's never been my *problem*, and you know that."

Jess leveled him with a dark stare that didn't match the bright-green dress she wore. "It's dangerous to be anywhere near her."

"I didn't start this. They did." Brett pointed into the darkness, not knowing where the truck had gone that had so carelessly dropped Thea at his feet. "I have to help her."

"This is ridiculous. It's a trap. It has to be. They know you'll go with her."

They. The Howards. Thea's own flesh and blood who had probably done this to her. Or his family, the Pattons? Both possibilities were equally terrible.

"Then let them come. I have a few things to discuss with them," Brett spat.

Jess raised a finger at him. "Don't you dare get caught up in this again."

"They started it, and I intend to finish it." The fury rolling inside him was enough to bring a storm to the Howards' doorstep. He'd burn the place down to protect Thea, and he'd dare anyone to try to stop him. He'd do the same for any woman who needed help, but Thea was different. He could be furious with her for leaving him, but he couldn't let her go alone like this.

Jess turned and huffed, stalking away like she was fed up with the lost cause.

Brett focused his attention back on Thea as he climbed into the back of the ambulance. Jess had a point, and he understood her concern. It just didn't measure up to the help Thea needed right now.

And always, if he were being honest. He would come running every time Thea called, now and any other time.

Brett settled into the small seat as the doors closed behind him. The paramedic checked the straps holding Thea to the stiff board they'd placed her on and extended another hand over her middle. "I'm Matt."

Brett took the hand and gave Matt his attention for the required two seconds of the greeting. He looked to be a good twenty years older than Brett. Hopefully, those extra years had been used honing his healing skills. "Brett Patton."

"What's her name?"

"Thea Howard." It had been years since he'd uttered the name, but it still flipped his stomach the way it used to.

Matt looked up at Brett, and the pieces of the puzzle clicked into place. "A Patton and a Howard? I've heard of you."

Of course, his reputation preceded him. He'd never get away from it. "It's not what you think. I wouldn't do this to her."

Matt turned his attention back to Thea. "What happened here?"

Scanning Thea's bruised and swollen face, Brett sighed. "I have no idea. A truck pulled into the parking lot, dropped her out, and left."

Brett reached out and brushed his fingertips over Thea's limp hand. Her skin was icy cold. He slid his hands around hers, pressing his warmth into her. "She's freezing."

Matt finished taping the IV to Thea's arm and reached behind him to pull a plastic-wrapped blanket from a compartment. He tore the plastic open and spread the thin blanket over Thea. Brett wrapped it tighter around her arms and legs.

"You have any idea who did this to her?" Matt asked without looking up.

Brett's ears burned as he rubbed a hand over Thea's arm to create friction. "I have a hunch."

The Howards did this to her. He had more than a hunch. But what had she done that would make her own family turn against her when they were so busy killing off his kinfolks? He'd thought the loyalty lines had been drawn in ways that would protect her from her evil family.

A deep ache settled in his chest. Of all the Pattons and Howards, Thea was the only innocent one. Who could leave her helpless, cold, and nearly dead and not give a second thought?

"How good is your hunch, and is there any chance the church would have security footage?"

Apparently, Matt was going to be an ally, and Brett latched onto the thread of hope.

"My hunch is ninety-nine percent sure but I don't have a shred of evidence. The church doesn't have security footage, as far as I know, but I'll ask one of the deacons."

Matt turned his attention to the vitals monitor and stared at it. "Stay with me. Stay with me," he muttered.

Brett's nostrils flared as he searched the monitor

for whatever warning Matt saw. “Is she gonna be okay?”

“She should be, but if she has internal bleeding, she’s in trouble. We’ll do everything in our power, but our healing abilities only go so far. Best to consult the Big Man for further assistance.”

Brett nodded and looked down at Thea. She’d been in his prayers in one way or another for years, but never like this. He closed his eyes and wrapped his hand around her thin wrist. “I’m right here, Thea. I won’t leave you.”

Surely, the Lord hadn’t brought her back to him just to rip her away again, but if prayer was all he could do for her, he’d give it his all the entire way to the hospital.

CHAPTER 3
THEA

A small slit of light burned Thea's eyes as she opened them. She quickly pressed them closed again as the pain shot to the back of her head. Then, it was everywhere. Her chest, arms, stomach, legs–everything hurt.

It hurt to breathe–a sharp and shocking pain that cut into her side. She had to get up. An urgency pushed her to get up. She had to run.

Why was she running? Wait, why *couldn't* she run? Why couldn't she get up? The pain in her chest was unbearable.

Opening her eyes again, the brightness stung again but not as badly this time.

A banging in her head had her eyes closing again.

"Did you do it?" a man shouted. His angry voice bellowed around her.

"Get your hands off me!"

She was dreaming. Had to be dreaming. Confusion followed the conversation in a dream-like world.

"Did you do it?" one man asked, lower and deeper than before.

Pain. The weight on her chest became heavier. Everything was uncomfortable. Different parts of her body vied for attention.

"I didn't touch her, but I don't answer to you. You probably did this to her."

"I would never hurt her," the other man said with a low warning.

"But you killed our dad. You didn't have a problem hurting her then, did you?"

That voice was familiar. Gage? The thought of her brother carried fear and longing in its wake.

"I didn't do it!"

A deep laugh. "I don't believe you for a second."

Another bang. "Who did this?"

That voice demanded attention. It was desperate and irate, but a broken sadness covered the words.

"You don't have any business here. Get out."

Gage? Who was he shouting at? Who did the other voice belong to? Something deep in her chest told her she already knew, but she didn't let herself believe it.

Thea tried to lift her head, but it was too heavy. She opened her eyes again and fought through the blurriness. It took a few blinks before she focused on the two men. Her gaze darted back and forth between them, sending a shock of pain behind her brow every time her eyes moved.

It *was* Gage. It didn't make sense. He was in Wyoming.

Oh. *She* was in Wyoming. How had she forgotten? She was back in the place where her family had loved and hated her.

Gage lived here. She was the outsider.

The other man–the source of the voice she'd once known well–couldn't possibly be Brett Patton. Not the man she'd run away from. Not the man who'd broken her heart and stolen everything from her.

But it *was* him, and Thea's heart beat wilder by the second as she tried to process the scene. She let out a low grunt as she tried to lift her head again. Big mistake.

The voices stopped, and Brett and Gage turned toward her. They stumbled over each other in their attempt to get to her bedside.

Thea jerked as she scrambled to move back. The pain in her side and chest was sharp enough to narrow her vision. *No. No. No.* The room came into focus, and the tubes taped to her tugged as she lifted her arms to cover her face.

She was in a hospital room, but nothing made sense—Brett, Gage, the pain, the beeping.

Gage was standing over her, his formerly youthful face hardened and almost covered in a dark beard. He'd been handsome when they were in high school. All the girls had followed Gage Howard around. Now, all traces of his boyish innocence was gone, replaced by a stone-cold warning.

"Nurse!" Brett shouted from somewhere else in the room.

"Thea, are you okay?" Gage asked. The kindness in his question didn't match the stern expression he wore.

She could barely pull a breath past her lips. Had he done this to her? Or was he still the brother she remembered who had a heart?

He was the one who encouraged her to leave–to save herself. If she could trust anyone, it had to be him. But so much had changed since then. Allegiances were everything to their family. Did a higher-ranking Howard have his loyalty now?

Gage's shoulder jerked back, and Brett came into view.

Which was worse? Gage or Brett?

"Thea."

That one word shattered what was left of her heart. There'd been a time when she'd foolishly trusted him more than her own flesh and blood. There'd been a time when he'd kissed her sweetly and told her he'd move mountains to be with her, do whatever it took to keep them together.

All he'd done was rip them apart. The cruel irony slashed through all of those good memories.

Her throat burned as she tried to speak. The words came out shaky and raw. "Get away from me." She wasn't sure if she was talking to Gage or Brett. Mostly both.

Brett was on her other side now, closing in on her and leaving her cornered. He wore a nice white button-up shirt, but the front was stained with dark-red blotches. "You're safe. I promise." He shot Gage a warning look that had her shoulders curling in.

"You're not safe either," she whispered toward Brett before looking back to Gage. "None of us are."

Brett scoffed. "If your brother feels froggy, he can jump whenever he's ready."

Gage stared at Brett. "My fist would love to meet your face again."

"How's the jaw these days? Last time I saw it, you were talking out of the right side of your face."

The tension in the room pressed down on her as the men leaned over the bed toward each other. Brett and Gage had been at odds for as long as Thea could remember, but their rivalry had seemed tame back then.

Back before Brett had been a part of her dad's death. Back before the feud between their families turned deadly.

Brett's appearance had changed too. The white

shirt stretched tight over his shoulders and arms, and the sleeves were rolled tightly to just below his elbows, showcasing strong forearms. His hair was a shade darker, his chest was broader, and the softness in his features was nowhere to be found. It seemed the last five years hadn't been easy on any of them.

Hate could do that to people–strip the goodness from them, inside and out.

Gage bowed up, and every muscle in his upper body tensed. It was like watching a Jack-in-the-box wind up before exploding out in a rush.

"Stop!" She tried to raise her voice, but the word came out hoarse.

Both of the men looked at her.

"Get out."

Brett's shoulders slumped. "Please, don't make me leave you. You had a partially collapsed lung, and it scared the life out of me."

A collapsed lung? No wonder her chest hurt so bad. What did that even mean? Some of the fear in her heart dissipated at Brett's softness.

Why did he want to stay? They were at odds now, born on different sides of the war lines. The last time she'd seen him, he was being questioned by police with his hands cuffed.

She could still see the flashing lights from that night. The eerie glow had cast his face in shadow. Sometimes, that's how he appeared in her dreams.

Sometimes, he was the sweet boy who'd made her believe in love.

Did any of that boy still exist? She'd really thought so before he got his hands bloody. The lines between witness and suspect had blurred that night, but did it matter which category he fell under? He'd been there when her dad took his last breath. He'd been the *reason* her dad had never taken another one. What was innocence when everyone was at fault?

There wasn't any innocence when Gage had basically overheard Brett's confession, moments after he'd been legally found innocent. He himself had admitted to killing her dad. What defense did he have after that? He even had a motive. All signs pointed to guilty, despite what the judge and jury had decided.

Brett crouched beside the bed and slid his hand under hers. The warmth crept from her hand up her arm, and she pulled away.

A shock of hurt flashed across Brett's features. "I don't know why you left, but I've been looking for you ever since."

The tug-of-war started fresh in her mind. The sweetness of his voice said he didn't mean her harm, but had he been looking for her for the same reason as the other Pattons and Howards? Did he see her as another Howard to destroy in the name of revenge?

No. He'd killed her dad in a misguided attempt

to help her, and despite her dad's evil ways, she couldn't think murder had been the solution to her abuse.

Brett rubbed a hand over his face. "Thea, I would *never* hurt you. Ever." He threw his hands in the air. "And despite what your brother would have you believe, I didn't hurt anybody!"

Gage narrowed his eyes and scoffed. "My jaw begs to differ."

"You know what I mean. I didn't have anything to do with what happened to your dad. If that's what you're unsure about, this is me assuring you that I didn't have a part in that." Brett's volume started to fall toward the end, and he looked back to Thea. "I'm sorry."

Her dad and the man she loved had been on starkly opposing sides that night five years ago. She'd been so shaken up about her dad's death that she hadn't stopped to reason. Innocent until proven guilty had briefly crossed her mind only to be overpowered by her family's bias.

Another piece of the ancient puzzle clicked into place. Brett's dad had been killed first, throwing gasoline on the fire burning between their families. Her dad had been a casualty of retaliation. An eye for an eye.

The whole concept was ridiculous now, but it hadn't always been that way. Thea had grown up in a home where loyalty to the Howards was prided above all else. No one ever told her to love her neighbor or do unto others as she would have them do unto her. No, the Howards knew how to fight the Pattons, just as their parents had taught them.

She had to be careful. If she tried to defend Brett again like she had back then–before she knew his true guilt–Gage would run back to their family and label her as a traitor.

Once a traitor, always a traitor.

Gage crossed his arms over his broad chest and lifted his shoulders. "You gonna keep looking at her like that, or am I going to have to escort you out of here?"

Brett rolled his eyes and leaned toward Thea to whisper, "His bark has always been worse than his bite."

Thea's cheeks had already started to lift in a smile before she remembered the pain. The thin skin under her eye stretched, and she winced.

"If you two are going to dance, can you take it to the parking lot?" It hurt to talk past the swelling in her face. "And maybe send a nurse this way while you're at it?"

Brett stood and fumbled for the bedside remote. "I hollered for someone when you first woke up."

Gage took the opportunity to question her. "Do you know who did it?"

Thea held his gaze for a few seconds. Was he asking because he wanted to know how much she knew? Or was he asking out of concern? "I don't know."

"Come on, Thea. Was it us or them?" Gage jerked his head toward Brett.

"Why would it be a Patton?" Brett asked. "I had no idea Thea was even in town, and I guarantee you the other Pattons never give her a second thought when Tommy, Bruce, and Cain are out there."

Thea's stomach rolled. Was it the pain or the mention of her uncles and cousin? Either way, she was about to be sick. It was all too much, and she was tired of fighting the dizziness.

Her mom was dying. Two men had run her down in the forest and beaten her senseless. The man she'd foolishly thought she loved was standing beside her, but he'd broken her heart just as thoroughly as he'd appeared to treasure it. She didn't know if she could trust her brother. Oh, and she apparently had a collapsed lung and really didn't have the money to spring for an extended stay at the hospital inn.

Gage's thick arms flexed. "Why would it be a Howard?"

"It wasn't me or any of the minions I could have at my beck and call. I'll tell you that for free. The only ones you needed to worry about are either dead or in prison. I'm here because I care!" Brett said. "You'd have to be stupid to think I did this."

"At least I'm not stupid enough to hang out on the wrong side of the battle line," Gage shot back.

Brett narrowed his eyes at Gage. "What are you even doing here? Did you get orders from the dark lord, or are you here to finish what you started?"

Thea closed her eyes and rested her head back against the pillow. She'd come back to the place she'd once called home with one goal–see her mom. Now, she'd found herself right in the middle of the Hatfields' and McCoys' latest rumble.

It had been so long since she'd seen Brett, but five years and hundreds of miles couldn't erase the memories. He'd been good to her for the short time they'd been together, but it had all happened so fast. It couldn't have been real. She'd never met another man like him–before or after their whirlwind romance. He'd had a huge part in pushing her out of Wyoming, kicking off the worst time of her life.

She peeked up at him again, and his attention was focused on her, not Gage. Brett had always been handsome, but the boy he used to be had outshined the good looks. He'd been chivalrous, kind, thoughtful, selfless. He'd been the perfect friend and boyfriend–one worth risking the wrath of her family over.

And then he'd stepped into the armor he was born to wear and took up his place in the battle.

Here they were again–face-to-face–and she

probably looked like she'd been through the meat grinder. Swollen face, matted hair, and all.

She'd known coming back was a huge risk, but she'd thought the worst she could encounter was her family. Turned out, it was her family and Brett in the same room.

Thea sucked in a deep breath as all energy seeped out of her. "Can you both leave? Please?"

Brett looked back and forth between Thea and Gage. "I don't want to leave you. I'm sorry we were fighting." Brett rubbed the back of his head. "I can sit quietly in the chair. Please."

A short nurse walked in and greeted them with a smile that was out of place. "Hello, Miss Howard!"

"I want to make sure you're okay," Brett said, leaning down to whisper. "And I don't want anyone to hurt you again."

So, he was here to protect her? It didn't make a lot of sense, but the part of her heart that still remembered the boy he'd been wanted to latch onto that hope and hold on.

He killed my dad. It was the only thought she needed to remember. Even if he'd done it to protect her, she could never condone killing.

The nurse stepped up to the foot of the bed and propped her hands on her wide hips. "How are you feeling?" she asked with too much pep.

"Tired. Everything hurts." Nothing made sense, and she didn't have the strength to care.

"Well, I'm about to give you a once-over." She pointed to Brett and Gage. "One of these handsome men your hubby?"

She shook her head as Brett and Gage said "No" at the same time.

"Then you best be making yourselves scarce. The sheets are coming off."

Thea's eyes widened, and she reached for the thin blanket. She didn't care how bad the damage was to her body, but neither of these guys were about to see her in a hospital gown.

Brett jerked his thumb over his shoulder. "I'll be in the waiting room." He turned to the nurse and extended a hand. "I'm Brett Patton. Please let me know if anything changes."

The nurse eyed him for a moment before glancing to Thea. "Wait a minute. Brett *Patton*. Thea *Howard*. Who are you?" she asked, pointing at Gage.

"Gage Howard."

The nurse threw her hands in the air. "Everyone out. I'm here to treat the patient, not play referee."

Gage ignored the nurse and turned back to Thea. "Why did you come back?"

Thea remembered her mom, and the stinging tears welled behind her eyes. "Emerson told me about Mom."

"That was stupid. They could have killed you," Gage whispered.

So, Gage believed the men were Howards. Did he

know which ones? She hadn't been able to see in the darkness. "I know. Looks like I made my bed, and I have to lie in it, presumably until the doctor discharges me."

"You have to leave," Gage said. Nothing in the stern tone of his voice left any room for debate.

"*You* have to leave," the nurse repeated. "Don't make me call security."

Gage turned and headed for the door. Brett took a few steps and stopped. He turned back to her and took a deep breath that lifted his shoulders. "Don't worry. I won't leave you."

With that last word, he walked out the door in front of Gage.

No, Brett hadn't ever been the leaving type. That was her.

CHAPTER 4
BRETT

Brett strode out of the hospital room and focused on the thudding of his footsteps as well as those of the enemy behind him. Brett had been unprepared for visitors today. Thea or Gage. Welcome or unwelcome. Well, the horrific night had bled into the early morning, so it was all one big, long, bad day.

When Gage had followed Brett past the nurse's station and to the double doors, he turned and faced the music, as ominous as it was.

"Who did this to her?" Brett asked.

Gage's lips thinned, and he looked over both shoulders before responding. "I don't know."

"That's not a good enough answer."

Gage lifted his hands in the air before letting them fall again. "Take it or leave it. Truth is, I didn't know Thea was in town. When Emerson told me she thought..."

"Don't stop there," Brett said. "Spit it out."

"Was it one of the Pattons?"

"Very unlikely. With my dad dead and my uncle in prison, the others are too lazy or drugged up to care about the Howards. That leaves your side. Who do you think did this?"

"I don't have to tell you anything," Gage said.

The guy's scowl didn't scare Brett. He wasn't leaving until he got some answers. "Listen, I don't know what you think you know, but I didn't kill your dad. This doesn't extend to the rest of my family, but *I* am not capable of murder. End of story."

Gage pushed a hand through his hair and sighed. Was the guy putting on an act, or was he ready to start kicking in doors for answers like Brett wanted to?

"Emerson said Thea came to town hoping to see Mom. She got another diagnosis. It's in the lungs this time, and the docs said she won't see next Christmas without a miracle."

Brett slumped against the wall behind him. Thea's mom had less than a year left. Now her sudden appearance made sense. Thea would run through fire for her mom, but coming back to Blackwater might be worse than facing flames.

Thea had to be crushed. After all she'd lost, losing her mom was just another stab in the back.

Brett hung his head and stared at the bland tile hospital floor. "I'm sorry."

"You and me both," Gage said. "Mom never deserved any of this."

"But who did this to her?" Brett pointed down the hall toward Thea's room.

Gage planted his feet shoulder-width apart. "I'm pretty sure I know who it was."

Brett's fists clenched at his sides. "Care to share with the class?"

"Nope."

"Tommy, Bruce, and Cain?" Her sadistic uncles and cousin had been Brett's first guess.

"I'm not telling you what I think."

"You don't have to. I can make my own assumptions." Brett had gotten a taste of the untruth of "innocent until proven guilty" when he'd been in the cross hairs, but it was hard to apply that courtesy to whoever did this to Thea. "I'm assuming it's them, but what do they have against her? She's their family. I thought their fight was with us."

Gage stared at Brett for an extra second. "What happened that night?"

"I thought we were talking about Thea. Someone just beat her to a pulp, and you want to chat about ancient history?"

"Just tell me. The answer is relevant."

How many times had Brett recounted his statement? Dozens and then some. In front of judges, juries, investigators, therapists, and even his friends. They'd all wanted to know if he'd really offed Thea's dad. The truth was plain and simple.

"I didn't kill him. I was trying to stop him."

"Stop who?"

"Mark." Brett's family tree was riddled with just as many holes as Thea and Gage's. Mark was the worst of the Pattons, and Brett had held onto hope that the family feud would die when they locked him up half a decade ago.

Unfortunately, whoever did this to Thea was keeping the fire well stoked. That man would never give up on the revenge he wanted for his brother's death.

"Wrong answer. I overheard you after the trial," Gage said with a scowl.

Brett narrowed his eyes at him. "What are you talking about?"

"You told your sister you did it. You admitted it. You did it, and you got away with it. Thea might have hated our dad, but she'll never forgive you. She swore up and down you were different, but you're just like the rest of us."

"That's bogus. I didn't do it, and I never admitted to it."

"You said the bullets hit their target just like they were meant to. Your sister tried to shut you up because the people around could hear you. You said it was true. Now, tell me you didn't mean to kill my dad that night."

"I didn't mean to kill your dad because I *didn't* kill your dad. I hated your dad. He abused Thea and your mom. I hated him, but I didn't kill him."

Gage stared at Brett, and the tension in his jaw didn't ease. "Fine. I didn't expect you to admit it."

"I didn't do it!" Brett shouted.

"Keep your voice down, idiot," Gage said.

"I'm not an idiot or a murderer. I was there that night because I knew Mark *was* there to kill your dad. I was trying to stop him."

Gage scoffed.

"It's true. Abusive or not, Thea wouldn't wish her dad or anyone else dead. She's not like the Howards."

"Or the Pattons," Gage added.

"Fair enough. She's good down to her bones. At least, she was. I don't have a clue who she is now. She up and left like everyone else when the fingers started pointing at me. She knew me better than that."

Gage looked to the right, then left before crossing his arms over his chest. "So, you're saying you weren't there that night to kill my dad?"

Brett threw his head back against the wall. "No, I wasn't there to kill your dad." The words sounded ridiculous. Killing someone–even hurting someone outside of self-defense–made everything inside him cringe. “I was there because someone has to put an end to this. Unfortunately, I got there too late, and then I was prime suspect number two right behind my uncle Mark.”

Gage twisted his lips as if weighing the words. “Why can’t Tommy and Mark have it out with each other?”

“Because if they’re going down, they’re taking everyone with them,” Brett said.

“How did you know Thea was hurt?” Gage asked.

“Whoever did this to her pushed her out of a truck into the church parking lot. I was at a wedding.”

Gage pointed at Brett’s collar. “I was wondering about the nice getup. Looks like you won’t be wearing that again.”

Brett looked down at the blood on his white shirt. Thea’s blood. “Absolutely not. I’ll be burning this as soon as I get home.”

“You brought her here?” Gage asked.

“There were two paramedics there for the wedding. They took care of her until the ambulance arrived.” Brett covered his mouth. He’d be reliving that panic in his nightmares for a while. “Then I rode here with her. I’m not leaving her. They’ll come back to finish what they started.”

“They went after her because she defended you.

Mom and I convinced her to leave. She promised she'd never come back, and as far as I know, this is the first time she's broken that promise."

"She defended me? Of course she would!" Brett straightened and threw his hands in the air. "We were together. She knew me back then, and it shouldn't have been a question, but I wish she hadn't said anything."

"I overheard you."

"You didn't overhear me confessing. Yes, I always hated how your dad treated Thea and her mom, but I didn't pull the trigger or help in any way."

"Your fingerprints were all over the gun, man."

He was tired of this argument. Fingerprints didn't equal murderer, and Brett wasn't a killer. "I picked it up before Mark took it. I tried to hide it from him, but he found it. I'm fairly certain he hoped to pin it on me with that piece of evidence."

Brett pushed a hand through his hair. "I sent my own uncle to prison. Got him life without parole."

"You could have been saving your own skin," Gage pointed out.

"Whose side are you on?" Brett shouted.

"I don't know!"

Brett chuckled. Gage tried to hide his own grin by rubbing a hand over his mouth.

"Are we on the same side?" Brett asked.

Gage shook his head. "I plead the fifth."

"You know what they did to Thea is inexcusable." Brett didn't leave room for arguing that point.

"That we can agree on. Trust me, they won't get away with it."

Brett kept his gaze firmly locked with Gage's as he extended a hand. "I'm not saying this is a truce, but if anyone tries to hurt Thea again, they'll have to go through me first."

Gage slowly shook his head as he eyed Brett's hand. "I'll do anything for Thea. I'm not sure I want to partner up with you though."

Brett laughed–one short, loud burst. "I'm your only choice. I'm so caught up in this, I'll never get out."

"I'm also not sure I can trust you," Gage added.

"Same."

Brett's hand still hung in the air between them. Gage looked at it once more. "Maybe we can make a deal."

Brett pulled his hand back and crossed his arms over his chest. "I'm listening."

CHAPTER 5
BRETT

"You keep her safe, and I'll make sure they pay for what they did to her." Gage's brows lifted. "Sound like a plan?"

Brett searched Gage's eyes, looking for any sign of deceit. Did he want to believe Thea's brother could be an ally so badly that he was overlooking duplicity?

God, give me a sign. Is this the way I can keep Thea safe?

Gage extended his hand. "I'll do anything for Thea. What about you?"

Well, the best way to get Brett's attention was to question his word. His hand was clasping Gage's before he realized what he was doing.

"Deal."

Gage glanced back toward Thea's room. "They

might come here. They'll claim they want to see her 'cause they're family."

Brett smirked. "Not on my watch."

"How long can you stay?"

"As long as it takes." That much was sure. Plus, he had a few questions for Thea when he got the chance.

"You'll have to leave at some point."

"Nope. Jess can bring whatever we need, and I have a few friends who can stand watch if I absolutely need help."

Gage narrowed his eyes. "You have friends?"

Brett threw his hands out at his sides. "I'm a very friendly guy! Not that you ever cared about getting on my good side."

"Can you trust them? And they can't be Pattons." Gage said, all joking aside.

"I trust them with my life." That was an easy truth too. He'd trust any of the guys on the ranch with his life and Thea's any day.

Gage looked back again. "I have to get to work. I'll be back this evening."

"Where are you working now?"

"Beau Lawrence's shop."

Brett knew Beau enough to trust him with some things, but did he trust the guy's wisdom when Thea's safety was at stake?

"The ranch is in the off-season, and there are

enough of us who stuck around to handle things that need to be done."

"Let me give you my number. Only use it if you have to, but keep me posted about her."

Brett pulled out his phone and saved the number. Gage left without much of a good-bye, and Brett took up pacing the hallway. Being on guard twenty-four-seven would require a lot of diligence, but he'd be ready if any of the Howards showed up.

His phone beeped, and he checked the text from his sister.

Jess: Where are you?

Brett: Hospital.

Jess: You need a ride?

Of course, Jess would be ready for him to part ways with Thea for good.

Brett: I'm staying.

When Jess didn't reply, he slipped the phone back into his pocket. He'd need a change of clothes if they didn't release her soon, but Jess probably wasn't the person to ask for help right now. He'd call his roommate, Linc, in a few hours and get him to pack up a bag for the hospital stay.

After all these years, he still felt the same loyalty to Thea as he did when they'd been together. Had she really defended him? If so, why had she seemed scared of him? Had the fear been because of Gage? Brett kept flip-flopping between trusting Gage and keeping his guard up.

If she'd initially thought he was innocent all those years ago, why did she leave without telling him where she was going? As much as he wished they could have run away together, he'd been a person of interest in a criminal case and hadn't had the liberty to leave.

But their relationship had been going great until their families decided to ruin everything. They'd been head over heels in love. At least, Brett had been in love. He'd known she was the one for him, and he'd let her know. He was too outspoken to leave people wondering what he was thinking. Thea hadn't gone a day without being reminded of his love for her.

Her voice had echoed in his head from years ago, and he'd questioned everything since she left.

Gage had delivered the news when Brett came looking for her, and the resulting fistfight hadn't been his brightest moment. Though they'd both grown up in families that hadn't guided them to use their words instead of their fists, Brett wasn't a violent guy. He could still say he'd never started a fight, but he'd made sure to always be the one to end it.

Thea had done a fantastic job of hiding all these years. Brett had looked for her more than once, only to come up empty-handed. He hoped she'd been hiding from her family and not him, because Brett wouldn't dream of laying a finger on her.

The nurse stepped out of Thea's room, closing the door behind her. Brett headed her off before she got to the nurse's station.

"Hey, is she okay?"

The nurse took a step back, pursed her lips, and narrowed her eyes at him. "I know who you are. Friend seems like a stretch."

"I really am. I didn't do that to her." Was this going to be the song he kept on repeat? A woman had been beaten, and it was easy to blame the nearest man. He'd learned that the hard way back when his uncle Mark killed Thea's dad.

The nurse took a deep breath. "She needs rest. Without fighting," she clarified. "I don't know you, and I'm not going to disclose her medical information unless she gives consent. If you want to know how Thea is doing, you'll have to ask her." She raised a finger at Brett. "If I hear you so much as pinched her, I'll have you thrown out of here."

Brett held up his hands. "I would never hurt her. Ever."

The nurse's guard didn't lower. He couldn't blame the woman. Five years ago, the feud had solidified itself into Blackwater notoriety. Even folks in neighboring towns had heard of the Pattons and the Howards.

"I'm here to make sure no one comes to hurt her again. If I'm not in her room, I'll be in the waiting room. If she needs anything, will you let me know?"

She didn't agree, but she also didn't tell him to get outta town. She looked both ways before turning back to Brett. "I hope they find whoever did this to her. People are cruel."

Injustice swelled in Brett's chest. "You have no idea. Thanks for what you're doing to help."

The nurse nodded once and stepped around him, heading to her next patient.

Brett slumped against the wall and tucked his chin to his chest. Thea was beaten and bruised from head to foot, and he was completely useless. He'd been angry with her off and on since she left, but seeing her in pain was turning him into a nervous wreck.

How could he help her? Having his hands tied behind his back brought on a new cadence of breathing as panic rose in his throat.

Lord, what do I do? How can I help her? Please. Help her. She's in pain, and she doesn't deserve this. It wasn't her fight. She was one of the good ones.

Thea wasn't just good. She was a complete contrast to her family. It hadn't ever made sense to him how she could have come from so much hatred. She must have gotten her kindness from her mom. Sharon Howard didn't belong in that circle of corruption either.

And now Sharon was dying. Thea had to be crushed. It was hard to be mad at her for leaving him when she was already suffering so much.

The old need to console her rose inside him. He understood Thea's relationship with her mom. If she needed a shoulder to cry on, could he put aside his pride and help her when she was broken?

He turned to the door and knocked. When he didn't hear anything from the other side, he slowly pushed the door open. The lights were dim, but Thea's eyes were open. The stark colors in her face kicked him in the gut.

"Can I come in?"

"Yeah," she squirmed a little, but she didn't try to crawl away from him like she had earlier.

Brett pulled up a chair next to her bed. "Did they give you something for the pain? Do you need anything?"

"Yes, and no. I'm okay."

"It's okay to not be okay," Brett said, though it gutted him to see her so broken down. Her brown hair was still matted, and her left eye was bloodshot, obscuring the pale green he'd memorized. She still held the thin frame from before, but her arms were thickened with muscle. She looked healthy aside from the bruises and cuts.

Had she been happy all these years? Had she made a life she loved away from all the noise she grew up with?

Had she made a happy life without him? That was the part that hurt most. He wanted her to be happy, and he selfishly wanted to be a part of it. But she'd cut him out, left him stranded and alone when he needed her most. Anger climbed up his neck, choking him with heat and pressure.

A warning flashed in the back of his mind. Neither of them had been raised in church, but Brett had given his life to Christ in the years since Thea left. He was supposed to rise above the anger. He was supposed to be able to forgive and give second chances. Too bad he hadn't perfected those virtues before now.

Had she found that faith too? If she hadn't, maybe now was his chance to help her find her faith, but he needed to get his anger in check first.

"What are you doing here?" she whispered.

"I was going to ask you the same thing."

She chuckled a little. "Well, I really don't know how I got *here*."

"They dumped you off at the church. Pretty much kicked you out of the truck. I was there for a wedding."

Thea closed her eyes. "Please tell me it wasn't yours."

Brett laughed. "I couldn't get married without you, cupcake."

The smile in her eyes faded and was immediately replaced by a swell of tears. Why had he said that? He hadn't stopped to think first, wanting the old, comfortable peace between them to come back so badly.

He propped his elbows on his knees and rested his head in his hands. “I’m sorry. I shouldn’t have called you that.”

She slowly raised her hand to wipe the back over her eyes, dragging tubes with it.

The hope that had been growing in his chest clogged in his throat. He had no idea if the nickname meant as much to her as it did him, but she would always be his cupcake. He could be mad at her all he wanted, but he’d loved her, and he still remembered what that was like. Those old feelings wanted to take the stage again, despite the wrongs.

“So they dropped me off at a church. I’m surprised they knew the way.”

“It appears they still keep tabs on me.”

“I’m sorry you got dragged back into this.”

Brett lifted his head. “As long as you’re in the fire, I’ll be there too. That won’t change.”

“You killed my dad. We’re not on the same side anymore.”

“That’s not true, and you know it. I never killed anyone. You know me better than that.”

“Gage told me–”

“I don’t care what he told you. I didn’t do it.”

“He said he heard you say you did it.”

“He didn’t hear that because I never said it.”

“I don’t know who to believe,” she said.

That confession cut Brett more than it should.

"There was a time when you would have believed me. You really trusted your brother more than me?"

"He was so sure! He said I was so hung up on you that I would have believed you no matter what, and he didn't want me building a life with someone like that."

"Someone who would have done anything for you? Someone who would have loved you more than anyone else in this world? Yeah. Sounds like a terrible situation." Brett's temper was rising. He was still mad at her for leaving, and hashing it out was just opening all those old wounds.

"Someone who would have killed a man to keep him from hurting me again," she whispered.

Brett shook his head. "I wouldn't have let him hurt you again, but I wouldn't have killed him unless I had to."

"I know how much you hated him. Unfortunately, I've seen too much of that hate in my life, and I know what it's capable of doing."

Brett stood, pushing his hands through his hair. "What's it going to take for you to believe me?"

"I want to believe you. I wanted to believe you then. I wanted to stay, but I..."

"But you thought I could be just as bad as them? I'm not like the others. You should have trusted me."

Thea closed her eyes. "I wanted to. I was terrified. When Gage said you did it, he was so convinced. I knew you had a motive–a strong one. I panicked. I left, and then I was afraid to come back."

Brett faced her and crossed his arms over his chest. "You doubted me, and you left me. I've been mad at you for years, but some stupid part of me is still a glutton for punishment. I still wanted what we had. I'm stupid, but I still love you."

Thea gasped, then reached for her side.

Apparently, no amount of anger could make him heartless when it came to her. He felt everything so clearly when she gritted her teeth against the pain.

He was at her side again. "What can I do?"

"It just hurts." She tried to move, but even little shifts seemed too difficult. She settled and looked up at him. "Promise me you didn't do it," she whispered.

"I didn't, but I shouldn't even have to defend myself to you. You should have known me better. You should have trusted me."

"I wanted to. I wanted to so bad. Gage convinced me I was being a vapid, lovestruck idiot."

"Gage is on my list," Brett said.

"He was trying to protect me."

Brett pressed a finger to his chest. "I would have protected you."

"I wanted to believe that."

"Then you should have trusted yourself over Gage."

Thea looked out the window into the bright

morning. She stared as if the answers were waiting just outside the hospital walls. "I'm sorry." She bit her lips between her teeth and closed her eyes.

Brett let out a deep breath. He'd wanted answers, and now he had them. He even had an apology. Why did it still hurt so much that she hadn't trusted him? He rubbed a hand over the back of his neck. "Listen, I'm not going to leave you. Whoever did this might come back and try to finish what they started. I didn't kill your dad, I'm still upset that you left, and I'll never hurt you. Those are the most important things right now."

Thea nodded slowly, looking straight up at the ceiling. "This is a trap," she whispered.

"Probably, but I still won't leave you. I haven't actually been hiding from our families all this time. I work at Wolf Creek Ranch."

She pressed the heels of her hands over her eyes. "I can't believe they dropped me off where you were."

"I can. They left you with me because they don't care two cents about you, and they know I do. I understood the assignment, Thea."

She sniffed and wiped her face, wincing when her hand brushed over her swollen cheek. "I'm an assignment."

Brett looked at the floor, unsure how to feel or react to all the news. "You were never an assignment. I thought we were on the same page once. Then, I wasn't sure."

He couldn't blame her for getting out. It was definitely the best option for her. Still, if she could have waited until the case was closed or told him where she was headed, he could have come for her later.

Brett lifted his head and sighed. "I'm still trying to get over why you left without me."

"They wouldn't have stopped hunting us. You were..."

What had she been about to say? A murderer? An accomplice?

"We knew too much," she said.

He'd worn his heart on his sleeve his whole life, and Thea had known he'd do anything for her. He would have jumped in the car with her without a second thought, but he wouldn't have killed anyone unless he had to make a choice. If it came to her or them, he would always choose her.

"You need to go. They'll come for you."

"Not a chance. I'm not leaving unless you give me a direct order and say you don't want me here. But if you do that, I'm going to send someone else I trust to look after you. So, if you don't want that, you're stuck with me. Gage and I will make sure they don't come back for you."

Thea shook her head slowly, rolling it back and forth over the pillow. "It's not safe."

"I never signed up for a safe life when I decided to stick by you. I knew what I was getting into, and I don't regret it for a second."

Thea's jaw tightened, and her lip quivered. He'd gotten so caught up in wanting answers that he'd forgotten why he'd originally come.

"Gage told me about your mom."

Thea looked away, tucking her lips between her teeth.

"I'm sorry. Sharon's a good woman, and I know how much you love her." He reached for her hand, and she squeezed it back. That little show of strength was an answered prayer. The fury inside him was quickly dying.

"I don't know what you've been doing all these years, but I've changed. For the better. I go to church for more than weddings, and I'm the leader of the men's prayer group."

Thea turned to look at him, and a little bit of the sadness fell from her expression, replaced by peace. "I've been in church for a while too. I wouldn't be here now if God hadn't... What I mean is, I found the way home long before I came back to Blackwater."

Brett lifted her hand, cradling it in both of his as he propped his elbows on the side of her bed. "Can I pray for you and your mom?"

Thea's lip quivered as she whispered, "I'd like that."

He rested his forehead against their joined

hands and closed his eyes. "Lord, I come to You on my knees today. Thea has been through so much, and I pray You'll give her healing, strength, and peace as she goes through recovery and the stress of coming home. Her mom needs You too, Lord. I pray You would wrap Your loving arms around their family and give them comfort and understanding."

"Thea!"

Brett recognized that high-pitched shout and wanted to push it out of the room. So much for a focused prayer time.

"I lift up Thea and her mom to You. In Jesus's name we pray. Amen."

"What happened?" Emerson shouted.

Brett raised his head, not giving Thea's mouthy cousin the benefit of his attention.

Thea adjusted herself on the bed, wincing at the pain in her side. He'd broken ribs before, but a collapsed lung could be serious.

"You can probably guess what happened," Thea said. The sadness in her words held little hope.

Emerson stepped to the other side of the bed and finally noticed him. She jerked back when she recognized him and pointed a thin finger at him. "What's he doing here?" she shouted.

"You don't have to yell. We're all in this same three-foot space," Brett said, trying his best to keep the bite out of his words.

Emerson crossed her arms over her chest. "I

need to talk to Thea alone."

Brett mirrored Emerson's posture. She was just like all the other Howards. Except Thea. "That's up to Thea."

Thea looked up at him and opened her mouth a few times before the words actually came out. "Um, could we have just a minute to talk?"

Brett nodded and cut Emerson a warning glare. He might not be afraid of Emerson, but she was still a Howard–one of the people who'd done this to Thea. She was too small to have done the actual beating, but Emerson looked out for Emerson and no one else. He didn't trust her as far as he could throw her.

"I'll be right outside. Holler if you need anything."

Emerson huffed as soon as he turned to leave. "What's he doing here?" If she'd been trying to whisper, she needed more practice.

Brett pulled the door behind him, leaving a small crack. He didn't care to eavesdrop, but he wanted to hear Thea if she called for him. Emerson was trouble, but Thea had always had a bleeding heart for her wayward cousin.

Brett just hoped Thea kept her guard up. The first thing Emerson would do when she left would be to let her dad, Bruce Howard, know who she'd seen at the hospital, and they all needed to be ready for the storm coming to their door.

CHAPTER 6
THEA

The tightness in Thea's chest returned as Brett walked out the door. If he was rational and logical, Emerson was a tornado without a warning.

"Can you believe he had the nerve to show up here? Wait till Dad hears about this."

Thea reached out for Emerson's hand. "You can't tell him."

Thea's uncle, Bruce, was just as awful as Tommy, and Emerson had suffered the abuse of her dad much more than Thea had. Bruce was especially cruel to Emerson and always had been. He'd wanted sons, not daughters, and Emerson bore the brunt of his disappointment. It was a miracle she'd survived as long as she had.

Emerson's dark brows pinched together. "You better believe I can! It's just like a Patton to show up when one of us is down and defenseless. When are they gonna get it through their thick heads?"

"None of this is Brett's fault." Thea said the words without thinking, and now she wanted to shove them back in her mouth. Defending Brett had gotten her into this mess to start with, and she'd let her family turn her against him back then.

She'd wondered over the years whether or not she listened to the right voice. At the time, the louder won out, but now, she was almost sure the still small voice that kept urging her to choose Brett was the one she should have listened to. She'd been so positive he was innocent, until Gage pointed out all the reasons he wasn't.

"You're trying to tell me that the Pattons didn't do this to you." Emerson huffed and propped her hands on her hips. It was her signature pose–one that sometimes made her five-foot-two stance look more like five-foot-ten.

Thea and Emerson had grown up together. They'd been born six weeks apart, but they were as different as night and day. Emerson was loud and didn't care what anyone thought about the opinions she spouted. Thea shied away from any confrontation, often choosing the path of least resistance just to keep the peace.

Thea swallowed hard. Her mouth had gone bone dry. "I don't know who it was. It was so dark." Though, she was almost certain it hadn't been the

Pattons. They wouldn't step foot on the Howards' lands without expecting an all-out war.

"You mean this happened last night? What did you do?"

"I went to see Mom."

Emerson threw her head back and grunted. "I told you not to go last night."

"You said Tommy would be gone."

"And I'm sure he was, but if you'd waited one more day he would have been in Cody."

"Does it really matter how far away he was? I got caught anyway."

Emerson turned to pace along the bedside, stomping and huffing with every step. "Those Pattons are gonna be sorry they ever set foot–"

"I don't know who it was," Thea said. She reached for Emerson's arm again when she paced closer. "Promise me you won't tell anyone Brett was here."

"They're gonna know!" Emerson smarted.

"I know, but I...I need some time to heal. I don't want to get caught up in the kind of mess they bring until I'm out of the hospital."

Emerson's nostrils flared, and her lips thinned into a line.

"Please?" Thea begged.

Emerson rolled her eyes. "Fine, but they're not gonna get away with this one. We'll make sure they pay for what they did to you."

Thea's stomach turned. It was starting up again–the kindling that always grew into a wildfire when the Howards and the Pattons pointed fingers at each other. Emerson hadn't even asked about Thea's injuries. Emerson had always been driven by revenge instead of compassion.

It made sense to keep from getting emotionally attached to the people in their family. Her dad hadn't been the only casualty they'd endured. Hate ripped the people you loved right out of your arms.

"Please, don't say anything. Who told you I was here?"

"Nobody! I called Gage to find out if he'd seen you when I realized you hadn't come home last night. He wasn't even going to tell me!"

Gage's secrecy confirmed Thea's fears. Her brother probably knew the Howards were responsible for her injuries. It was the only reason he'd keep quiet.

Emerson flopped down onto the bed beside Thea's throbbing ankle. "I shouldn't have told you about Sharon."

"No, I'm glad you did. Now that I've seen Mom, hopefully I can get out of here without starting any more trouble." The thought of leaving her mom for good still gutted her, but what choice did she have? The old fires were still burning around here.

"I don't want that guy hanging around here,"

Emerson said, jerking a thumb over her shoulder toward the door.

Thea didn't have a good response. She didn't exactly want Brett to leave. She'd missed him so badly over the years it had physically hurt, but she also still grappled with the circumstances around her dad's death.

Brett had been with Mark that night, and his presence implied some kind of involvement. At least, she'd thought so until today. Hearing Brett's side almost broke her heart.

He couldn't have done it.

"I'm sure I'm safe here. It's not like the nurses aren't in and out every half hour. Someone is always close by." The argument was feeble, even to Thea's own ears.

"Whatever. Don't come running to me when he uses you to get back at us."

"Back at us for what?" Thea had never known which side had been the first to fire shots, but during her lifetime, the uproar began when Bruce killed Brett's dad and got away with it. The specifics were still a blur. Something about property lines. For all she knew, it could be the truth or a coverup.

A triple knock sounded on the door, and Thea and Emerson looked at each other.

"Um, who is it?" Thea finally asked.

"Officer Scott and Officer Freeman," a male voice said.

Emerson's brows lifted as she stood. "Well, that's my cue to scram. I'll call you later."

Thea looked around. "I don't have my phone. At least, I haven't seen it since I woke up."

"Miss Howard?" the officer asked again.

"Come in," Thea said. Pain vibrated in her throat at the high volume.

Emerson rolled her eyes. "I'll leave my number with the nurse." She gave a curt wave and a half smile as she hiked her purse strap higher on her shoulder. The officers came in, and she strode toward the door.

Thea recognized Jennifer Freeman, who was apparently known as Officer Freeman now. She'd been a year older than Thea and Emerson in school, and the looks Emerson and the police officer gave each other said they clearly remembered those high school days when they'd been at odds.

Thea recognized Asa Scott too, but she wasn't as familiar with him. His mom had given Thea her first job at the antique store in town when she was only sixteen. He'd been a few years older than her, and they hadn't run in the same circles.

Jennifer closed the door behind Emerson and the officers stood at the foot of the hospital bed.

"Am I in trouble?" Thea asked.

"That's what we're here to ask you," Asa said.

The urge to laugh crept up her throat. Of course, she was in trouble. With the Pattons and her own family. Though, she couldn't really put her finger on anything she'd done to hurt anyone. She'd spoken up for what she'd thought and hoped was right, and it had earned her a bright-red target on her back–one she'd carry forever.

Thea looked back and forth between the officers. "I'm not sure."

Officer Scott pulled a small notepad out of his chest pocket. "We'd like to get a statement from you. Have you had any medication recently?"

"Yes. Maybe half an hour ago."

"We can come back later. Do you know when you'll be due for another dose?"

"I'm not sure."

"Did you suffer any head injuries?" Jennifer asked.

"They said I have a concussion." She'd certainly been feeling off all morning. How long would the concussion symptoms last? Had they already explained it to her and she'd forgotten?

Jennifer pulled out her own notepad. "Did you lose consciousness at any point during or after the injuries?"

"Yes." She remembered enough to know how her ribs had been broken. She'd be suffering from those nightmares for a while. "I don't remember being left at the church or how I got here."

Officer Scott scribbled something on his pad. "I ran into Brett Patton in the hall. We'll be getting his statement while we're here. Is it okay to ask him to notify us regarding a good time to come back to talk to you?"

Thea rested her head back against the pillow, feeling the exhaustion of the morning. "Yes, that would be fine."

Apparently, having Brett around had more perks than she realized. Her head was spinning, and her eyelids were growing heavier by the second.

"Thank you, Miss Howard. Is there anything we can do for you while we're here?"

The question injected a little life back into her. She'd grown up in a family who despised law enforcement and the controlling hand of authority. Asa and Jennifer weren't here to dole out punishment; they were here to serve and protect. Considering the mountain of trouble waiting for her outside the hospital, she appreciated their concern.

Though, telling them anything, with or without pain meds, would only make things worse.

"I'm fine. I appreciate you coming by, and I'll let you know when I'm not taking the medicine."

Jennifer nodded once and reached out a hand for Thea to shake. "We'll be in touch."

Thea shook the hand. "I don't know where my phone is, but you can get my room number and call here."

Asa stepped up beside the bed and clasped his hands behind him, showcasing the loaded belt he wore. "I spoke with Brett on our way in. He's worried about you. Right now, I'd like to know if you believe yourself to be in further danger."

Thea stared at the officer. He hadn't asked for any names. Could she get in trouble for answering honestly? "Possibly."

Asa nodded. "Is anyone else in danger?"

She glanced toward the door. "Brett."

Asa nodded again and extended a hand for Thea to shake. "I figured as much. Thank you, Miss Howard. I'll be praying for your quick recovery." He laid his card on the side table. "Call me if you believe yourself to be in any danger here or if you need anything."

"Thank you."

Thea stared at the card as the officers left the room. She was always in danger, but calling for help wasn't an option.

Less than an hour after the police left, the doctor came in to explain the extent of her injuries. It seemed they were most concerned about her collapsed lung and concussion. She had an ankle brace due to a sprain, and she had brand new stitches from the gash in her arm.

Brett came back in shortly after she spoke with the doctor, but they didn't have much time alone with the nurses flowing in and out of the room.

Thea's recovery would take weeks. That was the part that gnawed at her mind throughout the morning. How was she going to get back to Alabama? Without her phone, how could she let her boss know what was going on?

Worse than the recovery was the question of where her phone had been lost. It was pass-code protected, but if someone were able to bypass it, they'd easily be able to find out where she'd been hiding out all this time. Depending on who got that information, it could mean an end to the fresh start she'd worked so hard to protect.

The nurse left again, promising to be back soon, and Brett pulled up a chair beside her bed.

"You okay?"

Thea shook her head. "Not even a little bit." She cleared her throat. "You need to go home and change clothes."

He looked down at his blood-stained shirt. "I'll have Linc bring me something when he gets off work."

"Who's Linc?" There'd been a time when they'd known all the same people. Now, she had no idea who Brett spent his time with.

"Lincoln North." Brett grinned and shook his head. "We live in one of the wranglers' cabins at the ranch. I'm currently shopping for a new roommate."

"You don't like him?" Thea asked, desperate to

find out all of the things she hadn't known in the last five years.

"I do. He's a good guy. He'd do anything for anyone, but he does all of his good deeds in secret."

Thea chuckled, and her chest burned like fire. No more laughing.

"Are you okay?" Brett asked, wide-eyed and worried.

"I'm okay. It just hurts. A lot. All the time. Tell me about Linc. I need something to distract me."

Brett wore his heart on his sleeve and spoke his mind. Being secretive wasn't in his makeup.

"I bet it's frustrating for you that he's so private," Thea said.

"He's a closet softie! Someone should know that that grumpy wallflower is really a big teddy bear."

Laughing through gritted teeth, Thea looked out the window. The midday sun was high, but they'd come to take her for more tests soon. What would the sky look like when she was finally able to leave?

"What's on your mind?" Brett asked.

"Nothing."

Lie. That's a lie. Intrusive thoughts were running rampant. Where to begin?

"You don't have to worry about this happening again. I'll be here."

Of course, he would. Brett had always been protective of her, even when the feud between their families had only been a grudge. That protective nature had eventually convinced her he might have resorted to murder to help her.

"You scared me," he said. "You scared me so many times."

She opened her mouth to ask why, but he kept going.

"I thought they'd done something to you. I didn't know if it was my family or yours, but I thought they'd done something to try to keep you quiet." He brushed a hand over his short beard. "I went a little crazy after you left."

Thea's chest hurt, but it had nothing to do with a collapsed lung now. If he was really innocent, she'd done the unforgivable by leaving him. "Is that what Gage meant about his jaw?" she asked.

"No one in my family knew anything about where you went. At least, they weren't telling me anything if they did. When I showed up at your house, Gage was ready to fight." Brett clicked his tongue. "But he didn't accuse me or my family of having anything to do with your disappearance, and that was all the confirmation I needed. Wherever you'd gone, he knew about it."

"You're right. He convinced me to leave."

Brett snarled. Then his features relaxed as if he could exhale the anger. "I know a little bit about fear, but leaving? I can't understand why you left without me. I–"

He stopped short and shook his head. "I guess now isn't a good time to talk about that."

He hung his head, and the intense pang of her remorse stung worse than ever. She'd messed up whatever good they might have had, and she'd hurt him beyond repair.

She wanted to cling to him. She'd wanted to latch onto him back then and never let go. When she left, she hadn't been sure which way was up or who she could trust. Now, she knew. A whisper grew in her mind, saying that Brett could be trusted.

"They said they'll have to monitor my lung for a while. I definitely can't get on a plane any time soon, and they gave me something for nausea earlier. I don't want to think about how bad it would hurt to throw up right now, but they said that was par for the course with the concussion."

"Don't worry. We'll get you the best treatment, and I'll be right here with you."

Finally, someone to confide in. She should have known Brett would not only guess her worries but offer a shoulder to lean on in the same breath.

"It's hard not to. The broken ribs hurt so bad, and I'm terrified of making the collapsed lung worse if I vomit."

"What about your ankle? Did they say you need a new one? Did you pick out the replacement already? Make sure it's not a lefty. You'd go broke just buying double the shoes."

Thea grinned and let her head roll back against the pillow. The sprained ankle was the least of her concerns, and Brett had effectively turned it into a joke. "I'm not getting a new ankle. This one is just fine."

"Ain't that the truth." He propped his chin in his hand and rested his elbow on the bed railing. "You always had beautiful ankles."

Thea gently pushed at his arm, knocking his chin off his hand. "Stop joking and flirting."

"It's not flirting. It's honesty. It's an admirable quality. And those ankles are really–"

The door opened, and the friendly nurse walked in, halting Brett's praise of Thea's figure.

"It's time to shine! You ready?" the nurse asked with way too much pep.

Thea pulled the sheet up and gripped it in both hands. "No. What are we doing?"

"X-rays and an MRI. Doc wants to make sure your noggin is okay."

She'd never had an MRI before, and her first instinct was to shy away from the unknown. "Can we do it tomorrow?"

The nurse propped her hands on her hips. "Don't be scared. Doctor Wideman is the best around. He knows what he's doing, and you'll be jumping for joy before you know it."

Thea groaned. She didn't have much use for joyful jumping, but if she had to do it, maybe it was best to just rip the bandaid off and get it over with. "Okay."

Brett rested a hand on her shoulder. "Hey."

She looked up at him and fought back the tears. Her emotions were running high, and the nurse had told her to expect that. Apparently, medical testing was one of those things Thea didn't know she was afraid of until it was staring her in the face.

Brett leaned in and whispered, "You're going to be fine. I'll be right here, praying the whole time. You won't be alone."

Thea stretched her mouth into the best smile she could. It was completely fake, but she needed to put on a brave face.

The nurse unlocked the bed and wheeled her toward the door. "Don't worry. I'll bring her back as good as new."

CHAPTER 7

BRETT

Brett propped his elbows on his knees and bowed his head. He intended to make good on his promise to pray. Seeing Thea scared like that gutted him. Praying would at least ease the helplessness. After a few minutes of chatting with the Lord, he stood and looked around. His shirt was bloodstained–a reminder of the terrible night.

The door opened, and Gage walked in.

"Where is she?"

"X-rays and an MRI. They just took her back."

Gage surveyed the room. "She doing okay?"

"She's emotional."

"No wonder," Gage said. "I took the rest of the day off. You need to go home."

Brett held his ground. "I'm not leaving."

"I mean you need to go change clothes." Gage's

jaw twitched. "You look like you just came from a knife fight."

"I'll have someone bring clothes later."

"Just go," Gage said. "I'll be here till you get back."

Brett didn't move. This was the guy who'd stolen the last five years of happiness from him. He didn't want to make nice and pretend everything was okay.

"I'm starting to think you really didn't do it. Okay? Are you happy?" Gage threw his hands out to his sides. "I was trying to protect her."

"I would have protected her," Brett said, pushing a finger to his chest.

Gage laughed. "You were under investigation. Barely out of high school. No glorious career waiting for you. You were very unequipped to give her a fairytale life."

"I never promised a fairytale life, but I would have loved her."

Gage shook his head. "That's not enough, man."

The ringing in Brett's ears stopped. That was Gage's truth. None of them grew up with love and safety, so it made sense he didn't see the value in those things alone.

Brett might not have had anything to offer her except those two things–then and now–but they were big things.

After a few tense seconds, Gage took a seat on

the firm couch by the window. "Go get a shower. You smell like garbage."

He rubbed a hand over his itchy jaw. The stubble was longer than he liked. He probably did stink. Thankfully, Blake and Ridge had dropped Brett's truck off at the hospital after the wedding. "I'll be back in two hours. Tell her that when she gets back."

Gage rested his head back and closed his eyes. "Fine."

Brett made his way to the nurses' desk and waited until a young brunette woman gave him her attention.

"I'm visiting Thea Howard in room 508. She's having some tests right now. I'm going to shower and grab some things from home. Can I give you my phone number in case you need to get in touch with me while I'm gone?"

"Sure." The nurse took down the number and promised to note it in Thea's chart.

The freezing wind outside jolted Brett out of his exhaustion. He'd dozed for half an hour during the night while Thea was resting, but he'd been too on edge to relax. The nurses were in and out every hour, and each visit had brought hope of news about her condition.

The collapsed lung scared him the most. He'd heard about a guy in the rodeo who hadn't survived a collapsed lung. They said Thea's was minor, but he'd been screaming on the inside since the doctor explained things last night.

The sun was moving toward the west and shining right in his driver's side window as he drove to the ranch, which only drained the last of his energy. When he pulled up at his cabin, Linc's truck was gone and the silence of the secluded part of the ranch had his eyes threatening to close.

Fifteen minutes later, Brett was showered and shaved. In another five minutes, his duffel bag was packed and ready for a few days at the hospital. He climbed back into the truck with a little extra pep after the quick shower. The clock on the dash said he had a few minutes before he needed to head back. Plenty of time to get things sorted out around the ranch.

Starting up his truck, he called Hadley.

"Hellooo," she sang.

"Hey. My friend, Thea, is gonna be in the hospital for a little bit. She's having some tests done right now, so I can't ask her what she might need. Can you put together a bag for her?"

"Sure thing. Come on by."

When he pulled up at her cabin, Hadley was waiting on the porch with a bag. She tossed it through the open window into the passenger seat. "You're all set. I hope she's doin' okay."

Hadley moved from Tennessee to the ranch last year, and she and Brett had become fast friends. She was young, funny, and pretty, but there had never been a spark between them.

"Thanks for this. I'll make sure you get your stuff once Thea is back on her feet."

Hadley waved a hand in the air. "Don't worry about it. Call me if you need anything else."

"Will do." Brett shifted the truck into reverse and headed toward the main house. He parked out front and gave a quick double knock before letting himself inside. "Mr. Chambers!"

"In the office!" the older man shouted.

Brett stepped into the office just as his boss was standing up.

Mr. Chambers held up his mug. "I need a refill."

"That's exactly why I'm here."

Mr. Chambers was creeping into his eighties, and he'd had a few health scares in recent years that kept him hanging around the house more and more. Despite the doc's orders to cut back on the caffeine, Mr. Chambers could be counted on to have a fresh pot in the kitchen every few hours.

Brett went straight to the cupboard where the disposable cups were stacked. "Is this the good stuff or the fake stuff?"

Mr. Chambers pointed a finger at Brett. "The good stuff, but if you tell Ava, I'll make sure you regret it."

Brett held up his hands. "My lips are sealed."

The front door opened and closed. “Boss!” Colt yelled.

“Kitchen!” Mr. Chambers shakily poured the coffee into his cup. “I need a megaphone or something.”

“Does it bother you that we stop by all the time?” Brett asked before taking the first sip of the hot coffee. His boss might be old enough to be his grandpa, but Brett and most of the men working at the ranch liked to hang out with Mr. Chambers.

Colt walked in and pointed at Brett before grabbing a ceramic mug. “Dude, you have a story to tell.”

Brett settled back against the counter. “Well, I was born in the late eighties. It was the sunset of the age of hair bands and–”

“Tell me about the woman from last night,” Colt cut in. “Is she okay?”

“She has a concussion and a collapsed lung. They did some stuff for her lung last night that I didn’t understand, but they said she needed to be careful for a while. She also has a sprained ankle, so she might need crutches for a little bit. It seemed pretty bad. I came home to get a shower and pack a bag. Sorry about the commotion at the wedding.”

“Don’t worry about it. Jess said you know her,” Colt said as he poured a cup of coffee.

“You could say that.” Brett frowned. “Shouldn’t you be on your honeymoon?”

"It's my honeymoon every day. Plus, Remi couldn't stay away from the kids."

Brett laughed. "That sounds like her. So, your staycation is pretty much just sending the kids to sleep over at Stella and Vera's house all week?"

"Right. And that means it's too easy for Remi to just walk over there and hang out with them."

"You mean she doesn't want to hang out with you?" Brett asked, trying and failing to keep the chuckle out of his voice.

"She said she hangs out with me enough. Can you believe that? We've been married for twenty-four hours and she's already tired of me."

"To be fair, you've been legally married for six months."

"True, and she's stuck with me for life. Now, back to the woman in the parking lot."

Mr. Chambers jerked his head toward the back door. "Let's take this to the porch, fellas."

Brett followed Mr. Chambers and Colt outside where they each took a seat in the rocking chairs that faced the rolling expanse of Wolf Creek Ranch. Brett had called this place home for years, and he hoped to be an old man sitting on his porch drinking coffee somewhere close to here when he turned eighty.

The ranch would never belong to him in name, but he'd gladly put in a hard day's work here until the day they kicked him out.

"So, tell us about the mystery woman," Colt said. "You know her?"

Brett scoffed. "Know her? Yeah. I know her. Her uncle killed my dad five years ago."

Coffee spewed from Colt's mouth, but Mr. Chambers didn't bat an eye. Brett had suspected that the old man might have heard about his family, but they'd never talked about it outright.

Colt brushed his shirt sleeve across his mouth. "Excuse me. Please continue."

"Then my uncle killed her dad. Oh, and I was also a prime suspect in that murder case, until my uncle was proven guilty."

"So, your uncle was going to let you take the fall, or at least try to pin it on you, if the judge or jury didn't find him guilty?"

Brett lifted his cup. "You hit the nail on the head."

"Whoa. That's heavy," Colt whispered.

Brett had known his uncle Mark was capable of anything, he'd just been crazy enough to overlook that danger when he'd followed his uncle that night. He'd hoped to stop Mark before he did something stupid, but Brett had been too late.

"Yeah, he hasn't been on Santa's nice list since he was a toddler. Thankfully, the jury found him guilty, and he's been in prison ever since."

"Good thing," Colt said.

"As for Thea? I do a little bit more than know her. We were together when all of that went down."

"Nooo," Colt drawled. "No way. Why in the world?"

"Thea is different. She doesn't have a malicious bone in her body. Our families hated each other, but we were the black sheep of the families."

"What are they fighting about?" Colt asked.

Brett shrugged. "The story has been twisted a lot over the years. At first, I heard it was about property lines. The family lands share a border, and there's a pond that crosses over that line. Both families raised cattle, and while they both wanted access to the pond so they wouldn't have to pump in water for the livestock, the Howard side of the pond always froze early in the winter and dried up early in the summer. Thea's family claimed that my great grandpa had allowed them access to more of the pond, but my grandpa didn't want to honor that easement when he inherited the land."

He paused there, running a hand over his head. "There's also a rumor about someone in my family having an affair with one of the Howards, but I never could figure out who it was. I definitely didn't ask."

"Basically, it's a lot of he said she said?" Colt asked. "Might be easier to keep your distance from her, don't you think?"

"Might be easier, but I've tried that. It's not

gonna happen. Thea left town five years ago, and I haven't had a serious relationship since."

"I figured you'd say that, but it was worth asking. It was like that with Remi too. It was her or no one," Colt said. "I couldn't picture myself with another woman. It always felt–"

"Wrong?" Brett added.

"Exactly."

"I've flirted with plenty of women, but there's always something missing. I could go on a date and tell the woman in all honesty that she was great and all, but I wouldn't be asking for another date."

"Yep. I know that feeling."

"It's completely different with Thea. I've been looking for her for years because no one could hold a candle to her. I knew back then she was the one for me." Brett stared down into the black depths of his coffee. "I thought we were on the same page."

"So, she left and didn't tell you anything?" Colt asked. "And you still feel the same way about her?"

"I thought either my family or her family had done something to her. Then I heard enough clues that her family had probably sent her away. Still, I wish she'd told me where she was going. When she was out of sight, she wasn't out of my mind. I knew things were dicey with our families, but I couldn't believe she would leave without telling me."

Mr. Chambers hummed low in his throat. "Love is sweet 'til it's sour."

Brett fought the urge to glance at the old man. Mr. Chambers spent three-fourths of his life with a wife who loved him and stood by him day in and day out only to be forced to live out the end of his life alone.

Well, Mr. Chambers wasn't really alone, but it must be hard to live without the woman he loved.

"So, what are you gonna do?" Colt asked.

"Go back to the hospital. Her brother came by and pretty much confirmed my suspicions that her family did this to her. I don't want them to get the chance to finish what they started."

Colt sucked in a breath through his teeth. "Yikes."

"Yep." Brett stood and took a gulp of his lukewarm coffee. "Looks like I'll be hanging around as long as she'll have me. At least, as long as my boss will let me."

"Things are slow around here, and we have plenty of help," Mr. Chambers said with a wave. "Go be with your honey."

Brett grinned at the outdated endearment. "I'll do that."

"What about when she gets released from the hospital?" Colt asked.

"I don't know the specifics, but they'll have to go through me to get to her again."

"Just remember," Mr. Chambers said as he slowly rocked back and forth, "you can respond to hate with an eye for an eye or you can meet the injustice with the new command we've been given—love thy neighbor."

Brett frowned, knowing the old man was imparting wisdom he wasn't ready to accept. "I'm still working on that one, boss."

"It might take some time, but you'll have to be the one to take the first step. And probably the next one and the next one too."

"Sounds like a long row to hoe," Brett said. Knowing that Mr. Chambers was right didn't make the task any easier. "But I'll keep it in mind. I need to head back to the hospital. I left her brother there, and I'm not sure I trust him, even if we did make a deal to put our differences aside to protect her."

Colt lifted his mug in farewell. "Does Thea need anything? Remi can send something."

"I appreciate it. Hadley gave me a bag of stuff to take to her, but I'll ask her when she gets back if she needs anything else. Maybe keep her in your prayers? She's a little overwhelmed with all the injuries and the pain. She was pretty upset before they took her back."

Colt gave a sharp salute. "Will do."

"We can take care of that," Mr. Chambers said. "I'll tell Jameson to take you off the schedule for the week."

"Thanks. I'll be back to digging ditches and

building fences soon." He reached up to tip his hat before remembering he wasn't wearing it.

Funny how going two days without the thing seemed odd. He'd definitely had the feeling he was missing something a couple of times.

He walked back into the house and refilled his coffee cup before heading out. After a stop by Sticky Sweets for Thea's dessert, Brett walked back into the hospital ready to spend the duration of Thea's stay sitting by her bedside. The thought of being cooped up in a room all day would normally have him itching for freedom, but something settled inside him, allowing his mission to solidify.

Thea needed him, and she came first.

Brett's phone dinged with a message as he entered the hospital. He put the bags down and checked it.

Asa: Is Thea awake yet?

Brett: I'm not sure. I'll let you know when I get to her room in a second.

Asa: I'll text you in the morning to see how she's doing and if she's had any meds.

Thea would probably be tired after all the pain from today. How long would it be before she could forgo the pain relievers?

Brett: I'll let you know. Thanks.

Asa: We haven't heard anything from your family or hers since she was assaulted, but keep your eyes and ears open.

Wasn't that like preaching to the choir? Brett knew how to watch out for trouble. He'd lived with it for too long.

Brett: Will do.

Knowing he at least had a few of the local officers on his side, he rested his head back against the wall, closed his eyes, and prayed. Mostly asking for guidance as he and Thea navigated the dangerous unknown ahead, but there were moments of gratitude that snuck in.

Sure, he'd spent a bitter five years without Thea, but she was back now. They were two smart adults. They could figure out how to make this work if they both wanted to, even if it meant skipping off to another country to hide and live out the rest of their lives together.

If she'd have him. There was a chance she hadn't loved him the way he loved her.

Maybe they could get past it. The Lord had given him plenty of patience over the last twenty-four hours, but the allotment was running out. Whatever had pulled them apart could be erased. They could start over.

Brett's head jerked up without warning. What if she had a boyfriend?

No, she was single. For sure.

Though, he couldn't imagine how some lucky guy hadn't put a ring on her finger yet. The idea of her not wanting to get married seemed unlikely.

They'd talked about running away to elope all those years ago, and they'd nearly done it. Her dad's untimely death had left them stuck in Blackwater while the criminal investigations were going on.

His phone rang, and he groaned at the sight of his sister's name on the screen.

"This better be good," Brett said in greeting.

"I don't want to fight. I just called to see if you needed anything."

Brett's shoulders relaxed. At least he'd get a pass this time. "Thanks, but I went home a little bit ago."

There was a slight pause on the other end of the line before Jess spoke again. "Is she okay?"

Brett hid his surprise at his sister's sudden interest in Thea. "I don't know yet. She's got a collapsed lung, a pretty nasty concussion, and a sprained ankle. Give or take some cuts and bruises."

Jess groaned. "Listen, I'm trying not to be mad at Thea for the way she left you."

"Then don't be," Brett said. "It's that simple."

"Maybe you're right. Maybe I should just forget she left you when our dad had just been killed and you were a prime suspect in another murder case. Maybe I should just forget about how broken you were when you found out she'd left. Maybe–"

"Stop," Brett said. The one word held enough authority to quiet his sister on the other end of the line. "You don't know why she left, and now that I do, I'm trying to make peace with it because it wasn't her fault. She's still Thea."

"Ugh. I don't know if I should hug her or throttle her."

"You'll have to go through me if you try to throttle her," Brett said.

Jess sighed. "It's a blessing and a curse that you're a good guy."

"You're one of the good ones too," Brett reminded her.

Jess had always been straight to the point and firm in her convictions. She'd known the fighting their family did wasn't right before either of them had left home.

When they found Wolf Creek Ranch and learned about the Lord, things had clicked into place for both of them. They didn't want to be a part of their past, but Jess had a harder time forgetting the pain they'd endured along the way.

"Yeah, well, I might be on the fence until the Howards get what they deserve."

Mr. Chambers's words from earlier replayed in Brett's mind. "I want justice too, but we're not meant to be the judge, jury, and executioners."

"Maybe you're right. Just keep me posted."

Brett and Jess had always been on the same side. Their personalities were opposites, but their convictions often aligned. They'd made the decision together to leave their family and the mess they created behind, and neither of them had ever regretted it.

Now, Thea was back, and Brett couldn't run away from the past when it was staring him in the face.

"I will. Thanks for calling. Love you, sis."

"I love you too."

Brett grinned at the flat tone of Jess's words. They were the strongest words known to man, but her abrupt personality seemed to drain all emotion from them. Even without the emphasis, he knew she never said anything she didn't mean. If anyone didn't believe the things Jess said, it was their own fault.

He made his way through the hospital, winding through the elevators and corridors to Thea's room. When he knocked, the door flew open. Gage gave Brett a once-over before stepping to the side.

The doctor that Brett hadn't seen since the night before stood at the foot of the hospital bed. "Be patient with your recovery. I know this is a lot to take in, but pushing it could cause complications."

"How long?" Thea asked.

"I wouldn't expect to feel completely like yourself again for at least four weeks."

A month. Brett stifled the panic that threatened to rise in his chest. He wanted her healthy and strong for basic reasons, but every minute she was immobile made her a sitting duck. He'd just have to stay close as much as possible.

"I'll be back in the morning. Let one of the nurses know if you have any questions or issues."

"Thank you," Thea said as the doctor excused himself.

Brett stepped to the side of the bed. Thea's color was pale, and her eyes blinked slowly.

"Did you miss me?" Brett asked. If she could just laugh or smile, he'd have some small assurance that she'd be okay.

Thea turned her head to look out the window. "You didn't have to come back. Have you even slept?" Her words were hoarse and slow.

"A few hours last night."

Thea tried to sit up before Brett picked up the bed remote and raised the upper part of the bed.

"Is that okay?" he asked.

"Much better." She glanced at Gage.

Her brother rolled his eyes and straightened from the wall he'd been slouching against. "Fine. I'll go. Call me if anything changes. I'll be back tomorrow."

"You don't have to do that. I'll be fine," Thea said.

Gage looked back and forth between Brett and Thea. "I'll call in the morning." He picked up his worn-out baseball cap and headed for the door.

As soon as they were alone, Brett asked, “So, how was it?”

Thea slowly tilted her head from side to side.

“Let me guess, it was nothing,” Brett said.

Thea grinned and rolled her eyes. “I know it was silly to worry, but I’ve never done any of this before.”

“Not silly,” Brett said quickly.

“I’m so tired,” she whispered.

Brett stepped to the edge of her bed. “Then rest. I’ll be here when you wake up.”

Her eyes drooped, not closing all the way before opening again like she was trying to fight sleep. She looked as if she could sleep for a year, and the way her bruised eye was changing to a deeper mix of purple made Brett’s chest seize with a wave of fresh anger for whoever did this to his girl.

His girl? Where had that come from? It’d been a long time since she’d been his.

“Brett?”

“I’m here.” He jerked out of his daze and stepped closer, careful not to jostle the bed but needing to take her hand.

She looked out the window at the darkening sky again. “It’s getting late. You better head home.”

“If it’s okay with you, I’d like to stay. I don’t want to leave you alone.”

Thea’s gaze locked with his. Would she send him away?

Finally, she said, "Okay. You can stay. For the record, I think it's a bad idea."

Brett jerked back. "What are you talking about? All of my ideas are good ideas."

"No, all of your ideas are extravagant and half baked," she said.

He scratched his chin and made a show of thinking. "I don't know how you could possibly get that idea."

She raised her hand and ticked off on her fingers. "You bought a car when we were seniors that was falling apart because you said it just needed some TLC, you asked me to go on a date with you after the first time we sat next to each other in biology class, you wanted to run away and get married the weekend before we graduated."

"Hey, I stand by all of those ideas," Brett said. "Especially the last one."

Thea sighed. "Who knows where we'd be if we'd gone through with it," she said softly.

"Probably better off than we are right now."

He'd never regretted asking her to skip town with him. There would have been a Texas-sized mess to deal with when they came home, but they would have been family–in the eyes of the state and God. Even without the confirmation of a marriage license, Thea was his one and only.

She always would be.

Her lips curved into a small smile as she finally

let her eyes close all the way. "Thank you for staying."

And before he had the chance to tell her she didn't need to thank him because she already had and because there was no way he'd have been able to make any other choice after what she'd been through, her head tilted to the side, and she finally drifted into sleep.

She'd thanked him for staying, and it was a simple thing since he'd just told her he'd be there when she woke up. But he couldn't help but wonder if she meant it in a bigger, more important way. Like thanking him for staying after finding out her reasons for leaving. Thanking him for understanding, and for not walking away.

The only question was, now that everything was out in the open, where would either of them go from here?

CHAPTER 8
THEA

"Miss Howard, I need to get your vitals."

Thea squirmed and immediately froze at the painful tug in her muscles. She squinted against the bright sunlight shining in the hospital room. Looking up at the young nurse, she blinked a few times.

"Good morning!" The nurse's smile and high cheekbones accentuated her heart-shaped face. "I'm Shayna. I'll be your nurse today."

Every inch of Thea's body radiated pain, and her cheek throbbed. A small grunt escaped as she tried to sit up.

Brett stood and made his way to her bedside. So, he hadn't been a dream.

"Sorry to disturb you, but I need to get some numbers. I think you'll be taking a stroll around the hallways today. On crutches, that is. Then the doctor might release you. You'll have some follow-up appointments, but at least you'll be out of here."

Heat crept up Thea's neck as she glanced between the pretty nurse and Brett. As if she needed a reminder that she looked like a train wreck, the nurse had to be a gorgeous runway model, and the one who got away had to be front and center first thing in the morning.

"Do you need anything?" Brett asked.

"Um, I don't know," Thea said, trying to wipe her eyes without upsetting the bruise on her cheek.

"Isn't that the sweetest?" the nurse said. "I bet you're getting the husband of the year award."

"I wish," Brett said.

"So, y'all are not married? Could've fooled me. How long have y'all been together?"

"I've loved her since we were seventeen," he said without missing a beat.

The heat was spreading into her face now. "What?"

"That's the sweetest!" The nurse's pitch hit an all-time high as she clutched the front of her scrubs.

"But we're not together." Thea's chest constricted as she said the words.

The smile on Brett's face died. Why had she corrected the nurse? Brett used to be the romantic type. He was the kind who promised her the world in sweet words, but had he meant them?

No. He liked to say extravagant things to get a

reaction out of people. He hadn't loved her since they were seventeen. If that happened to be the truth, what she'd done to him was truly unforgivable.

Thea had done little dating since leaving Blackwater, but it hadn't taken long to figure out that sweet words were a dime a dozen and men like that often had empty promises. The disappointments hadn't crushed her, but she'd learned to guard her heart. They'd say anything to get what they wanted. Too bad she hadn't learned that lesson before Brett came along. She might not have fallen so hard.

But she hadn't gotten the smarmy vibe from Brett. Ever. In fact, the outrageous things he said were mostly true, or at least he believed them to be true. He felt things deeper than any man she'd ever met.

"Oh no! I'm so sorry. I just assumed."

"It's fine," Brett said. "Thea moved away a long time ago, and this is the first time we've seen each other in almost five years."

The nurse perked up. "That's exciting." She winked at Brett. "You'll have to let me know if the old flame rekindles."

Thea wouldn't be rekindling any old flames. The magnitude of the last few days was settling in. She had a collapsed lung. It was one of the major, essential organs, and her worries over that were never far from her mind.

She also had a concussion that was making her emotional. To top it all off, she didn't have health insurance. She hadn't even talked to her boss. When would she be able to get back to Alabama? She'd expected to be gone a few days at the most, but how in the world was she supposed to get back to the other side of the country when the doctor said flying was out of the question due to the collapsed lung?

"Will do." He turned to Thea with a soft smile. "How are you feeling?"

Her throat constricted as she tried to speak. Why had she opened her big mouth and pointed out that they weren't together? She cleared her throat and tried again. "I'm okay."

Okay was an overstatement. Everything hurt from her head to her toes.

"Can she have breakfast?" Brett asked the nurse.

"She sure can. They'll come by and give her an order form in just a minute. I think I have everything I need. Call if you need anything."

"Thanks," Brett and Thea said in unison.

When the door closed behind the nurse, Brett pulled the chair beside the bed. "I got you something."

"What is it?"

"A strawberry cupcake from Sticky Sweet's."

Thea looked up at him and tilted her head. "What?"

"Isn't that what you like?" His brows pinched together in a flicker of uncertainty.

"How do you even remember that?" she asked with eyes narrowed.

"You're the only person I've ever met who lit up like a kid on Christmas morning whenever someone mentioned strawberry cupcakes. It was hard to forget."

Thea looked down at her hands. She'd made a huge mistake in leaving him.

Brett sat on the side of her bed. "Hey, what's wrong? I'm sorry if you don't like the cupcake. I can get you something else."

She chewed on the inside of her lip and didn't look up at him. "No, it's great. Thank you. I haven't had a strawberry cupcake in a long time, and I want it. It just brings back a lot of memories that I don't know what to do with."

Brett's furrowed brow eased. "I know what you mean. Seeing you has really churned up the old muddy waters."

Thea squirmed and winced as the pain and discomfort vied for her attention. "Everything hurts."

"I'm sorry," he said.

"You didn't do it. There's nothing to be sorry for. I'm the one who's sorry. I–"

Brett picked up her hand, and she didn't pull

away. “Let’s not talk about it now. It’s over. We can move on.”

But she couldn’t move on, and she didn’t believe he could either. “I’m just as confused as ever. Not about you. I believe you. But Gage and Emerson...”

“I don’t know the answers. I still want to rip Gage’s head off for his part in all this, and I definitely won’t trust Emerson.”

Thea pinched the bridge of her nose. “I’m not sure trusting anyone is a good idea.”

“Gage gave me his number. I’ll only use it if necessary. Right now, you don’t need to worry about anything else. You’re perfectly safe.”

“Thanks for staying. And for bringing me things. And for not hurting Gage.”

Brett grinned. “You think I could take him?”

She laughed, and it left her ribs screaming. “I don’t know, but I would bet good money you’d both end up with broken bones.”

He cleared his throat. “Actually, I think we were on the same page by the time he left. We both just want you to be safe and happy.”

Another punch in the gut. She’d been so wrong for so long.

“So, what do you want for breakfast?” he asked.

“She said they’d bring a menu,” Thea said.

“I can get you anything within sixty miles of here with one phone call. Say the word.”

“We’re at least forty minutes from Blackwater.”

Brett brought his hands together as if he were praying and made a dramatic show of begging. “Please tell me what you want. I’ll do anything.”

“Okay, okay. I’d like some pancakes, please.”

“And coffee?” Brett asked.

“Yes. Just black.”

Brett pulled out his phone and started texting. “Got it.”

“You act like you have a crew of people ready to do your bidding,” Thea joked.

He tucked his phone back into the chest pocket on his shirt. “No. I just have friends.”

That was believable. Brett had always been the guy everyone loved. He hadn’t belonged to any certain circle in high school. He’d floated effortlessly between groups, and he’d been accepted wherever he went. Brett had a way about him that incited loyalty and trust. Probably because he’d come whenever a friend called.

The nurse popped back into the room, and she had a friend in tow this time. “Miss Howard, we need to get some more x-rays.” She started unlocking the bed wheels and bundling tubes.

Thea gave Brett one last look, and he met her gaze with a wink. That simple wink had her stomach flipping like an acrobat. He’d always been handsome, but he’d filled out since she’d last seen him. The butterflies in her stomach were having a pep rally, but the cautious voice in the back of her head warned of the heartache in her future.

Things with Brett couldn't work out. It had been the same story when she left whether he killed her dad or not.

A nurse walked on either side of her bed as they made their way down the hall. The pretty nurse, Shayna, gave a little hum in her throat.

"You sure the two of you aren't together?" she asked sweetly.

Thea nodded, unsure of her voice when she wished the opposite were true. Brett was one of the best men she'd ever met, and he was completely off-limits. Sure, they were adults and could make their own decisions, but their choices always left someone they loved hanging.

Would Brett leave Jess and come with Thea to Alabama? Would he want to leave Wolf Creek? Would she even have a job waiting for her back home?

Home. She wasn't even sure the place existed.

"He seems like a catch. What's wrong with him?" Shayna asked.

Thea chuckled. "Absolutely nothing."

"Okay. I'll stop pestering you." There was about a three second pause before she continued. "But he's just so sweet, and the way he looks at you just makes my heart melt."

"I saw it too," the other nurse said.

Thea flopped her head back onto the pillow, sending a jolt of pain down her spine. "It's not him, it's—"

"Don't say it's you. You're a catch too," Shayna said.

"Well, it's not really either of us. It just wouldn't work."

The other nurse hummed. "Sounds like an excuse."

Thea swallowed and closed her eyes. "It is. He might think he wants to be with me, but I doubt he's thought about all the things he'd have to give up to be with me."

Shayna sucked in a breath through her teeth. "Yikes. Okay, maybe it's more complicated than I thought. I'll leave you alone about it." She patted Thea's shoulder. "I'm just glad you have someone here for you. It's sad when we have patients who never get a visitor."

"I'm really glad he's here," Thea whispered.

Shayna brought the bed to a stop outside a room. "Let me see if they're ready for you."

Thea waited patiently until it was her turn for x-rays. The movements reminded her of all kinds of aches and pains she'd hoped were subsiding. They x-rayed about half of her body before wheeling her back to the hospital room where Brett waited.

The sweet smell of syrup greeted her as they entered, and Brett stood to greet her. That handsome grin had her stomach flipping, and knowing she was the reason he smiled had her cheeks heating.

"Welcome back. Did they take good care of you?" Brett asked.

Thea wanted to roll her eyes at his overdone greeting, but Brett had always been outspoken and over-the-top. "I was treated like a queen."

"As you should be. Thanks for looking out for her, ladies."

The nurses exchanged knowing looks before directing their mischievous smiles at Thea. "You're so welcome. Give us a shout if you need anything."

As soon as they were alone, Brett rubbed his hands together. "You ready for breakfast?"

"I'm starving." When had she eaten last? Two days ago?

Brett placed the tray in front of her, adjusted the bed, and situated her coffee and pancakes.

"What did you get?" she asked, pointing to the other bag.

"Biscuits and gravy with a side of bacon."

Thea hummed. "Bacon sounds good."

He pulled the containers out of the bag. "It's yours if you want it."

"I'm not taking your food. I have plenty. Thanks for getting this."

"No problem. You want me to bless the food?"

Blessing the food. It was something she always did, but she ate almost all of her meals alone. "Sure."

Brett bowed his head, thanking the Lord for the food and asking for guidance through Thea's recovery. As soon as he said, "Amen," he reached for her plate. "You want me to cut it up for you?"

"No way. I can feed myself."

"You have ten stitches in your arm. I can help."

She picked up a fork and started working on the mushy pancakes. "There will be plenty of things I can't do on my own, but pancakes won't get the best of me."

"That's my girl."

Brett's deep words were a balm to old wounds. What did it say about her that she was basically wallowing in Brett's adoration? She dove into the pancakes and tried to swallow her feelings for the man waiting on her hand and foot.

"So, when did you start going to church?" she asked.

Brett closed the empty container and tossed it into the trash. "Not long after you left."

There it was. Another reminder of what she'd done to him.

"My attorney went to church, and she invited me to join her and her husband after the trial. I'd been showing up for a month or so before I dragged Jess through the doors. She quit her kicking and screaming after a few weeks. We met Mr. Chambers there. He was looking for more help on the ranch, and the rest is history."

"Sounds like a good gig." Thea twirled the fork in her fingers before jumping into the part that bothered her the most. "How's Jess?"

Brett reclined in the chair, resting his hands behind his head. "Same as always."

Thea kept her gaze down as she continued. "She didn't like me very much. I imagine she liked me less after I left the way I did."

Brett sat forward, propping his elbows on his knees. The position stretched the fabric of his shirt over his broad chest and thick arms. "I don't really care what Jess thinks. I liked you enough for the both of us."

If they stayed on the same topic, tears would be coming soon. "Do you like working at the ranch?"

"I love it. You remember the place?"

"I do. I bet it's awesome working there." It was a job she would've liked to have herself if things had worked out differently.

"Where have you been?" Brett's question was soft, but it was clear he was trying to ask it casually.

"Alabama."

Brett's eyes widened. "Really? What made you settle there?"

"Before I left, I found a job posting online asking for help at a barn. The place was in Pell City, and since I'd never heard of it, I figured no one else here had either."

"A barn? You work with horses?" Brett asked with a gleam in his eye.

"Yep. The owner, Misty, is amazing. She let me stay in the old room at the barn. She taught me how to take care of the horses. They have lots of boarders there. Then she taught me how to train them."

"You're training horses? No kidding. That's what Jess and I do at Wolf Creek."

Thea laughed. "What are the odds we ended up doing the same thing?"

Brett shook his head. "I don't have a clue, but it's awesome. I was ready to get out of the cattle business, and horses were a much better option in my opinion." He fidgeted in his chair a little and scooted closer to her bed. "I've been thinking about something I want to run by you."

Uh-oh. The warning before the announcement had her ears heating up. If whatever he had to say was no big deal, it didn't warrant an intro like that. "Um, okay."

"What are your plans after they discharge you?"

Oh. That sneaky thought she'd been rolling over in her head was demanding attention now. What were her options? "I guess I need to figure out how to get home."

Brett scooted closer again. "I have an idea. I

know you have a life there. You have friends and a job, I know. But what if you stayed here?"

Thea gasped, sending that invisible knife stabbing into her chest. Anything other than a slow, regular breath was torture.

He handed her the drink on her tray, and she took a sip. Once the pain had subsided, she gulped. "I can't stay here."

"But you can. Jess and I have been talking to our boss about adding another hand at the barn. It could be you. They offer housing on the ranch. The pay isn't much, but when you don't have any living expenses, it adds up. Plus, all meals are free for employees."

Free meals. Housing. Brett sure knew how to sell it. But it was a crazy idea.

"You could stay there. At least until you heal."

"No way. I'm not staying with you," Thea said.

"Gee. Tell me how you really feel."

"I'm just saying it would cause more trouble." A lot of trouble. So much trouble.

"I didn't mean stay with *me*. I was thinking about my friend, Hadley. She's staying in one of the newer cabins, and they have two rooms." He lifted his hands and shrugged.

"I figured you didn't mean to ask me to live with you. I just mean they'll find out if we're..."

"We're what?" Brett asked, daring her to continue.

And the heat in her face was back. If they were together. That was what she'd been thinking. But he'd offered her a temporary place to stay, not a relationship.

He used to tell her such sweet things, and she'd lived for that kindness. Other than her mom, that kindness had been absent from her life, until Brett came along and promised her the world.

But they'd been so young and unchecked. It hadn't been real, had it? She could hear his words in her memories and dreams.

You're the only one for me. He'd told her often enough that she'd wanted to believe it.

But that promise wasn't hers now. She'd given it up a long time ago.

"Brett, I don't know what to think when you're around."

"I know things weren't always perfect, but it was pretty close," Brett said.

Thea took a deep breath. "Right, but I made mistakes."

"Maybe we could do things better this time. We're older and wiser and all that jazz. I–"

Thea laid her hand on his. "I know. You're a great man. I've never doubted that, but... what if the past we remember wasn't real?"

"Oh, it was real. I remember all of it very vividly. I'd have to be dead to forget you."

Her mouth hung open slightly as she stared at him.

"What?" he asked. "Did I say something wrong?"

"I just can't believe I'm here and all this is happening. I never thought I'd see you again. I had no idea I was so wrong." She covered her mouth as her chin shook.

"Why are you upset? Tell me, so I can help."

"A lot happened back then. It's just a lot to relive."

Brett looked around the room until he found a box of tissues and handed it to her. "You okay?"

Thea dabbed at her eyes and wiped her face. She didn't want to relive her mistakes anymore. "Hadley? Is she your girlfriend?"

Brett made a dramatic show of falling back in his chair. "Heaven help me. If I had a girlfriend, would I have been hanging around you like a lost puppy for two days?"

"Okay. That's a good point."

"No, I don't have a girlfriend, nor have I had anything close to one in the last five years."

The look he gave her had a fire roaring in her middle. His piercing gaze locked with hers, daring her to look away.

All right. So he didn't have a girlfriend.

"Hadley is a woman who is strictly a friend. She's the one who sent the stuff for you."

"Stuff?"

Brett slapped his palm to his forehead. "I forgot to tell you. She sent a bag of clothes and stuff you might need. I just trusted her to know what to send." He picked up a duffel bag and brought it over to Thea. "You fell asleep soon after I got back last night, and it slipped my mind this morning.

Thea opened the bag and looked inside. Clothes, a toothbrush, deodorant, shampoo and conditioner, lotion, and the works. "Oh, that's so sweet. Will you thank her for me?"

"I was hoping you could thank her yourself. I already asked her if she'd be okay living with you. She said yes, and she's hoping you'll say yes."

"You already asked her!" Thea shouted. The deep breath pulled in her chest.

"I was hoping you'd really consider it. I can be close in case you need me. You'd have time to heal. I can keep an eye out for anyone who might try to hurt you again."

Anyone who might try to hurt her. Who did that include? She didn't even know the answer.

"Hadley is great. You'd like her."

She twirled the bed sheets between her fingers. "I'll think about it. Thanks for putting enough thought into this to put a plan together for me."

Brett rested his big hand over hers. "Anytime. And I know all of this is a lot for you. So, if I'm..."

"You're what?" she asked.

"Coming on too strong. Just say the word, and I'll back off. Okay?"

All of this was a lot to take in, and having Brett beside her, reminding her of the past and her still uncertain thoughts about it was confusing.

But did she want him to stop? Not really. She wanted that safety and kindness he offered. "Thanks. I'll let you know."

"So, back to Wolf Creek. Think about it, okay."

She'd known about Wolf Creek Ranch before she left, but she'd never been there. It was well known in the area, and curiosity was pushing her forward.

"I'll think about it."

The door opened, jolting Thea out of the moment with Brett. The nurse walked in, smiling as always. "How are you feeling?"

"I'm fine." Though, Brett's offer left her reeling.

"Good. I'm just checking vitals. The physical therapist will be in shortly."

"Thanks."

Was there a guide to navigating a hospital stay while your handsome ex is being incredibly charming? If she accepted the offer to stay with Hadley until her injuries healed, how was she going to resist falling for Brett Patton again?

CHAPTER 9
BRETT

Thea tossed the dice onto the tray table. She leaned over to study the roll. "Two, three, four, six, six." She let out a heavy sigh. "I already have a straight."

"Go for sixes?" Brett offered. They'd played every game they could think of at this point, but she definitely favored Yahtzee.

"Do you like to read?" Brett asked.

They'd been trading questions and answers after every round, and he'd learned more about her in the last two days than he'd learned about anyone else in his life. Her green eyes practically sparkled when she talked about the things she loved, so Brett's mission was to stumble upon those passions and explore them.

"Love it," Thea said.

"What do you like to read?"

Thea narrowed her eyes at him, but a smile tugged on her lips. "That's two questions, but I'll allow it since they're related. I love romance."

Brett grinned. Of course, she would be a romance lover. He would have been surprised if she'd enjoyed thrillers, given the state of their past. "Like, the stable boy falls in love with the princess?"

"Romance novels are a dime a dozen, but I'm pretty picky about what I read. Thankfully, there are lots of books now without the...um...sex scenes."

Brett pinched his lips together and stared at his scorecard, once again feeling incredibly lucky that Thea had given him a shot the first time. He'd have to work on being a much better man before he could ever come close to deserving another chance.

"I like the ones about emotional connections. You know, the ones where they save the world together and come out stronger on the other side."

"I wish I'd asked that question sooner. I could have gotten you some books."

Thea shrugged, clearly moving easier today than she had over the last few days. "I didn't need a book. You've kept me entertained."

That he had. He'd kept her so entertained that he'd been terrified of asking the questions he really wanted the answers to for fear of disturbing the lighthearted fun.

A knock sounded at the door, and a gray-haired nurse walked in. "Hello, hello!"

"Hey, Gladys," Brett and Thea said in unison. Gladys had been Thea's nurse for the last six hours, and they'd made fast friends with her.

Gladys stepped to Thea's bedside and propped her hands on her hips. "You ready to blow this popsicle stand?"

Thea's eyes widened. "Really? Now?"

"Really now," Gladys confirmed. "The doctor just put in the discharge order. Do you have clothes?"

Thea tried to sit up straighter and sucked in a sharp breath. The broken ribs were still giving her fits, and Brett's stomach turned every time she moved and winced.

"Yes. I have clothes."

Brett grabbed the bag Emerson had sent and brought it to Thea's side. Her cousin stopped by earlier to bring Thea's luggage. She'd also offered to return Thea's rental car.

While Brett hadn't been thrilled to see Emerson again, her attitude had been much better the second time she stopped by. She'd probably offered to help out with the rental because she felt bad about whatever she'd said to Thea the first time she visited. Brett hadn't asked, and he wasn't sure he wanted to know.

Thea dug in the bag, pushing through clothes. "Um, can you help me change, please?" she asked Gladys.

"Sure thing."

Brett clapped his hands. "Sounds like my cue to leave. I'll be outside."

He stepped out and looked up and down the hallway. The days were starting to run together.

Thea had agreed to stay at the ranch after the discharge. She'd be bound to crutches for at least a week. Hadley's mom was in a wheelchair after a major stroke, so the cabin already had a ramp that might make it easier for her.

Pulling his phone from his pocket, he called Jess. She'd probably brush him off again, but one last try to get through to her wouldn't hurt.

"What's up?" Jess answered.

"She's getting discharged."

"Good."

Brett took a deep breath before begging. "Please come to the ranch."

"No."

"I know you can take care of yourself, but what if they come looking for you? They've already hurt Thea."

"I'm not Thea," Jess said sternly.

"But you're in danger just like she is. If you come to the ranch, I can keep an eye on both of you."

"Sorry, bro. I'm staying here," Jess said in her typical monotone voice. "I like my house, and I worked too hard to get this place."

Jess was a hard worker. He loved that about her.

But she was being stubborn on this point. Living on your own was great until there wasn't anyone around when you called for help.

"But you don't have a roommate now. You're paying the whole rent. Housing at the ranch is cheaper."

"I don't want to. End of story."

Knowing he'd lost this one, Brett sighed. "All right. Just be careful, okay?"

"I'm always careful."

She was. Everything was literal with Jess. She took things at face value and did what was logical.

Brett's attachment to Thea was irrational to his sister. He understood her qualms, but he knew how to make up his mind and stick to it too.

"Okay, then. I guess this is the last time I'll bring it up."

"Good. You'll be at work tomorrow, right?"

With Thea getting discharged, he needed to get back to the barn. Hadley was off work during the winter season, and she'd be able to help Thea with anything. Other than staying with her mom at the assisted living facility, she wandered around the ranch offering her help wherever it was needed.

"I'll be there." Maybe he could even get Thea to the barn soon. Being around the horses would be good for her.

Jess said a quick, "Bye, bro," before ending the call.

Brett had just stuck his phone back in his pocket when Asa called.

"Hey, man. How's Thea?"

Brett scrubbed a hand over his jaw. He needed a shave in the worst way. "Breaking out as we speak."

"Good to hear. I know she's still recovering, but we need to get that statement. Sooner, rather than later."

Brett looked back at the door to Thea's room. "I know. We're heading to the ranch in just a minute. Let me run it by her, and you can meet us there."

"Thanks, man."

Gladys stepped out of the room and closed the door behind her. "She's all ready. I gave her the discharge papers, but you'll need to wait for an attendant to come by with a wheelchair."

"Oh, she's gonna love that," Brett said. Thea was already complaining about the immobility and helplessness.

"They all do, but it's standard procedure," Gladys said. "I hope I don't see you two here again."

"Same. Thanks for all you've done."

"You take care of that woman. She's a good one."

Brett smiled. "You don't have to tell me twice."

Gladys patted his shoulder as she stepped around him.

Brett crept back into the room to find Thea dressed and sitting on the side of the bed. She wore baggy sweatpants and a thick gray sweater, and she had a heavy-duty brace on one leg.

"You ready to run?" Brett asked.

She rolled her eyes. "Ha-ha. Very funny. I don't know when I'll be running, but it won't be today."

He sat on the chair beside the bed and propped his elbows on his knees. "You'll be running again soon. I'll help you."

Thea looked away and swallowed hard. "You don't have to do all this for me," she whispered.

"I don't have to. I want to."

Brett's heart had always been soft for women, children, and animals, and seeing Thea struggling and in pain had him searching for ways to help. Anything. He'd do anything to make Thea's life just a little easier.

She looked at him then. There was skepticism in her raised brow, but she didn't press him. "Do you need to go get the truck?" she asked.

"I'll wait until your chariot arrives." He didn't want to leave her alone. It was ridiculous, since he'd have to leave her at some point once she got settled at the ranch, but he hadn't gotten his fill of her yet. He'd been starving all this time, and a few days of her wasn't enough.

"Knock, knock," a man said at the door. He wheeled the chair in, and Brett helped Thea move from the bed to the chair.

When she was all settled, he jogged ahead to get

the truck. The day was sunny, but the warmth didn't reach his skin. The chill of winter still hung too thick in the air. He found the truck in the parking lot, pulled up to the curb at the hospital entrance, and got out.

Thea started to push up with her arms.

"Wait," Brett said. He leaned down and tucked an arm behind her knees and the other behind her back. "Put your arm around my shoulders."

"You don't have to pick me up," Thea said.

"I would really like to help you into the truck, if you'll let me."

After a few tense seconds, she wrapped an arm around him and held his shoulder with the other. He easily lifted her from the chair and gently placed her in the passenger's seat.

"All good?" he asked.

She squirmed a little. "All good," she confirmed.

Brett thanked the man and rounded the truck. Once they were on the road, Thea started squirming more.

"Are you sure you're okay?" he asked.

"Yeah. I'm just not used to sitting up like this. But it feels great to be free."

Freedom. Was that what this was? It sure felt like some kind of bond had been cut away. He had Thea beside him, and they were heading home. Well, to the home he'd made since leaving his family behind. She had her own home, and she wanted to get back to it.

Was he selfish to want to keep her? If she didn't want to stay, would she let him come with her? He'd eased up on the flirting, and they'd settled into a companionable friendship. While he loved spending that time with her, he'd been suppressing the part of his heart that wanted more. If she wanted that same thing, she hadn't let on.

"Asa called while you were getting ready to leave. How do you feel about giving a statement today?"

"I totally forgot about that. Yeah, that's fine. Do we need to go to the sheriff's department?"

"He said he could meet us at the ranch. He knows his way around. I'll let him know which cabin you'll be in."

"Thanks. I can't believe I forgot to call him back. I don't even remember where I put his card."

"It's fine. He's not upset. He knows you've been through a lot lately. Are you sure you're ready to do this? Do you need to rest some more?"

"Ready as I'll ever be, I guess. I'd rather just get it over with."

She'd avoided all talk of their families the last few days, and he couldn't blame her for wanting to pretend that twisted reality didn't exist. "Do you know what you're going to say?"

Thea sighed and sank down farther in the seat. "I have no idea."

"They got my statement. The first morning at the hospital," Brett confessed.

"They did? Oh, I remember Asa telling me that now. What did you say?"

A tinge of panic laced her words, and Brett lifted his hand to reach for her. He'd barely moved before returning his hand to the wheel. He'd been doing a good job of keeping his hands to himself lately, despite the constant urge to touch her. "Nothing that would put you in more danger."

"What about you? If they find out you told the cops anything, they'll come for you."

"What could I tell them? Unfortunately, I don't know who deserves all this anger." He gripped the steering wheel and savored the burning in his palms as he pressed and twisted the hard leather.

"I don't either. Actually, I might not know any of them if I met them on the street. People change a lot in five years."

"Some don't," Brett said. "You haven't."

"How do you know that?" Thea whispered.

"I just do. You're still the girl who cried while I dissected a frog in biology class. You're still the girl who stayed up late helping me study for tests. You're still the girl I..."

Brett's throat constricted, cutting off his words. She was still the woman he wanted to spend his life with. The last few days had reassured him of that fact, but her feelings hadn't caught up yet. Would they ever?

Thea cleared her throat, saving him from the hasty love confession. "There's still a lot about me you don't know," she said quietly.

"Will you let me get to know you?" He glanced at her in the passenger seat. She was beautiful in ways no other woman could be. Her dark hair was pushed behind her ears, and the swelling of her cheek couldn't touch the softness in those sea-green eyes.

They'd been young and dumb back then, but there were things about their relationship he couldn't regret. Giving his heart to her was one of them. She deserved more than he could ever offer her, but for now, he'd allow her the time she needed to make up her mind about what she felt for him.

And if she didn't hold the same feelings for him anymore, could he go on with his life as if the best part of his heart hadn't been shattered?

"I need some time," she whispered.

There it was. The tip of the knife pierced the skin of his chest. Would she drive it deeper and twist, or would she pull back and save him?

"Whatever you need." He turned and winked at her. He could pretend on the outside while he was screaming on the inside.

"Thanks. I just don't know what's going on. I

don't know when I'll be able to walk again or when I'll be able to go home."

The knife hit its mark and twisted. She still wanted to leave, and could he blame her?

"Is it okay if I hang around to help? I know it'll be hard for you to get around for a while, and you'll have lots of doctor appointments. I'd like to be your personal driver."

There. That was logical. She needed a ride. He had a truck.

"I'd like that." She played with her hair and turned her attention to the road ahead. "So, this is the ranch?"

There were still so many uncertainties between them, and as much as he wanted to push, he couldn't beg for more when she wasn't ready to give it.

After all, he'd waited years for another chance; he could wait a little longer.

CHAPTER 10
THEA

Brett parked the truck in front of the cute cabin. It wasn't big, but it had the look of a new construction. Smoke billowed out of the chimney, and a purple car was parked out front. The homey scene pulled Thea's attention from the pain in her chest and face.

"This is Hadley's place, which makes it your place for now," Brett said as he turned off the engine. "You ready?"

"As ready as I'll ever be."

Truly, she was ready. Seeing the ranch and the cabin had hiked up her excitement, and meeting her new roommate had her uninjured heel tapping on the floorboard.

Brett jumped out of the truck and jogged around the front, opening her door before she had time to grab her crutches out of the back seat.

"I'll take those," Brett said as he extended a hand.

"Why? You don't need them."

"Trust me, cup–" His eyes widened, and he cleared his throat. "Just trust me."

Trust. Wasn't that the one thing she'd always been short on? Fortunately for him, Brett had barreled over her walls a long time ago.

She handed him the crutches, and he propped them against the truck. He turned back to her and rested his hands on the top of the open doorframe. Leaning in, he gave her that heart-melting grin.

"Now, can I carry you inside?"

Thea rolled her eyes, but her stomach did a little happy dance. "That's unnecessary."

"I'll let you hobble on your own if you want, but please let me do this for you. The doctor said you'd have swelling for a while, and you haven't had it elevated in over an hour. It's a long drive from Cody."

Well, Brett had certainly been working on his persuasion skills because she had zero rebuttal. Maybe she didn't want to protest. "Okay, but we're not making a habit of this. I'll never get back to walking if you carry me around all the time."

Brett didn't try to hide his triumphant grin as he slid a hand under her knees and positioned the other behind her back. His grip on her leg and side was strong and sturdy as he lifted her from the seat as if she weighed as much as the duffel bag she'd brought. She grunted a little as the familiar pain shot up her side. The heavy brace weighed her down, but Brett didn't miss a beat.

"Don't worry. You'll be dancing on that leg again in no time," Brett said.

"Dancing?" Thea laughed. "These legs weren't dancing before the incident. I don't think I'll miraculously figure out how to do it once my ankle heals."

"Really? I figured you'd be a natural. We open up the dance hall in the evenings sometimes. Maybe you'll want to give it a try someday."

Someday? How long would she be here? Until the doctor released her to travel? Long enough to figure out how to get around on her own? Until she could navigate an airport with her luggage?

But the thought of leaving Brett was one she continually pushed from her mind. Things wouldn't work between them, and it was all too easy to forget that when he was being so nice.

Brett held her tighter to his chest, and the warmth seeped through her thick winter clothes. His strength settled into her bones, calming the anxiety she'd been carrying. If nothing else, his steadfast strength made her want that for herself. She could overcome this setback. She could dedicate herself to healing.

The cabin door burst open as Brett took the first

step onto the porch. A young woman with a long ponytail threw her hands in the air.

"You're here!"

"In the flesh," Brett said. "You ordered a roommate?"

"I'm Hadley. Welcome home!"

The pull in Thea's cheek begged for relief from the smile, but there was no way to stop it. She'd have to get used to the screaming bruises on her face if Hadley was going to be so cheerful.

"Thanks for letting me crash here for a little bit," Thea said.

"I've been dying for a roommate," Hadley said. "Come on in."

Brett carried Thea inside and walked straight to the couch in the middle of the main room. He lowered her to the seat with amazing gentleness before pulling the worn coffee table closer to her. Hadley grabbed a throw pillow and tossed it to Brett, who positioned it under Thea's brace.

The place was small, but it had all the makings of a cozy home. Thin curtains hung over the window in the main room, a low fire danced in the fireplace, and an upholstered ottoman overflowing with blankets sat beside the recliner.

Definitely homey.

"You comfy?" Hadley asked.

"So comfy. This is way too much. You definitely

don’t have to do anything for me. I can use the crutches.”

Brett snapped his fingers. “I’ll go get your crutches and the bags.”

And he was off again, doing everything for her in the same way he’d been doing for days. She released a heavy sigh as he disappeared out the door.

“I promise I’ll give you some space. I’m just excited to have someone here,” Hadley said as she sat on the coffee table.

“Thanks. I’m grateful for the help, but Brett won’t even give me a chance to do anything for myself.”

“Oh, yeah. Extreme is his default. You know, you can just tell him to ease up. If you don’t, he’ll keep on.”

Thea glanced toward the door where Brett might reappear any moment. “I know. He’s just trying to be helpful, and it's been great having him around when I’m still hurting.”

Hadley shook her head. “I’m so sorry this happened to you. I can’t understand how some people are so cruel.”

“I wish I could say the same,” Thea whispered.

She’d learned a lot about what people were capable of over the years. Some were evil to their core, but others were inherently kind. It was the difference between Uncle Tommy and Brett. They were complete opposites, and Thea's discernment had gotten a workout over the years. She could generally tell if someone had the potential for hatred or if they knew how to choose good, even when it was the tougher path.

"You're safe here," Hadley said. "Brett might be a tad on the intense side, but you can rest assured he'll do anything to protect you."

Thea nodded. How had they gotten here? The war between the families had a new team. She and Brett were the enemy of both sides, which made them the easy, vulnerable target.

Brett returned with her crutches, her bag, and the bag Hadley had sent. He closed the door against the cold wind and shivered. "Asa just called. They'll be here in a minute."

"The police officer?" Hadley asked.

"Yeah. He came by the hospital, but I'd been on pain medicine. He wants a statement about what happened," Thea said.

Hadley's eyes widened. "Man, I bet it'll be hard to talk about it."

Brett sat on the couch beside Thea. "Are you sure you're up to this?"

"I'll be fine. I just hope I say the right thing."

She'd been so focused on physical healing that pushing thoughts out of her mind had been easy lately. Had she thought about it enough? Too much?

Would the information help or hurt her? The headaches from the concussion left a lot of confusion behind.

A firm knock at the door told them the officers had arrived.

Hadley jumped up and opened the door. “Come in, officers.” Her chipper tone held none of the uncertainty of a moment ago. She’d transformed into a welcoming hostess. “Have a seat. Can I get you something to drink?”

Asa held up a hand. “Nothing for me, but I appreciate the offer.”

“Same,” Jennifer said.

Thea scanned their badges, refreshing their formal names. Officer Scott and Officer Freeman. It had been a long time since she’d known them as acquaintances, and despite their kind visit at the hospital, she was still flip-flopping over whether they were friends or unknowing foes.

Thea tried to push up onto her good foot, but Asa held up a hand. “No need to get up. Just relax.”

She settled back into her seat, thankful she wouldn’t have to balance to shake hands. “Thanks for coming. I completely forgot to call you back.”

“It’s understandable,” Officer Freeman said. Her tone was direct but not unfriendly. “You’ve been through a lot, and we want to make sure you’re safe.”

Thea stretched her mouth into what was probably a ridiculous grin. Safety hadn't been available to her for a long time, and she wasn't sure it would come to her now. "I appreciate that."

Brett and Hadley had moved to stand behind the couch, allowing the two officers to choose their seats. Asa took the recliner, and Jennifer took a seat beside Thea on the couch.

Jennifer rested a tablet on her lap, unfolding the attached keyboard. "I'll be transcribing as you talk. We might interrupt with some questions, but feel free to start at the beginning.

"I'll do my best." Thea wrung her sweaty hands and looked over her shoulder.

Brett was standing behind her. "Do you want us to leave?" he asked.

"No. I think it's good that you're here. This involves you too, and Hadley needs to know what she's getting into." Thea gave her new friend a smile. "Feel free to change your mind about letting me stay here after you hear this."

Hadley turned to Brett and jerked her thumb at Thea. "She doesn't know me very well."

Thea lowered her voice. "I'm serious. It's okay if this is too much, I told Brett it wasn't safe for you."

Hadley patted Thea's shoulder. "He told me enough. Consider me warned."

Thea wrung her hands in her lap. "I grew up

here, and almost everyone in my family has a criminal record. The ones who don't are too young. My family has been in a long-standing disagreement with Brett's family."

"Can you state your family name and Brett's family name?" Jennifer asked.

"Howard. And Brett's family are the Pattons."

Asa leaned forward. "I heard about the incidents that went on a while back. I was working at the jail, so I wasn't part of the investigative team. Does that have anything to do with your current injuries?"

Thea shrugged. "It's possible. First, Brett's dad was shot. And killed."

She swallowed the bile that crept up her throat. Brett had been confused. He didn't have any love for his dad, but he'd been angry at the injustice. Everyone knew it was probably Bruce who killed Oscar, but no one had ever been convicted.

She'd been helpless. She'd been seeing Brett for months when it happened, and watching the man she loved struggle with anger and grief, despite his feelings for his dad, had permeated every corner of her life.

"They never found out who did it, but most people thought someone in my family was to blame."

"But no one was convicted?" Jennifer asked.

"Right."

"Can you state his name?"

"Oscar Patton."

"And he died in Blackwater?"

"Yes."

"Five years ago?"

"Yes."

"I'm sorry for the interruption. Continue."

"A few weeks after Brett's dad died, my dad was killed." The lead weight dropped in her middle. There were reasons she avoided thinking about all that happened back then. The violence made her physically ill.

"Can you state your dad's name?" Jennifer asked.

"Wesley Howard."

"And his death was ruled a homicide?"

Thea nodded. "Yes."

"Was the murderer prosecuted?"

Thea kept her gaze on Jennifer, but Brett's presence behind her held her attention. "Yes. At one point, Brett was believed to be an accomplice."

"Who was convicted of the murder?"

"Mark Patton."

"Did you have any relation to Brett Patton at the time?"

Heat crept up Thea's neck, constricting her throat. "We were in a relationship."

"And Brett Patton was eventually found not guilty?"

"Yes. He was only there when my dad was killed because he was trying to stop Mark."

Jennifer nodded as she typed. "Please continue."

"I left town after my dad was killed."

"Before or after Mark Patton was convicted and Brett was found not guilty?"

"Before."

"Did you believe yourself to be in danger then?" Jennifer asked.

"Yes."

"Was that the reason you left town?"

"Yes."

"Did you believe the danger to be from the Patton family?"

"Yes." Another confession rose in her throat, but she choked it back.

If she told them she'd been afraid of her own family back then, they would ask for her reasoning. It was all a big web of loyalties and broken ties.

"Did you believe the danger to be from Brett specifically?"

"No."

Jennifer turned to glance at Brett over her shoulder. "Would you like to continue this conversation alone?"

"No. I know Brett didn't do this to me, and I know he wouldn't have hurt me back then either."

Jennifer nodded, signaling for Thea to continue.

"I've been living in the Southeast for the last five years."

"Did you believe yourself to be in danger there?" Jennifer asked.

"No."

"Why did you come back?"

The flashes of pain and betrayal were fresh in her mind. Coming home had done her no favors. "My mom is sick. She's been battling cancer for years, but she got news from the doctor recently that the treatments aren't working the way they should. I wanted to see her."

"I'm sorry to hear about your mom," Asa said.

Thea bit her lip and nodded once. The wound from her mom's diagnosis was still too raw.

"My cousin, Emerson Howard, called me last week and told me. I asked for time off work and flew up here. I saw my mom on Saturday night."

"Last Saturday?" Jennifer asked.

"Yes. The incident happened right after I saw Mom."

"Where were you?"

"Emerson's house is located on the property that borders my mom's. I had planned to stay with Emerson. I walked through the woods between the houses."

Thea's breath halted in her lungs. Would she be accused of trespassing? Her mom would never charge her, but if Uncle Tommy found out or already knew, would he use that against her?

"I spoke to my mom then started back toward Emerson's house. I was walking along the road on my way to the woods when a truck drove past. The truck stopped just ahead of me, and two people got out."

"Could you tell whether they were male or female?" Jennifer asked.

"Male."

"Can you describe the vehicle?"

"It was an older pickup truck. It was a dark color, but I couldn't tell you exactly what it was."

"What happened when they got out of the truck?"

"They started toward me, and I ran for the woods."

Jennifer asked for the address of Thea's mom's house and a few other location details before they moved on to the attack.

"I'll be honest, I don't know who it was or what they looked like. They were much bigger than me, and they didn't speak. It was dark, and I couldn't see anything."

"What happened next?" Jennifer asked.

"They carried me to the truck. I was in and out through a lot of that. The pain in my chest and head was terrible." Thea didn't want to linger on those memories. The dizziness and pain were things she hoped to never experience again.

She glanced at Brett to find him standing with his arms crossed over his chest. The intensity in his stare left her breathless. As hard as it was for her to relive the attack, Brett was probably having a tough time hearing about it too. The fire in his eyes said he was ready to punch through walls.

"You didn't recognize anything in the truck?"

"No."

"And you didn't see where you were going?"

"No. I didn't even know how I ended up at the hospital until Brett told me."

Asa gave Brett a nod. "We got Brett's statement already, so he filled in a lot of those blanks."

"I'm glad," Thea whispered.

Whoever had hurt her probably hadn't realized they'd saved her life by dropping her off at Brett's feet. He'd taken care of her when she hadn't been able to care for herself.

"Has anything suspicious happened since the attack?" Jennifer asked.

"Nothing I'm aware of. I was in the hospital for days, and I didn't have many visitors."

"Is there any other information that may be helpful to us?"

"I don't think so."

Jennifer turned the tablet around and faced it

toward Thea. “Can you read this and sign at the bottom if the information is correct?”

Thea took her time reading the report, and everything was as she’d said. She used her finger to sign the screen and handed it back to Jennifer.

“If you think of anything else, please give us a call.” Jennifer handed over her business card. “I wrote the case number on the back. You can pick up a copy of the incident report at the department in a few days.”

“Thanks for coming out here,” Thea said.

“We can’t make any promises...”

“I don’t expect you’ll find who did it,” Thea interrupted. “I’m still glad you followed up with me. It feels good to have it documented.”

The report might seal her fate, but she had to have faith in the justice system. It was the only straw she could grab.

Asa extended his hand to her as he stood. “Let me know if you need anything. Mom has been asking about you, and she put you on the prayer list at church.”

Thea’s lungs were heavy. It was nice to know there were people praying for her, but would her name become a whisper in the town? Would word get back around to her family? Or Brett’s? Almost everyone in town knew about the deadly feud between their families.

Probably not. The Howards and Pattons weren't church-going folks. Nor were their friends.

"I appreciate that. I always loved your mom."

Asa's manly, bearded face took on a look of boyish innocence at the mention of his mom. "She loves you too. Here's her number if you want it." He pulled a card and pen out of his chest pocket and scribbled down the number.

"Thanks! I'd love to catch up with her."

It was the truth, but she had no intention of integrating into the community. Not when her welcome had been so loud and violent.

CHAPTER II
THEA

Asa and Jennifer said their good-byes and left quietly. Hadley closed the door behind them and slunk against it. “Whew. That was a lot to process.”

Thea winced. “I’m sorry.”

“It’s okay. I just hate that you’ve been through so much.” Hadley flopped into the recliner where Asa had sat. “So, I was thinking we could get you settled in today.”

Thea glanced at the bag by the door. “It’ll take all of five minutes.”

“Nap first?” Hadley asked.

Slumping into the softness of the couch, Thea sighed. “That sounds amazing.” She hadn’t done anything strenuous, but exhaustion had followed her like a dark cloud since the injury.

Brett stood and stretched his arms over his head.

"I'll let you get some rest. I promised Jess I'd help her out at the barn today."

Thea's attempt at a smile probably looked more like a grimace. What a nice reminder that she'd have to face Brett's sister at some point. "Good. I've been telling you to go to work for days now."

"And I still don't want to go."

"I thought you liked work," Hadley said.

"I do. I'd just rather be helping Thea."

Thea groaned. Brett's kindness was over the top, and she loved it. But he refused to look at their situation realistically. He forgave too easily. They couldn't have a normal relationship. Everything logical said it was a bad idea.

"Aww. You are just too sweet," Hadley said. "Don't worry. I'll take care of her."

"I appreciate that. I'll check back in later." Brett winked at Thea and turned to pick up his hat.

"Bye," Thea said quietly.

She hadn't been away from him much since she rolled into town, and the loss pricked in her chest. He'd been good to her. Too good. But she needed time to think about her feelings.

When Brett closed the door, Hadley whispered, "The mother hen is gone."

Thea chuckled. Brett *was* a lot like a mother hen.

Hadley moved from the recliner to the couch, bending her knee and facing Thea. "I'm so excited to have a roommate. I used to live with my mom and sister. I'm still getting used to having my own place."

"I promise I'll be out of your hair soon," Thea promised.

"Don't worry about it. So, you're from here?"

Thea adjusted her leg propped on the coffee table. Hadley seemed nice, but how far could she be trusted? "Yep. I just haven't lived here in a while. My mom has cancer."

Hadley dropped her gaze to her hands. "That stinks. My mom had a stroke last year, so I get it. She still needs a lot of help, but I'm glad she's still with me."

Thea pressed her lips together. Her mom was still alive, but the luxury of having her mom with her hadn't been a reality in a long time. It still wasn't.

"Any info about her diagnosis? Is it treatable?" Hadley asked.

"They told her at the last appointment that if she didn't go through with the intense chemo and radiation treatment, it was only a matter of time."

Time. The one thing everyone wants but can't seem to get enough of.

"The problem is, she doesn't have the money for all that. Plus, there isn't anyone here who really cares about helping her get to and from appointments or supporting her in the treatment at all."

"That's awful. I'm so sorry."

A single tear pushed its way out, and Thea wiped it. She'd done enough crying already. "I can't even go see her."

"Why not? I'll take you."

"No, you can't."

"Sure, I can."

Thea shook her head. "Family issues."

"Oh," Hadley drawled. "I can't believe it's that bad."

"It's that bad," Thea whispered.

"If they treat their family like that, I'd hate to see what they do to their enemies." Hadley looked around, and the silence settled between them. "I still want to help."

"That's incredibly nice of you, but it's dangerous." Thea waved a hand over her injured face.

Hadley leaned forward. "If you want to see her and help her, I'll help make it happen."

Tilting her head, Thea studied Hadley. They were practically strangers, and half of the dangerous truth had just been detailed for the police. "Why would you do that?"

Hadley shrugged. "If my mom was in bad shape, I'd do anything to be with her. If there was any way to help her, I would do it. My sister went above and beyond to help Mom and me. She put herself in danger to make sure we were cared for. After I found out what she did, I realized I would have done the same if I'd been given the chance."

"Who's your sister?"

"Cheyenne."

"Is she okay now?"

Hadley smiled. "She's great. Everything worked out, but she dealt with a lot of terrible things to keep us safe. And that's what's important–protecting the people we love."

"I would do anything for my mom," Thea whispered.

Hadley rested a hand on top of Thea's. "Me too. Having my sister to help me was an answer to prayer. If you don't have anyone else, you have me."

Hope and fear bloomed rapidly in Thea's thoughts. Could she see and help her mom? What would she have to do to make it happen? "I won't ask you to do that."

"You didn't ask. I volunteered."

Thea looked at Hadley's hand resting over hers. She'd been through some rough times in her life–times when she hadn't expected to pull out of the pit. But God had held her hand through all of those dark times. Had He sent Hadley to guide her through this limbo between fear and grief?

"Maybe I need to help her in a different way. If she could just get her doctor to set up the treatment plan, maybe you could help get her there and I could help pay for it."

"Sure, but do you have the money for that?" Hadley asked.

Thea let out a sarcastic laugh. “I don’t have much. Even less now that I’ll be getting a hefty hospital bill, but I’ve been training horses for years, and I saved every penny I could. I had plenty of time off to come here, but I didn’t expect to stay this long. My boss is understanding because I’ve never asked for anything, but I need to get back soon.”

“Why don’t you work here while you’re stuck?” Hadley asked.

“How?” Thea pointed to her injured ankle.

“We can always use extra hands around here. We can talk to Ava and Mr. Chambers about it. He’s the owner, and she’s his granddaughter. Ava’s pregnancy hasn’t been easy, and I’m sure she could use some help when she’s not feeling well and wants to just rest. Her morning sickness is brutal sometimes.”

“I’d love that. I need to earn my keep here, too.”

“You said you train horses? I bet Jess and Brett would love to have you at the barn too.”

Thea grimaced. “I’m not sure Jess will want my help.”

“Sure she would!”

“I don’t think you understand. I know Jess. She didn’t like me when we were teenagers, and I can guarantee she doesn’t like me now.”

“That’s ridiculous. Jess comes off as unfriendly, but she’s fiercely loyal.”

“That’s what I’m afraid of. Remember her dad? My dad? I left her brother? Ringing a bell?”

Hadley waved a hand in the air. "But you didn't do any of that. Well, except for the leaving Brett part. Why'd you do that anyway?"

"It's complicated."

"So I heard. I thought your family was dangerous. Why the mercy for your mom?"

"Mom isn't like the rest of them. She married my dad when she was young, and she loved him. My dad wasn't a good man, and he didn't grow up with a good sense of right and wrong. My uncles are the same. They don't have a bit of kindness in them."

"I'm sorry."

"I don't think Mom knew what she was getting into when she married Dad, but once she was in, it was like a life sentence. They couldn't get away from the family, and she basically spent her time trying to keep her kids out of danger."

"That's rough."

"I feel bad for her." It was the most Thea had voiced aloud about her mom's fate.

Her mom was a good woman, but for all her best efforts, she was going to lose what was left of her life without the hope of redemption. If Thea never got a chance to see her mom again, she would die without knowing what Thea had learned about God.

Pushing up onto her good foot, Thea reached for her crutches. "I need to get up. I can't take much more of this sitting."

Hadley was on her feet seconds later. "Sounds good. Let me show you to your new room."

The afternoon rushed by in a blur as Thea hobbled around the bedroom putting her things here and there. Hadley talked the entire time, and Thea only needed to respond every so often. Who needed a television when Hadley was full-time entertainment? She told stories about the kids at the ranch and the wild things that had happened since she moved to Blackwater five months ago.

When she'd been on her feet long enough that her ankle swelled in the brace, Thea eased onto the bed in her temporary room. She lay weightless with her eyes closed for ten seconds before her stomach rumbled.

"Ready for dinner?" Hadley asked.

"Starving."

"We have stuff to make sandwiches, or I could heat up a frozen pizza."

Thea grimaced as she rolled onto her side. "I need to give you some cash for groceries. I'll pay half of your rent while I'm here too."

"We'll talk about that later. We could go to the dining hall if you want. My meals are free, and I'm sure you can work something out with Mr. Chambers and Ava for meals. Especially if you'll be helping out around here."

Hadley's phone rang, and she pulled it out of her back pocket. "Hello."

Thea let her head rest back onto the bed, allowing Hadley to have some privacy.

"I'll ask her," Hadley said before pulling the phone away from her ear. "Brett wants to know if you're coming to supper at the dining hall."

"Do you want to go?" Thea asked Hadley.

Hadley nodded.

"Then let's go."

Hadley pressed the phone back to her ear. "We'll be there in a jiffy."

When she hung up the phone, she tossed it onto the bed and reached both hands out to Thea. Gently pulling her up from where she'd been lying on the bed, Hadley sang, "Up, up, upsy daisy."

Thea grunted through every movement. The pain in her chest wasn't easing.

"Do I look decent enough to meet new people?" she asked, looking down at her old sweater and sweatpants–the only pants she knew would fit over the brace. She could wear pants under it, but she hadn't taken the time to do that when she'd been so eager to leave the hospital.

"You look fine. Trust me, there isn't a beauty contest being judged around here. We're pretty casual."

With her crutches, Thea followed Hadley outside. The pain in her sides was amplified when she rested onto the crutches, but she couldn't go without them. Snow bordered the edges of the porch and covered the land as far as she could see. The only disturbed path was tire tracks where Brett had driven earlier.

The crutches sank a few inches into the fluffy snow, and keeping her braced leg lifted was a workout she hadn't expected. The bottom hem of her pants was soaked within minutes.

Of all the things she missed about home, the snow wasn't one of them. Thankfully, Hadley's car was parked close to the porch.

Thea sank into the passenger seat and gently lifted her crutches into the back. "How far is the dining hall?"

"Just over that hill. You drove close to it when you came in," Hadley said as she backed up and turned to follow Brett's tracks.

Three minutes later, they parked beside half a dozen other vehicles in front of a long building with a porch that extended from one end to the other.

"That's the main house," Hadley said, pointing to the left. "That's the check-in office. The admin offices are behind it. This is the dining hall, and the dance hall is connected on the back side."

Thea looked around. "It's nice to have it all right here together."

"It sure is. Let's go. I'll introduce you to folks. Looks like almost everyone is here."

Taking one step at a time, Thea pushed up one porch step after another. The pull in her chest was stifling. Maybe she should take Brett up on the offer to carry her more often.

Hadley held one of the double doors open, and Thea swung herself in. The inside of the dining hall was massive. Wide antler chandeliers hung from the open-rafter ceiling, a few tables were clustered near the serving bar, and the old wooden floor was scuffed and worn as if it had hosted hundreds of guests over the decades.

A high-pitched laugh pulled her attention to the nearest end of the serving bar where Brett held onto a little girl's hands while he swung her around. Her dark hair fanned out as Brett twirled in place. The girl couldn't have been older than four or five. When Brett sat her down, her smile was as bright as his.

"Again! Again!"

Thea stopped, captivated by the happiness in Brett's eyes. Seeing him playing with a kid was more than her fragile emotions could take.

"That's Abby. Colt and Remi's little girl," Hadley said.

Brett threw his hands in the air and bounced on his toes. "No, you do me this time. It's my turn."

The little girl laughed. "Mister Brett! I can't swing you!"

Brett looked up, and his eyes locked with Thea's in an instant. It was almost as if he'd felt her gaze on him. His bright smile didn't falter as he grabbed the little girl's hand. "Come on. I have someone I want you to meet."

It was going to be harder than Thea had expected to live this close to Brett and contain her feelings.

CHAPTER 12
BRETT

Brett swung Abby up into his arms, and her giggles turned into full-on belly laughs. Thea stood just inside the dining hall, watching him approach.

There was a magnet between them–a pulling force dragging him to her. It had been that way between him and Thea since the first time they met. He'd taken up his place beside her in their last semester of high school, and that connection didn't waver until she left.

Now, he didn't know what to do with that instinct.

He could understand the leaving. What he hadn't understood was why she hadn't trusted him. Now that she was here, he hated knowing he'd lost that time and possibly any chance of making a life with her.

Brett stopped in front of Thea and cradled Abby in his arms. "Thea, meet my main girl, Abby. Abby, this is my second favorite, Thea."

"Hey, Thea! Oh, you have a boo-boo."

Thea raised her hand to the bruised side of her face. The constant reminder of what Thea had gone through kept a fire burning in his veins. Maybe it was a good thing he didn't know who was responsible. He'd be all too tempted to give someone the fight they'd been asking for.

"It's just a bruise. I'm okay," Thea said.

"Oh, good." Abby pointed to Thea's crutches. "And you have four legs!"

Thea looked down at the crutches before smiling up at Abby. "I do. Hopefully, I'll get back to just two soon."

"Miss Cheyenne and Miss Hadley's mom has a carriage. It has wheels. You should get one of those. Then I could push you around!"

Thea tapped her finger on her chin. "That sounds like a good idea."

Hadley stepped up beside Thea and wrapped an arm around her. "Let's get to the food before Abby has you bedridden."

Brett flipped Abby over his shoulder, and she squealed in delight. "We're ready to eat. Let's see what's on the menu."

Abby giggled and kicked her legs as he strode

toward the serving bar. When he set her on her feet, she bounced up and down. "That was fun!"

Brett reached for a plate and handed it to Abby. "You can make your plate yourself?" Abby's independent streak had been showing out lately, and that usually meant he'd be trailing behind her to pick up the mess she left.

"Yeah," Abby said.

"That's yes, sir!" Remi shouted from the other end of the buffet line.

"Yes, sir," Abby whispered.

Brett took another plate and moved to stand between Abby and Thea. "I'll make your plate."

Thea took her hands off the crutches and flopped them back down to her sides, realizing she couldn't hold a plate and move both crutches. "Thanks. I hadn't even thought of that."

"I want to help Miss Thea!" Abby said.

Brett's brows lifted, but he stepped back, letting Thea stand near Abby.

"Thanks so much. You're sweet to help."

Abby brushed her long hair behind her shoulder. "I like to help." She pushed up onto her tiptoes to see over the bar. "What do you want first?"

Thea scanned the bar. "I don't know. It all looks so good. What's your favorite?"

"The blackberry cobber. It's yummy," Abby said.

"Cobbler!" Ben shouted from the closest table. "There's an L in it."

"Who is that?" Thea asked as she bent down closer to Abby.

"That's my brother. His name is Ben."

"Will you introduce me later?" Thea asked.

"Yeah! I can tell you everybody," Abby said.

Thea reached for a serving spoon in the mashed potatoes, but Abby reached up at the same time.

"I can do it!" Abby said.

Thea pulled her hand back and let Abby wrestle with the big spoon.

Brett piled food on his own plate and watched Thea and Abby. It seemed he wasn't needed. He took a seat at a table next to Colt and Remi, and Thea and Abby joined him a few minutes later.

Abby held Thea's attention through the whole meal. Without a chance to get a word in, Brett's plate was clean first, and he waited while Thea listened intently to Abby's chatter about living at the ranch.

"And Mommy says I can start learning to ride the horses this year. I want to ride the little ones. The big ones scare me."

Thea nodded. "I get that. I was scared of the big ones at first too. But horses are all different. Sometimes, the little ones are tougher to handle than the big ones."

"That's what Daddy said." Abby leaned over and lifted a hand to whisper in Thea's ear, but the whisper wasn't very quiet. "Colt and Remi aren't our real Mommy and Daddy, but they said we can call them that."

Thea's eyes widened as she looked up at Colt and Remi.

Brett leaned over to whisper in Thea's other ear. "They're Colt's brother's kids. He and his wife died in a car wreck about six months ago."

Thea gasped, then quickly controlled her expression. The wreck and the kids had been a shock for all of them last September, but the kids seemed happy to be at the ranch with Colt and Remi.

They'd all done their best to make the kids feel at home. It couldn't replace their parents, but Colt and Remi adopted the kids just before Christmas. Ben and Abby didn't miss out on any love, that was for sure.

Remi pulled out her phone and read something on the screen. "Miss Stella is on her way to pick you up. Take your plates to the trash if you're finished," she said pointing to the kids.

Abby jumped up, dragging her plate with her. "I gotta go, but we'll have more fun tomorrow, right?" she asked Thea.

"Definitely. Thanks for introducing me to everyone."

"I'll let you meet Miss Stella later. We're in a hurry 'cause we have cookies to make tonight."

Thea waved. "Sounds like fun. I'll see you soon."

Remi leaned forward with her elbows propped

on the table. "I think we're going to play some trivia in a little bit. Are you in?"

"I am!" Hadley said quickly

Brett looked to Thea. "You feel up to it?"

Thea shrugged. "I don't think I'll be any good at it."

"You never know. I'd pick you to be on my team anyway."

Colt scoffed. "What are you talking about? You gave everyone the silent treatment for a full day after you lost at Pictionary."

Remi put a hand up beside her mouth. "Brett is a sore loser."

"I am not! There's nothing wrong with *wanting* to win."

Thea held up her hands. "Maybe I can just be the judge or the host."

Brett bumped Thea's shoulder. "I'm a little competitive, but I'm mostly competing with myself. I just like to get better all the time, and if I don't win because I messed up a lot–"

"You get moody," Remi said.

Brett threw his hands in the air. "Okay, maybe I get moody. I'd still like to be on your team."

Everything was better with Thea by his side. Games, work, life–it was all a little brighter when she was around.

Thea glanced back and forth between Brett and

Remi. "Okay, I'll play, but I don't want any complaining when we lose."

"Shh. Don't say that. We're not going to lose," Brett said.

"What's the prize for winning?" Thea asked.

"Bragging rights," Colt said. "I think Jameson and Ava want to play too. Jess said she might come, and she could be on Hadley's team. I'll let them know we're ready."

Everyone tossed their scraps, and Brett picked up a rag. He wiped the tables before going back to help put away the leftovers. Thea was talking to Vera, the main cook, and helping cover everything with foil.

"I spent some time in Alabama when I was a kid," Vera said. "My mom was a nurse, and she got a job at a hospital there. We were in Birmingham, so it was a whole lot different from what I was used to."

"I see you met Vera," Brett said. "She's the genius behind all the good food around here."

Vera grinned and tucked her chin. The older woman was a total sweetheart. She had a heart as big as the west, but she couldn't take a compliment without turning bright red from the neck up.

"Oh, I just love cooking for folks. It's a blessing I get to do it every day," Vera said.

"Jess!" Hadley said.

Brett turned and waved a hand at his sister. She gave one look at Thea beside him and said something to Hadley before turning around and walking back out.

"I guess that means Jess still doesn't care for me," Thea whispered.

"Don't worry about her," Brett said.

"It's because she's afraid I'm going to lead the trouble back to your door."

Brett held Thea's gaze and resisted the urge to pull her close. He'd promised to give her space. "Let them come."

"But these people might get caught in the crossfire. I don't want to risk that. They don't deserve what's coming for me."

Brett turned so he was facing her. Why couldn't she understand? "Whatever comes for you has to go through me first, and I dare anyone to try."

Thea stared up at him, but there was still a swarm of indecision hidden in that look.

"I won't let anything happen to you. We'll be so careful, they won't have a chance to get to you."

With a sigh, she looked down. "Only until I can leave."

She was still talking about leaving. Clearly, she didn't care about him half as much as he cared about her. What had changed?

"Thea, I know you hate being here. I know why you want to leave." He sighed, ready to verbally admit his defeat. If she didn't feel the same way, they didn't have a chance at making things work.

"I don't hate being *here*. This place is amazing, and the people are too. I know why you love it, and I'm glad you found a home here. I just can't live the rest of my life in Blackwater, constantly looking over my shoulder wondering when they'll be back to finish what they started."

"I get that. What I don't understand is why your family hates you enough to do this to you."

The back door of the dining hall opened, and Jameson and Ava walked in. Thea carefully turned to look behind her, snapping the tension of their conversation.

So much for answers. He brushed a hand through his hair, fighting the urge to pull it all out.

Ava's pregnancy was showing now, and she always cradled her stomach when she walked. Kids were everywhere he looked these days. Ben and Abby, Ava and Jameson's upcoming arrival, and Colt and Remi were expecting too. Brett didn't mind. He'd always connected with kids. Jess always said it was because he was still a kid. Whatever the reason, he was looking forward to a new generation at the ranch.

Thea laid a hand on Brett's arm, effectively shutting off all other thoughts in his head.

"I need to talk to them about staying here and meals and stuff," she said.

Brett had already mentioned it to Jameson and Ava, but Thea would want to talk to them herself.

Ava had been excited about the prospect of having more help in the offices, at least until Thea's leg healed more. Jameson had been interested in Thea's equine experience.

Would she even stay that long? What would happen when she was ready to leave? Would she skip town without a good-bye like last time?

No. They would talk about it first. Conversations came easy between them now. They were older and wiser, weren't they?

Ava spotted Thea and made her way over. Thea took a few steps on her crutches to meet her.

"Hey. I heard you'd made it," Ava said. "I wanted to come by and introduce myself earlier, but I figured you'd be getting settled in."

"Thank you so much for letting me stay. I promise I'll be out of your hair as soon as I can travel."

Brett's heart sank to his stomach. Did she just need to get away from Blackwater, or would she be happy to be rid of him too?

"No rush!" Ava extended her hand. "I'm Ava, and this is my husband, Jameson."

Thea shook both hands and said hello. "I'm Thea. I used to know Brett when we were younger. And Jess," she added.

"Well, we're happy to have you here. I know you're not able to get around very well, but I'd love to have your help in the office. We're cranking up for the tourist season, and I could use some help with the phones and registrations."

"I'd love that. Just tell me what to do," Thea said.

"Great. We'll work out a contract position and the details in the morning. Until then, you can consider the meals and housing as a perk of the job."

"I can't thank you enough. I've been feeling useless lately, and I'm ready to get back to work."

"Brett said you trained horses," Ava said. "We'd love to talk about moving you to a position at the stables when your ankle heals."

Thea glanced back at him before turning back to Jameson and Ava. "Oh, I don't know. I need to get back to Alabama when I'm able to travel."

Ava waved a hand in the air. "Right. I understand. You already have a job. We're just happy to have you here for now. Make yourself at home, and let me know if you need anything. Here's my number." She pulled a card from her back pocket and extended it to Thea.

"Thanks again," Thea said as she studied the card.

"You're very welcome. Now, let's play some trivia!"

"I'll be the host," Hadley said. "Jess can't play tonight, so I'm the odd woman out."

Brett gently laid his hand on Thea's shoulder. "Let's get you a seat on the end so you can prop up your foot."

Turned out, Thea wasn't as bad at trivia as she claimed. Hadley proudly displayed the third iron horse statue in front of them.

"That's another round for Brett and Thea," Hadley said.

Thea's innocent giggle made her look eighteen again. "What are these?" she asked as she picked up the bucking horse.

"They're decorations from the check-in office. We don't get to keep them. But there was one time when the prizes were Slim Jims. Now that really felt like winning."

Thea opened her mouth and acted like she was sticking a finger down her throat. "Gross."

Brett leaned forward and pointed a finger at her. "Them's fightin' words."

Thea laughed again. "Bring it on then because that fake meat is disgusting. It's right up there with breakfast sausage."

Brett's eyes widened and he looked around. "Don't let Vera hear you say that. Her sausage is to die for, and her sausage gravy has won awards. *Awards*. Plural."

Thea clapped a hand over her mouth and glanced at Vera by the serving counter. She was busy chatting with Paul. The older wrangler only stopped by when he knew Vera wasn't swamped during meals.

Brett leaned in and whispered close to Thea's

ear. “I’ve been trying to get those two together for years.”

“They aren’t married?” Thea asked.

“No. They’re both too scared to make the first move.” Brett clicked his tongue. “It’s a shame because she’s the only person he’ll say more than two words to, and she turns red whenever he walks in the room.”

Thea reached down to pet the dog at her feet. Paul’s best friend was closer to a massive wolf than a house dog. Thane had taken up with Thea as soon as they’d been introduced, which Brett had always thought was a sign of trustworthiness. Dogs could sense those things.

Thane could probably also sense that Thea needed help. As far as Brett was concerned, he and the wolf were on the same team.

“One more round?” Hadley asked.

“No more for us. I’m exhausted,” Ava said.

“We’re calling it a night then,” Jameson said.

“I second that,” Remi chimed in. “I’m tired, but I didn’t want to be the first one to say it.”

Hadley shrugged with her palms in the air. “And I think that makes Brett and Thea our winners.”

Brett slapped his palms on the table and whooped. “I knew we were a winning team!”

Thea rolled her eyes, but her grin said she was pleased with the praise. “I think we just got lucky.”

“Luck? We won that game fair and square.”

Hadley stepped up to the table beside Brett and Thea. "I'm gonna stay a little bit and help Vera clean up the kitchen."

"Oh no. You go on home," Vera said. "I've got this."

"I actually wanted to talk to you about something," Hadley said quietly.

Brett chuckled. "Now no one is curious."

"I like secrets!" Colt said.

Hadley rolled her eyes and leaned in to whisper, "I wanted to talk to her about Ava's baby shower. Will you kids keep your voices down?"

Brett put a finger in front of his lips. "Sorry."

Hadley turned to Thea. "I know you're tired. This won't take long."

"I'll take her home," Brett offered.

Thea opened her mouth–probably to object–but Hadley was already heading toward the kitchen. "Thanks! I'll be there soon."

Brett grabbed the crutches and handed them to Thea. "You ready?"

"Thanks." She adjusted herself above the crutches and started toward the door without missing a beat, waving good-bye to everyone she passed.

Apparently, Thea was skilled in using crutches and making friends.

It was dark when they stepped out of the dining hall, and Brett walked in front of Thea, making sure the path was clear and the truck door was open and waiting for her.

When they settled into the truck, Thea shivered. "It's so cold. I'm not used to this anymore."

"Did you bring more layers? I can go into town tomorrow to get you a new phone and some clothes." He didn't glance at her in the dark cab. It had to be bothering her to hide out in her hometown. "I'd say you could go with me, but–"

"I know. Thanks for offering. I think I'll take you up on that if it won't mess up your day."

"Not at all. What size do you wear?"

"Medium, usually. I'll give you some money."

Brett shook his head. "It's on me. I don't have many reasons to spend money, and I'd like to help you out."

"You have been helping. Too much."

Brett sighed. Despite his efforts, he was still coming on too strong. "I'm sorry. I just want to make things easier for you. I can't change what happened, and I can't heal your injuries, so I'm just trying to do whatever I can."

"I know, and I'm thankful for everything you do. You're so sweet."

Sweet. He was sweet. It was a far cry from the "I love you" she used to say. He got it. They were different people. Older and wiser and all that. But if there was a part of the old Thea that still remained, it could only be better now. They'd both found

Christ and learned from a lot of mistakes. That had to equal something.

Brett pulled up in front of the cabin and parked the truck. "I'd like to come in and get the fire going."

Thea smiled, and the dim moonlight lit up her joy. "I'd really appreciate that. It's been a long time since I built a fire, and I'd do a lot of fumbling around with this thing." She pointed to her bulky brace.

He turned off the truck and jogged around to her side. He pulled her crutches out of the back and held them out to her. "Any chance I could carry you inside?"

She hesitated before that sweet smile lifted her cheeks. "I guess that would be okay."

Brett wanted to fist pump the air but contained his excitement. Leaving the crutches by the truck, he cradled Thea in his arms. He held her as close as possible, not knowing when he'd get the chance to be this close again.

Inside, he gently sat her on the couch, propping her foot up on the coffee table. "I'll be right back with your crutches."

He darted to the truck and picked them up just as his phone rang. It was Asa. It was a good bet that whatever was on the other end of the line wasn't good news. Brett answered just as he stepped back inside the cabin.

"Hey, boss."

"Hey. Are you with Thea?"

Brett walked around the couch and sat next to her. "I am. Want to talk to her?"

"If I can."

Brett handed the phone to Thea. "It's Asa."

She stared at the phone for half a second as if it might explode before taking it and pressing it to her ear. "Hello."

Thea listened for a few seconds before she said, "Can you hold on a second? I'd like to put this call on the speaker so Brett can hear too." She held the phone between them and pressed the button. "Okay."

"We heard from Tommy Howard today," Asa said. "He filed a missing person report for you."

CHAPTER 13
THEA

"A what?" Thea said. "Why? He shouldn't even know I'm here." Panic rose in her throat like claws scraping down the walls. Tommy knew she was here and wanted to find her.

"His statement says his niece, Emerson, claimed you came into town on Saturday and that she hasn't seen you since Tuesday," Asa said.

"Well, that's true that I came to town on Saturday, but she knew where I was."

"Until today when you checked out of the hospital," Brett added.

Staring at Brett, she scraped for words. They'd decided to tell Emerson Thea was going back to Alabama, but she hadn't come back to the hospital, and they didn't want to call her and stir up more trouble.

"She knows I don't have a phone. She returned

the car I rented, and she brought my bag to the hospital."

"This is ridiculous," Brett said as he stood and started pacing the room. He pushed his fingers into his hair and huffed.

The same nervous energy hummed in her limbs. Too many people knew she'd come back to town. They knew it was only a matter of time before Tommy found out and did whatever he wanted to mess with her. She'd stupidly thought she could get out of here without being noticed.

"They just want to finish what they started," Brett said. "You can't tell him where she is."

"We won't. Thea is an adult, and if she doesn't want to be found, we don't have to disclose her information," Asa said.

"Good. Then we don't have to worry about it," Brett said as he sat beside her.

Thea shrugged. "I guess not."

"He might try to cause a scene," Asa said. "I don't know what his plans are. Just keep your eyes open, and let us know if anything happens."

"We will," Thea said.

"We'll keep her completely out of sight until she's well enough to travel home."

Thea wrung her fingers in her lap. Could she get someone to drive her home? It was a long drive, and they'd have to stop often for her to elevate her foot.

"Thanks for letting us know. We appreciate the heads up," Brett said.

"Anytime. Have a good evening."

Thea ended the call and stared at the phone. "I hate this," she whispered.

Brett reached for her hand holding the phone and lowered it to the seat of the couch. "I won't let anyone hurt you."

"I don't know why they want to do this. I mean, I sort of know why, but not really."

"I guess siding with a Patton is incriminating enough."

She slumped against the back of the couch and wrapped her arms around her middle. She was putting all of these people in danger just by being here.

Brett stood and went to the fireplace. Would he figure out it was best to get her out of here? She had no car and could barely walk. Add on the hefty hospital bill she would be getting soon, and everyone might as well kick her while she was down.

The door opened, and Hadley walked in, letting in the cold. "Brr." She shivered and hung her coat on the rack by the door. When she turned to Brett and Thea, she came to an abrupt stop. "What's wrong?"

"My uncle filed a missing person report for me," Thea said.

Hadley's eyes widened. "Oh, no, no, no. The police didn't tell him anything, did they?"

"No, but it means he knows I'm here, and he's looking for me."

Hadley sucked a breath through her teeth. "That's not good."

Brett sat on the coffee table in front of Thea. His usual carefree demeanor was gone, replaced with quiet calculation. "I won't let them find you."

"I know you want to keep me safe, but they know I'm here. I'm sure they know where you live. They keep tabs on all of their enemies."

"But they can't get to you here. We upped security not long after they built the wedding chapel and started having public events here," Brett said.

"It's still not safe," she whispered.

"Would it be better to get you back to Alabama? There's a good chance they'd try to follow us," Brett said.

"I've thought about that. I'm sure they have someone watching this place, but I can't stand the thought of putting anyone else in danger."

Thea looked from Brett to Hadley. Her complexion had paled, and she was staring at the fire.

"I need to go," Thea said. "I can't do this to Hadley."

"Wait," Hadley said. "You can stay. I'm okay with it."

"I'm not," Thea said as she tried to push up from the couch. Her arms ached from the stitches and bruises.

"No." Hadley moved around the couch to stand in front of Thea. "You're still so beat up. It would be hard to ride in a car that far like this, and you're not released to fly. What if you got in the air and your lung collapsed? I think we need to be vigilant."

"I could stay."

Brett's deep words vibrated in Thea's chest. Of course, Brett had always put himself between her and danger. He hadn't known it back then, but he'd saved her years of this mess. He was the reason she left, but he was also the reason she wanted to stay. She'd desperately wanted to stay.

"Just during the night," Brett said. "I think if you stay around the main house or the barn during the day, you'll always have someone nearby in case something happens. I could sleep on the couch at night and leave first thing in the morning."

Thea looked down, shaking her head. "That's–"

"I think that's a good idea," Hadley interrupted.

Thea looked to Hadley and saw determination mixed with resolution. She was afraid but still willing to step up and help.

"I don't mind Brett being here. It'd make me feel better about your safety, and it can't hurt," Hadley said, lifting her hands in the air.

Thea looked back to Brett who watched her, waiting patiently for her answer.

"I promised to give you space, and I'll stand by that. You won't even know I'm here," Brett promised.

Hadley stepped across the room toward her bedroom. "I'll let you two decide. Just know I'm okay with it either way."

"Thanks," Thea said. Defeat settled heavy on her shoulders. Hadley had opened her home, and Thea had done nothing but disrupt her new friend's life.

The bedroom door closed quietly behind Hadley, and Thea waited for Brett to speak first. She still didn't have a clear decision.

"Hadley is honest. If she didn't want you to be here, she'd say so," Brett said.

Thea rested her head against the back of the couch. The day had been long, and she hadn't had the usual nap she'd gotten used to during her hospital stay. She'd also moved around a lot more, and most of her joints and bruises were screaming in protest.

"Okay." She rolled her head to the side and looked at him. The genuine care in his dark eyes made her want to reach for that safety. "I'd like for you to stay. If you're sure it's okay."

Brett gave her that half smile that sent flutters through her stomach. "I'd love to. And I promise I won't be moving in. Just sleeping here. I'll leave all my things at my place."

"You said you were looking for a new roommate," she said.

Brett chuckled low. "I wasn't expecting you."

"I wasn't expecting you either. Or any of this."

He stared at her for an extra heartbeat. That pause was enough to captivate her.

"I have a few things to wrap up tonight, but I'll be back shortly." He stood and checked the fire before stopping at her side. "Do you need anything?"

A new family. A new life. A leg that worked. A lung that wasn't ready to give out.

Brett. All the things she couldn't have.

"I'm fine. Thanks."

"See you soon."

He left without much noise, and Thea was alone with her thoughts. Had she made the right decision? Would she be able to keep her distance from Brett when he was always helping and doing things for her?

She didn't want to. Why not give in?

Thea groaned and tossed her head back. Things between them had been messy from the start, but they'd managed to tangle everything into a knot.

She closed her eyes and swallowed past the sting in her throat.

"Lord, what am I doing? Where do I need to go?" she whispered.

Then, the real crux of her desires floated back to the surface.

"Please help my mom. I don't know anything about cancer or anything else, but I know I love her, and I don't want to lose her. She's the only person who ever loved me, and I–"

That wasn't true. Brett had said he loved her back then, and she'd truly believed him. He'd been loyal to his core–willing to stand beside her in the face of their families.

But could that young love have survived? She didn't regret leaving Blackwater, but leaving Brett...

Hadley's bedroom door creaked, and she peeked out into the living room. "You okay?"

"Yeah. Just trying to solve all the problems," Thea said as she pushed to sit up straighter.

"No need to rush. They'll be waiting for all of us in the morning."

Thea chuckled. "That's what I'm afraid of. And every morning after that."

Hadley rested a hand on Thea's shoulder. "You need rest. It's been a long day. You're still healing."

"I should just go home," Thea whispered.

"What happens when you get there? Do you have someone to drive you to your follow-up appointments? Do you have someone who can help you shop for groceries?"

Hadley raised some of the questions Thea had been asking herself. She'd inevitably find herself stuck without help, and she'd probably mess up her fragile lung at the very least. The leg brace would be gone soon, but she'd really messed up her ankle when she continued to run for her life after twisting it. "Not really. I have friends, and some of the ladies at church would help, but they're mostly older. It's a small church."

"Then let's table those thoughts. At least for a few days. Brett won't let anything happen to you, and the ranch is truly safer now. There were some incidents this past year that brought up the need for heightened security. Jameson has been focused on it all winter."

Thea pushed up onto her good leg and grabbed the crutches. "I guess I need to get ready for bed before Brett gets back."

"He's a good one, you know?"

"I do. And there was a time when I thought that was a good thing. Now, it just makes it harder to pretend I don't care about him."

"Then don't pretend. What's holding you back?"

"Everything. The odds were always stacked against us, and for a while, I thought we were meant to weather that storm together. Then I started doubting his innocence, and everything got messed up." Thea rubbed a hand over her brow. The confusion was just as strong as ever. "It's almost like my feelings are being decided for me. Like, we were such a sure thing back then. Did I even think about it before falling headlong into love? I guess I didn't have much of a choice. You feel what you feel, right?"

Hadley shrugged. "I wouldn't know. I've never been in love."

Hadley stood and wrapped her arms around Thea. Resting into the comfort, she let the silent tears go. It didn't help anything to keep them bottled up, and pretty soon, the little bits of hope she kept collecting would make her want to believe she and Brett might actually be able to win, despite the odds stacked against them.

But that was a fool's dream. The happy life they'd imagined when they were younger had only been a vapor–a fantasy they'd made up when they'd been drunk on love and dreams.

"So, big question coming," Hadley said as she pulled out of the hug.

Thea wiped her tears and hardened her heart. "Bring it on."

"How are you going to shower with one working leg?"

A loud laugh burst from Thea's chest before she could rein it in, and she immediately clutched her chest. "I have no idea. Very carefully?"

"I'll help. We'll figure it out in the morning."

"Thanks. It's probably overdue, but I'm about

fifteen minutes from crashing. There's no way I could take on the shower monster tonight."

Hadley jerked her head toward the bathroom. "You can have the bathroom first."

"I won't be long."

Long was a relative term because it took a few too many minutes to brush her teeth and comb through her dirty hair. A shower was definitely the first thing on the to-do list tomorrow. One of the nurses had washed the blood out of her hair, but whatever shampoo they'd used made her hair feel like a horse's mane.

Maybe she'd get to the stables soon. Ava had work waiting for her in the main offices, but she'd been praying to catch a glimpse of the horses all day. She'd been lucky to snag the job at Lakeshore Stables when she moved to Alabama, and the horses had helped her through that dark time as much as the people. The silent friends had been all the therapy she'd needed.

She braved a glimpse at herself in the small mirror and regretted it. The bruises were purple along the crescent below her left eye. The split in her lip was closed but still looked gruesome. One thing she hadn't noticed before were the finger-shaped bruises on the side of her neck.

What a perfect visual of the hand that had held her down her whole life. Howards or Pattons, they'd choked the life out of her in more ways than one.

She stepped out of the bathroom just as Brett walked in the front door. He wore a thick jacket, red flannel pajama pants, and work boots. He shrugged out of the jacket and hung it on the rack by the door. Blankets and a pillow lay on the couch, ready for their nighttime bodyguard.

"Hey, I figured you'd be asleep already."

The gray T-shirt he wore hugged his chest and back in all the right places. She definitely liked the relaxed look on him. "I was headed that way."

He toed off his boots by the door and stuck his hands in his pockets as he approached her. "Good night. Sleep tight."

"Good night," she whispered back as she turned and hobbled to her bedroom.

With the door shut behind her, she rested all of her weight against it. A quiet peace settled around her. She *would* have a good night, all because Brett was standing guard right outside her door.

She'd prayed for help, and the Lord had sent her a protector–one she didn't deserve.

CHAPTER 14
BRETT

Brett's alarm vibrated against his hand under the pillow. He'd turned off the sound, afraid he'd wake Thea and Hadley before the sun. He'd always been a light sleeper, and thankfully, there hadn't been a single sound in the night.

Rolling over, he turned off the alarm and rested his arm over his eyes. Tommy wouldn't give up easily, and Brett wouldn't either. Thankfully, Hadley's couch was new and pretty comfortable. It had served him well the last two nights.

He took a few minutes to thank the Lord for another day, pulled on his shirt, and folded the blankets. After slipping on his jacket and boots, he faced the frigid morning. God really knew how to sprinkle the fluffy white stuff on Wyoming. They got their fair share, that was for sure. Winter wasn't his favorite time of the year, but maybe it would allow him to spend some time with Thea.

He pulled up at his cabin and found Linc already making coffee in the small kitchen.

"Morning, sunshine," Brett said as he took off his jacket and boots.

"Morning. All quiet on the western front?" Linc asked.

"All good. I think we'll at least have a few minute's heads up thanks to the security system Jameson put in. Tommy isn't the brightest bulb in the box."

Linc raised his mug of coffee. "It's not smart to underestimate your enemy."

Brett crossed his arms over his chest and leaned against the counter. "I hate that I have enemies. It's stupid. I haven't spoken to my family in years."

"Comes with the territory," Linc said.

"What territory? I didn't do anything wrong."

"You inherited a lot of hate. It's kind of stuck on you."

"Yeah, my parents weren't winning any awards for kindness. Mom was as mean as a snake before Dad died. She was worse after."

His dad had been the breadwinner, working long hours for a trucking company based in Cody. His mom had been free to sit at home and stir up trouble. When Brett's dad died, she moved in with her sister, who spouted enough hate to turn his mom's callous heart completely to stone.

Brett huffed, still ticked at his mom after all these years. "She didn't try to put on airs and pretend she was a good mom or even a good person. She hated everyone, and Dad was the same. They were the perfect pocket pair. It took a lot to get over all that anger. My anger at them. Their anger at the Howards and everyone else they decided to team up against."

Linc sipped his coffee. "Makes me glad I didn't have parents."

Linc was Brett's opposite. He was stern, quiet, and didn't go out of his way to be friendly. But there was a heavy second where Brett actually envied the guy. Would it have been better to be orphaned and at the mercy of the state or grow up being beaten and hated by his parents? Was that the reason Linc pushed people away? Probably.

Jess had dealt with their parents' abuse a whole lot differently than Brett had. She'd held in the anger until they were safely away from their parents before she lashed out on someone or something else. Brett had silently endured it, repressed everything, then hid the darkness behind a wall of humor. It beat giving in and letting the sadness take over.

"I don't know which one is worse, having terrible parents or no parents at all," Brett said.

"I didn't need any help being a screw-up. I did it just fine on my own."

That was another difference between Brett and Linc. Brett still had hope that he could be better than all the bad he'd seen. Linc talked like his fate was sealed.

"You turned out pretty decent. At least you have good taste in friends." Brett grinned and pointed to his chest.

"Who said we're friends?"

"I said. There was a meeting, and the vote was unanimous."

Linc poured out the last sip of his coffee and left the mug in the sink. "Great talk, but I've learned a few things the hard way."

"Oh, yeah? Like what?"

"Don't make friends. I'll keep my eye out for trouble," Linc said over his shoulder as he headed toward his bedroom.

"We're friends!" Brett shouted. "Like it or not."

Linc's bedroom door closed with a nice thud of wood on wood.

Whatever. Linc talked a lot of gloom and doom, but everyone knew they could count on him when they needed help. He just hadn't figured out that actions spoke louder than words.

By the time Brett was showered and dressed, the first signs of the sun were filtering through the windows. Hadley would be up, so he texted her.

He'd spent the day yesterday getting caught up on work while Thea slept most of the day and night.

Brett: I'm going to town to get Thea a new phone. Will you ask her if she has a cell plan and if she needs anything else while I'm out?

Hadley texted back with the name of the service provider and a request for comfortable pants for Thea. It had been a long time since he'd worn a leg brace, and he'd forgotten about that never-ending discomfort.

He climbed into the truck and checked the clock on the dash. He had a little more than an hour before he needed to be at the barn. The general store opened in fifteen minutes, and the cell phone store opened a little after that.

The store had a few pickup trucks in the parking lot, and he made his way straight to the trash bags. On his way to the register, he picked up a bottle of pain relievers.

A helium balloon attached to a display table in the bakery section caught his eye. Thea would like a cupcake too. Strawberry. She'd eaten the one he got her at the hospital like she was starving.

Half a dozen cupcakes it was, then.

A bouquet of pink and yellow flowers caught his eye. He didn't know what kind they were, but they were pretty, and Thea needed something pretty.

Ten minutes later, he checked out of the store ten pounds heavier and fifty dollars lighter.

The cell store was open, and he was able to get Thea a new phone after a bunch of back and forth about plans and contracts. He'd had to call Thea on Hadley's phone so she could give him permission to buy a phone for her while she couldn't be present. He gave himself a good pat on the back for keeping his temper in check when it seemed way too complicated to just buy a cell phone.

Back at the ranch, he found Thea in Ava's office. He knocked on the open door, but the women had seen him coming, or at least heard him. His boots thudded against the old wooden floor.

"You two keeping this train on the tracks?" he asked as he leaned against the doorframe. It was Thea's first day "on the job," and if things went well, maybe she could be convinced to stay.

"Always," Ava said. "Whatcha got there?"

Brett pulled the container of cupcakes from under his arm. "A mid-morning snack."

"It's still early morning, but feel free to come back at mid-morning with another surprise," Ava said.

He put the cupcakes on Ava's desk, handed the new phone to Thea, and sat in a chair. "Don't tempt me. I've been looking for a reason to sneak back over here later."

Thea slipped the phone into her pocket, said a quiet "Thank you," and looked down at the papers on the desk in front of her.

Ava reached for the cupcakes. "I know you brought these for Thea, but I'm having one."

Thea giggled. If she'd lift her chin, he'd get a chance to check her bruises this morning. And he'd get a look at her pretty face. He'd been imagining it wrong these last five years. She'd been beautiful back then, but she was gorgeous now.

She was hot. Bruises and all. No way around it. He hadn't seen her in makeup or with her hair fixed any way other than brushing it, and he had trouble looking away from her most times.

Thea reached for a cupcake and glanced at him for half a second. "Thank you."

"You're welcome. And my work here is done." He stood and tipped his hat at Ava before doing the same to Thea and adding a wink.

"See you at lunch," Ava said around a mouthful of cupcake.

His next stop was Hadley and Thea's cabin. He left the goodies on the table and found a tall glass for the flowers. If Hadley had a vase, he didn't find it.

He pulled up at the barn right on time. Jess's truck was already parked out front, and the barn doors were open. He ran into Jess in the tack room and stepped around her to get Vanilla's grooming supplies.

When he reached for the crate, Jess lifted her chin. "She's got an infection around her shoe. Tucker said to use that antibiotic on it."

Brett studied the new ointment in Vanilla's crate. "Did he look at Kiwi's leg while he was here?"

"He said it's arthritis. We'll probably retire her after this year."

Brett nodded and got to work. Jess wasn't on board with the Thea situation yet, and he knew enough to give his sister space. They'd done a fantastic job dancing around the elephant in the room yesterday, and it seemed today would be the same. He'd never been in the habit of telling his younger sister what to do, but there were times–like now–when he wanted to tell her to stop being stubborn.

Avoiding Jess was easier than he'd expected. She spent the morning training their newest horse, Geyser, and Brett took his time giving each horse a thorough check as he groomed them.

His phone dinged with a text as soon as he put Jethro in his stall.

Ava: Thea wants to know if you're coming to lunch. I think she wants to save you a seat.

Brett grinned down at his phone like a goof. The hearts at the end of the text said Ava was playing matchmaker.

Brett: I'll be there in five.

He put Jethro's grooming supplies away and washed his hands. Jess stepped out of a stall on the other side of the indoor arena.

"I'm going to lunch. You want me to bring you a plate?"

"No need," Linc said as he walked in. He held up a white container.

So, Linc would bring Jess lunch, but he wouldn't even be friends with Brett? They were roommates, for Pete's sake. If he didn't know any better, he'd say Linc was interested in Jess. Only, Linc and Jess never seemed to be interested in anyone, and they weren't even slightly affectionate to each other.

"Thanks," Jess said as she pulled off her gloves. "Put it in the office, and I'll get to it in a little bit."

Linc put the food in the office and walked back out. He wasn't going to stay and eat with Jess. Definitely not interested.

Brett followed Linc out. "What's on the menu today?"

"Fried chicken." Linc didn't spare a friendly second to elaborate. Not that Brett's question had required more of an answer, but a "See you later" would have been nice.

Brett found Thea in the dining hall chatting with Jameson and Ava. Thea and Ava wore matching smiles. Linc could use a lesson from Thea on how to make friends.

She was definitely a social butterfly. All the women at the ranch wanted to sit beside her, effectively crowding Brett out of the cool kids space.

"Your girl is popular," Ridge said as he took the seat beside Brett.

"I'm glad they're being nice to her."

"Why wouldn't they be?"

Brett shrugged. "It's hard to understand why some people are good to you and some people are bad to you when you grew up thinking you sucked."

"Her parents were just as bad as yours?" Ridge asked.

"Her dad gave mine a run for his money, but her mom is good. That's where Thea gets it."

"That's tough. My parents would have done anything for me. Still would. They traveled all over the country with me when I was a teenager and came to almost every football game I played all the way through the pros."

"My parents just wanted to tear other people down for sport. It was like they hadn't done a hard day's work if they didn't screw up someone's life."

Ridge stopped eating long enough to study Thea. "She must be tough if she can handle all that and still smile."

Brett watched her as she used her hands to tell Hadley some story. Her lips were moving a mile a minute, and her eyes were brighter than he'd seen them in days.

Seeing her happy was the only thing he'd been craving for almost a week now, but he hadn't thought of it in the same way Ridge had. He'd been thinking of her as a fragile flower, easily crushed by the first hoof to stomp on it. It really was a miracle she could still lift her chin and face the days knowing the evil that had beaten her down so many times.

"You're right. I haven't been giving her enough credit. She's been doing a good job of handling things on her own. I just hate seeing her upset. It makes me sick to my stomach."

"That's something they never told us about relationships–that we'll feel whatever they feel. When Cheyenne gets upset about her mom's health, it makes me want to either punch a wall or puke."

Brett gave his friend a side glance. "That is surprisingly accurate. I think living with Hadley will help Thea come to grips with what's going on with her mom."

"Maybe. Cheyenne and Hadley's mom has good days and bad days, so get ready for that roller coaster."

Brett rested his forehead in his hands. "She deserves to be able to see her mom. She's the one person Thea has always been able to count on. She's probably the one who told Thea to leave in the first place."

"You're not upset about that?" Ridge asked.

"Sounds like Cheyenne filled you in on our shared history. To be honest, I was mad when she first left. Livid. Then I was upset because I thought we were in it for the long haul, and apparently, she didn't feel the same. After a while, I got over it enough to be able to look back and admit that she needed to get out of here. We both wanted to leave, and I couldn't really blame her for doing it."

Ridge nodded. "I've thought the same about Cheyenne."

Ridge hadn't met his bride-to-be in the most conventional way. She'd come to the ranch to ruin his life, all for a hefty sum of money that would help pay for her mom's medical bills.

Come to think of it, that sounded a lot like Thea. She'd do anything for her mom, including put herself in danger.

Ridge stood and picked up his empty plate. "I've gotta run. I have to pick up my tux and make sure it fits."

"When is the wedding again?"

Ridge paused. "Dude, you're in the wedding. Please tell me you know when to show up."

Brett grinned. "I'm just messing with you. Can I bring a date?"

"I think Cheyenne already invited Thea."

"Good." Maybe if she'd already planned to go, she wouldn't mind being his date.

If she was still here. The wedding was over a month away.

Ava stood and headed toward the trash can. Brett jumped up to meet her.

"Hey, how's Thea been doing today?"

"She's great. She learns quickly, which is a relief."

"I was wondering if I could sneak her out to the barn for an hour or so. I think she'd like to spend some time with the horses."

"Oh, yeah. That's a good idea. She told me about her job back in Alabama. I can tell she's missing it."

"Thanks. I'll bring her back soon."

He approached the small crowd hanging around Thea and took a seat across from her. "Hey, Ava said I could take you out to the barn for a little bit if you want."

Thea's eyes lit up for a split second before the excitement faded. "Are you sure? We still have so much to go over."

"I'll bring you back whenever you're ready. She said she was okay with it."

Thea looked over her shoulder to search the room for Ava, who waved on her way out of the dining hall.

"Okay. I'd like that." She picked up her plate and started to stand.

Brett jumped up and ran to her side of the table. "Let me help you." He took the plate from her and handed over the crutches. After tossing her plate and drink in the trash, he met her at the door.

Paul's truck was parked next to Jess's outside the barn. It would be nice to have someone else around to cut the awkwardness with his sister, but Paul wasn't exactly a talker either.

"Your friend is here," Brett said as he turned off the engine.

Thea narrowed her eyes at him. "I'm not sure Jess considers herself my friend."

"Not her. Thane."

"Oh! Good."

Inside, Thane spotted them instantly and padded over to Thea. She rubbed the end of her crutch over the dog's side before they made their way down the right side of the stables.

"I think introductions are in order." He lifted his hand at the first stall. "This is Vanilla. Vanilla, this is Thea. We like her."

Thea stepped up to the palomino and lifted her hand for Vanilla to smell. "You're beautiful."

"She says you're pretty too. She likes your eyes."

"Is that what she said?" Thea asked.

"Definitely." He stepped to the next stall. "This is Lightning. She's feisty. No wonder she's Jess's favorite."

Jess led Burgundy out of a stall a few feet away. She looked up but didn't acknowledge them as she headed for the grooming station.

"I don't even know what to say to her," Thea whispered.

"Just give her time. She's busy being stubborn."

"I didn't want to hurt you," she said quietly.

Brett kept his attention on Lightning. She abandoned him during the worst time in his life. Hurt was an understatement. "I need to groom Kiwi. Want to supervise?"

"Sure."

Her agreement was soft, but he desperately wanted to change the subject. Horses he could handle. Feelings? Not so much.

He took his time greeting Kiwi and leading her out of her stall. At the grooming station, he found a bucket and flipped it over beside a chair. Thea took her seat near Kiwi's front end and propped her injured foot on the bucket. Thane lay at her feet, and she gave him plenty of attention.

He groomed Kiwi in silence, and Thea handed him each brush he needed. He was on the other side of the horse when Thea gasped.

Brett peeked around by Kiwi's neck. "What's wrong?"

Thea was staring at the phone in her hand, and Thane stood at attention at her side. "I just turned it on. There are twenty texts from Emerson."

It seemed the Howards weren't willing to give up. "Does she know where you are?"

Thea scrolled through the messages. "It doesn't look like it."

"But surely they know. Everyone in town knows I've worked here for years." He took off his hat and ruffled his hair.

"I talked to Hadley last night about whether or not I should leave. If I go back to Alabama, I can't work, at least not at my old job. I can't do anything physical for a few weeks. I don't have anyone who could drive me to doctor appointments, and I'm sure I'd be terrible at driving with my left foot on the gas and my right leg in the passenger seat."

Brett rubbed a hand over his mouth. This was not the time to laugh at the funny image of Thea trying to take care of herself. "Right. And you have plenty of help here."

Thea looked back at the phone. "She wants to know where I am."

"Tell her you went back to Alabama."

"It looks like I'll be staying for a while. I need to talk to Ava about that."

"I could go with you. To Alabama," Brett said.

He didn't have to hold his breath for her reaction. Her head whipped up.

"How? You have a job. You have a life. If you leave your job, then we go from one income between us to none."

Brett paced in front of Kiwi who was starting to pick up on his and Thea's anxiety. "You're right. I have savings, but–"

"We can't run away. When does it end?"

"When you get well. Then we could–"

Then *she* could go home. There was no *we* after she healed.

She shook her head. "There's no sense in talking about it now. I can barely walk across the barn without gasping for air and needing to elevate my leg."

Brett squatted in front of her and looked up. Her brows were pinched together, and her eyes drifted closed. He slowly reached for the phone, and she let him take it from her. He put it on the bucket beside her foot and took her hands in his. The skin on the tops of her hands was soft, but callouses were spread over the palms–a sign she didn't mind stepping up and working hard.

"They won't win. Don't give up."

She bit her lips between her teeth and lowered her chin.

"Hey," he whispered.

She lifted her gaze to him, but his encouragement had fallen on deaf ears. "We will win. You'll be free. If I have to burn everything down, go to the ends of the earth, protect you with my life, I'll do it."

Her eyes squeezed closed, and the sobs came. She gasped for breath, and Brett pulled her to rest against his shoulder. Every cry hit him like a whip on his bare back as he brushed a hand over her hair.

"Why are you doing this? Why are you helping me?" she asked through tears and sniffles. "I left you."

Good question. It would be really cool if he knew the answer. "I don't know. Because I can't do anything else. I can't leave you. I can't stand the thought of you hurting. I–"

He loved her. He'd known it since that first night in the hospital that the full force of that love had survived all these years. He just wasn't sure if she was ready to accept it yet.

He'd held her like this while she cried before. It was the first time her dad hit her mom after he started dating Thea. It hadn't been the first time, but Thea hadn't been able to see her mom hurting without falling apart. She cried as if she'd been the one to take the punches. And there were times in the past when she had.

Young Brett had immediately offered to level the guy–thirty-year age gap or not. Any man who could lay a hand on a woman deserved to get picked on by someone his own size.

"I'm sorry." Thea sniffed and wiped her nose on her sleeve. "I may have developed a hay allergy."

Brett laughed. "I think cracking jokes when feelings pop up is my job."

"Well, you were just being sweet, and that makes me feel worse about barging into your life with all my problems."

Brett cradled her face in his hands, rubbing the tears away with his thumbs. "It's you and me against the world."

Her bottom lip trembled before she wrapped her

arms around his neck, pulling him close. “Thank you,” she whispered against his neck.

He rubbed a hand over her back, soothing her through the last of her tears. “I’d do anything for you.”

CHAPTER 15
THEA

Thea woke to the sun shining brightly through the bedroom window. She tried to roll away from it, but the heavy brace on her leg pulled. Her arm and neck ached. Sleeping had been a pain lately, but she couldn't put all the blame on her physical injuries.

Flopping onto her back, she closed her eyes and prayed for sleep to take her again–just for a few minutes. At least she'd slept late enough that she'd miss Brett's worried looks. It was enough that he'd watched her with those pitiful glances after her breakdown in the barn yesterday. He'd tried his best to perk her up, but the emotional toll of everything was piling up at once.

He'd left her with Hadley for a few hours in the evening to pick up a load of lumber from the hardware store, but other than that, Brett had stayed dutifully by her side. Thea didn't understand the reasoning. She was a complete wet blanket, weighing everyone down.

The sound of clinking glasses coming from the kitchen told her Hadley was probably making coffee, and Thea needed some in the worst way.

Pushing slowly out of bed and stretching the protesting muscles, she got dressed and pulled her hair into a ponytail. She'd been right about the coffee. The warm smell lifted her shoulders and filled her with a spark of life.

"Morning, sunshine. How do you like your eggs?" Hadley asked.

"You're cooking?"

"I thought we'd skip the early morning social hour. You didn't seem too chatty last night."

Thea propped her crutches against the wall and practically fell into the chair by the table. Getting up and down with grace was out of the question these days. "You got me there. Sorry I've been a downer."

Hadley pulled a skillet out of a cabinet. "It's fine. Anything you want to talk about?"

"What are you up to today?" Thea asked.

"Hanging out with Ben and Abby while Colt and Remi enjoy some of their honeymoon at home. You?"

"I told Ava I'd help her in the office today. Can I get a ride?"

"Sure thing. You like bacon?" Hadley asked.

"Definitely. Anything I can do to help?"

Hadley grabbed a package of bacon from the fridge. "Just sit there and keep me company. After hearing from your lovely cousin yesterday, I don't think it's a good idea to meet up with your mom again."

"I know. It was a stupid idea in the first place. That's how all this mess started."

"Right, but maybe I could just get a message to her for you."

Thea thought about it for a moment before shaking her head. "I don't want to push the limits. We all know how dangerous this could be."

"I get it. The offer still stands. I could pretend to be a vacuum saleswoman, or I could act like I was the exterminator and just show up at the door."

"I definitely don't want you showing up at the door when Tommy could be there." Thea shuddered at the thought of sweet Hadley coming face-to-face with the devil himself.

"I told the kids I'd take them to Grady's Feed and Seed today to look around. They love that place. You need me to pick up anything for you? They have some winter clothes. You might need a thicker coat if this winter decides to keep up the unforgiving temps."

"I could really use a sweater," Thea said as she got up to get Hadley some money.

"Comfy and warm. Got it."

Thea laid the money on the table. "There's some extra for groceries."

That was the last of her cash, and while she needed money, she wasn't sure about trusting Hadley with her debit card yet. Maybe Brett would take it to the nearest ATM the next time he was in town.

Though, knowing him, he'd probably just try to give her money. His generosity was both sweet and frustrating. He trusted way easier than Thea did. How many times had he been taken advantage of in his life? Unfortunately, her name was on his list of traitors.

His uncle had tried to blame him for her dad's death. He probably had his own set of trust issues that he calculated in his spare time. Growing up with families like theirs made it hard to see the good side of anything.

The casual chat with Hadley over breakfast had turned Thea's mood around, and she was looking forward to the morning when they headed outside. Fog settled over everything in the cold morning. She could barely see her hand in front of her face, much less her future.

Hadley parked in front of the check-in office and reached into the back for the crutches. Thea took them, closed the door, and waved as Hadley rolled the passenger window down. "Call me when you need a ride somewhere. If I'm not around, I'm sure Brett will pick you up."

"I don't have his phone number," Thea said, pulling out her phone.

Hadley rattled off the number and waved as she backed out.

What did it say that she was happy to know Hadley would pick her up, but silently hoped she was busy? After Brett saw her get all snotty and blubbery over text messages yesterday, he was probably smart to run for the hills.

The check-in desk was unmanned, but Stella waved from the gift shop. The older woman had welcomed Thea to the ranch with open arms–literally. Stella had wrapped Thea in a big hug and gone on and on about quilting.

Despite her insistence that she didn't know how to sew or quilt or do anything crafty, Stella didn't want to take no for an answer about attending the Tuesday evening quilting circle. It looked like Thea's social calendar was filling up, despite her unknown end date at the ranch.

Thea hobbled into Ava's office. "Knock, knock."

Ava sat at her desk rubbing circles on her temples. She didn't open her eyes. "I'm so glad you're here. Can you answer the phones today? I'm feeling like a trainwreck this morning, and I can't shake the nausea."

"Sure."

"If someone has a question, and you don't know the answer, you can ask Stella or just leave a message and I'll return the call later."

Ava stood slowly, holding onto the desk. Thea had heard morning sickness could be brutal sometimes, but Ava's color was way off.

"Don't worry about anything. I'll handle things here. You just get to feeling better."

"Thanks." The soft word was barely audible.

"Do you need someone to drive you?" Thea couldn't do it herself, but she could ask Stella.

"Jameson can take me home. He's in his office. Thanks for the offer."

Alone in Ava's office, Thea sat in the padded chair behind the desk and looked around. Notes were posted around the desk. A cork board hung behind her next to the window looking out onto the ranch. It was filled with notes and memos. Even the filing cabinets had notes on them in various handwritings. Some had names below them.

Order sod.

Meet Joe at the south barn Wednesday at eleven.

Cabin furniture arriving Feb 24. Deliver to storage #3.

Survey of western border. Gerry Guthrie.

The notes went on and on. Ava had some kind of organized chaos going on, and Thea's fingers itched to tidy the paper scraps.

She pulled out the card Ava had given her and typed up a text.

Thea: You have a lot of notes here. Is there anything I can do to help?

She put the phone on the desk, not expecting an answer anytime soon. Ava might be puking up breakfast right now.

Pushing back up onto the crutches, she made her way around the room studying the notes, remembering a few she felt confident to handle that she could ask Ava about later.

The quiet of the offices was amping up her boredom. After staring out the window for a few minutes, she hobbled over to Jameson's office. The people still working during the winter stopped by Jameson and Ava's offices regularly, and Thea had yet to see their doors closed. Though, she'd checked the filing cabinets–those were locked. Probably containing bank information.

Jameson's office had two windows–one looking out the same way as Ava's and another showcasing the path leading in and out of the ranch. The mural-sized map of the ranch that covered one entire wall captivated her attention. Miles and miles of land, mapped out in elevation and terrain. Valleys, mountains, campsites, cabins, creeks, and rivers spanned thousands of acres.

So many places to hide.

No wonder Brett thought she'd be safe here. Was

that his plan? Did he think she could disappear into the wilderness if necessary?

She looked down at her injured leg. She wouldn't be going anywhere fast. She'd tested out the ankle last night, and she couldn't put weight on it. It kept her from doing simple tasks on her own, much less running for her life. She'd taken a shower on her own last night, and the half-hour ordeal had exhausted her.

Thea found the check-in office on the map and touched it with her finger. She knew how far the stables were and used that distance to judge how far away other things were. Storage houses, barns, cabins. Every structure was marked with a label and number. There was even a furnace somewhere east of the offices.

Brett probably knew this place like the back of his hand. She traced her fingertip along one of the horse trails. A permanent campground was marked at the end.

The creak of the door at the front of the offices pulled her attention from the map. Heavy boots thudded on the wooden floor before Brett spoke.

"Morning. Is Thea here?" he asked.

"Ava's office," Stella replied.

Thea waited until Brett appeared and stuck his head into Ava's office before she cleared her throat. "I'm in here."

Brett changed course and stepped into Jameson's office across the hall. "You okay this morning?"

"Better than yesterday. Sorry about all the tears."

"No need to be sorry. You've been through a lot." He propped his hands on his hips and looked up at the map. "So, do you see what I see?"

"You have a plan?"

"Of course, I have a plan. Don't worry. I know where we're going."

Thea inhaled a deep breath, but it did nothing to calm her nerves. He thought they'd need to implement the plan, and that wasn't doing anything for her fears.

"Don't worry about it." He rubbed a hand over her shoulder. "If you need to get somewhere safe, I'll take care of everything. I'm sittin' on ready, and the police department knows where we'll be and what to do if we sound the alarm."

Thea looked up at him, and a jolt of gratefulness surged through her chest. "You made a plan for me?"

"Of course."

"Is there anything I should know?"

Brett shook his head. "Not really. You'd have to take a horse, but I think we can ride together on one of the stronger ones."

Thea's eyes widened. She wanted to get back on a horse so bad she'd had fitful dreams about it the last two nights, but she didn't expect to get back in the saddle anytime soon. "You think I can?"

"If we don't have another option, you'll have to. Don't worry about that either. I can get you on and off a horse. Maybe keep a few things packed just in case. And when I say it's time, we have to go immediately. No questions."

Thea nodded vigorously. "Got it."

He'd come up with a solid plan, and she trusted him. The least she could do was make it easy to help her escape. He was doing all the heavy lifting–literally.

"I've been thinking about something else lately." She hesitated, preparing herself for his reaction. "Hadley said she'd be willing to get messages to my mom."

Brett shifted his weight from one side to the other but didn't say anything.

"I was thinking, maybe she could get a message to Gage, and he could tell my mom I'm okay. I'm sure she heard about what happened. Tommy knows I'm here, and he would have asked her if she'd seen me."

Brett stared at the floor for what seemed like a full minute before looking up. "I don't like anything that invites trouble."

"I don't either, but she needs to know I'm okay. And maybe I could get an update about her latest appointments. If I could get some more information about her cancer, maybe I could find a hospital that would be able to help her. We don't exactly have the world's leading research team out here in the middle of nowhere."

Brett rubbed the short beard on his jaw. He'd always been clean-shaven when they were younger, and the beard made him look older and much more rugged than he had when they were teenagers.

The new look took him from a solid ten to a twelve point five on the sexy scale.

"I promise to be careful."

"How exactly were you thinking this would play out?" Brett asked.

"Gage told you he's working at Beau Lawrence's garage. Hadley could show up and pretend to be Gage's girlfriend and pass along the message. She could drop off lunch for him and stuff. No one would question that, right?"

"You're assuming Gage doesn't already have a girlfriend," Brett said. "Who would want to date him?"

Thea chuckled. "Fair enough. I don't know if he does or not. I haven't spoken to him for more than ten minutes in the last five years. I don't know anything about him. But he's my brother, and he..."

Gage convinced her to leave Blackwater, and he kept her secret all these years. That meant he'd cared about her at one point.

It was more than she could say about her younger brother, Max. She didn't know if he was above ground or below it, and she wasn't about to ask Emerson or Gage. Max was addicted to violence–the gorier, the better–and she didn't want to be in his crosshairs when he got that evil twinkle in his eyes.

"He did seem really concerned about you at the hospital, and he promised he wouldn't spread the word you were here. It's a risk, but it's up to you."

"I think I want to do it," Thea whispered. The more she thought about the brother she used to know, the more she thought Gage would have surely leveled out and gotten smarter over time. "We can err on the side of caution. We could tell him I made friends with Hadley while I was here. I went back home, but I still talk to Hadley, and she wanted to help me keep up with Mom's condition."

"I'd feel much better letting him think that," Brett admitted.

"Will you see if he'll do it? Meet up with Hadley?"

"If you're sure."

"Well, let me run it by Hadley first."

Brett laughed. "Can you imagine? Hadley pretending to date Gage. It's comical."

"It's not like he's ugly," Thea said, swatting at Brett's arm.

"I reserve the right to think he's dumb just because I don't like him."

Thea rolled her eyes, but a smile played on her lips. She traced her tongue along her bottom lip, hyper aware of how close Brett was standing and all that he would risk to protect her.

"Do you think it's a bad idea?" she whispered.

"I don't necessarily think it's a good idea, but I'd do anything to make you happy." He lifted his hat and rubbed a hand through his hair before putting it back on again. "I know how much it means to you to talk to your mom. I'll make it happen."

She reached up and wrapped an arm around his neck, balancing the other arm on the crutches. He wrapped his arms around her, steadying her as he gently lifted her off the floor. The strength and comfort in his embrace warmed her inside and out.

"Thank you," she whispered.

"If anything happens–"

"We don't have to talk about it."

"We do. If anything happens, I'll do whatever it takes to protect you. Do you understand? I'm not like them, but if it's you or them, I won't hesitate, and I won't regret it."

Thea tightened her hold on him. The gravity of his devotion pulled her in. How could she have left this?

But that same determination to protect her had convinced her of his involvement with her dad's death. He would do anything for her, and she'd believed he'd been capable of killing her dad to keep her safe.

"I'm sorry. I'm so sorry I left, but–" Her voice

shook as she tried to gather her determination to give him the apology he deserved.

"I'm glad you left. It wasn't safe for you, and you were better off away from all this. I don't blame you."

Oh, but he should. Even though every facet of her family and his had pushed and pulled in a political battle that left her an easy target by both sides, she still should have stayed by his side.

The phone rang in Ava's office, and Thea pulled away to wipe her face. "I have to get that."

Brett gently wrapped a hand around her arm, getting her attention. "Can I come over tonight?"

The second ring sounded.

"You come over every night. You've been sleeping on the couch."

"I meant to hang out with you."

The phone rang again.

Thea nodded. There hadn't been a question of what her heart wanted.

It wasn't necessarily the best idea, but she'd had enough of trying to stay away from him. "I'd like that."

His fingers slid from her arm, but she hesitated.

The next ring jolted her out of the haze, and she turned for the office, looking forward to an evening with Brett.

CHAPTER 16
BRETT

Brett parked in front of Hadley and Thea's cabin and settled back into the seat. "You can hang out with her without scaring her off. Don't lead with your feelings." He gripped the wheel and huffed. "Don't force your feelings on her."

Thea went along with things to make everyone else happy, and he'd spent the afternoon questioning whether he'd imagined a connection earlier because he wanted it so badly.

Did Thea feel half of what he felt? Then, now, any time?

He shut off the engine and pushed the truck door open with more force than necessary. She'd agreed to spend some time with him, and he wasn't going to waste any more of that time hem-hawing about it. He stomped his snowy boots on the porch and gave a quick double knock.

"Come in!"

Thea sat up from the couch. "Sorry. It's much faster for you to let yourself in."

He hung his hat and coat by the door and toed off his boots. "Don't worry about it."

She looked him up and down. "You look ready for bed."

Glancing down at the gray sweatpants that had been tucked into his boots a few seconds ago, he shrugged. "Almost ready for bed. I don't sleep in this."

Thea's eyes widened. "Oh."

Let her mull that one over for a while. He sighed loud enough for her to hear.

"You okay?" Thea asked.

The little wrinkle between her brows was endearing. She did care about him, but how much?

"What a day," he said as he lifted her legs from the couch and sat, placing them back in his lap. "A hot mess of a woman needs my help all the time. It's hard being a knight in shining armor, you know?"

Thea relaxed and swatted his chest. "Stop it."

"It's true. She's ridiculously hot too. It's a problem, but don't worry about me. How was your day?"

She was smiling now, and his work was done.

"It was good. A super sexy cowboy has been doing everything for me, and I can't lie, it's fantastic."

"A sexy cowboy, huh? Should I introduce him to my fist?"

Thea rolled her eyes. "You can act like you're a caveman all day, but you're a total softie."

"It's true. I'm a teddy bear. I need lots of hugs."

This was what he'd been missing. It was like a bridge had been mended between the past and present and he could be himself again.

"I bet you do. Do all the women hug on you?"

Brett shook his head slowly, keeping his gaze locked with hers. Her determined stare did crazy things to his heart rate. "Nope."

Thea narrowed her eyes and tilted her head. "I find that hard to believe."

"One good thing about being the jokester is that no one takes you seriously. Expectations are low."

Thea tapped a finger on her lips.

Dang it. Why did she have to draw attention to her lips? He was already dreaming about them every night. Daydreaming too was enough to kill him.

"That's not how I see you. At all," she whispered.

"I made sure the expectations were different with you."

Thea sat up and rested her head against the couch, bringing them close enough that he had to fight the urge to wrap his arm around her waist.

"This feels like living in a bubble again," she whispered. "It was like that a lot when I first moved to Alabama. I felt safe sometimes, but then I would remember who I was running from, and the safe feeling would disappear."

Brett swallowed hard. Had she been running from him?

He knew in his gut it was mostly about their families, but had she been afraid of him all this time? Had she seen it as her chance to escape?

"And you feel safe here?"

"Mostly. Always when you're around."

He didn't stop himself from wrapping his hand around her waist. Every inch closer to her made him want more and more.

She glanced down at his hand but didn't move it. "Is Linc missing his roommate?"

Brett laughed. "Not at all. He likes being alone."

"But you don't," she said.

"I don't," he confirmed.

He didn't want to be with just anybody. He wanted to be with her.

"Do you miss your job?" he asked.

She threaded a hand through her hair, making his attention zero in on the movement. "I do. I love my job. Those horses are some of my best friends. Thankfully, Misty is giving me daily updates. She even let me talk to a few of them yesterday after I was moping around feeling sorry for myself."

"Oh, I talk to the horses all the time. Jess doesn't talk unless she has something important to say, so the horses are my only entertainment."

“They make the best friends. No judgment. No expectations beyond feed me and love me. It’s easy.”

“I’m easy too. I would be happy with feed me and love me,” Brett said.

“You’re a lot like a loyal horse. I’ll give you that.”

“Are they in a bind because you’re here?” he asked.

“Not really. My boss is teaching her niece how to be a trainer, so it’s okay that I’m away right now. She wants her niece to kind of be pushed into the job so she can get the full experience.”

“That’s kind of how Jess and I started here. The foreman had just let the barn manager go because he was stealing, and he needed someone fast. He spent a few hours a day telling us what to do before he walked away and just expected us to figure it out. Thankfully, Mr. Chambers checked on us every once in a while. Turns out we make a good team because we’re pretty much opposites and we trust each other.”

“I bet you’re great with the horses. Anyone would be lucky to work with you.”

“Why? I’m not doing anything special.”

Thea leaned forward the slightest bit. “Because you’re trustworthy. You don’t know how rare that is. I trusted you from the beginning, even though I shouldn’t have. I still wanted to trust you when all the evidence said you were guilty.” She pushed her fingers through her hair again before settling back against the couch, closer to him than before. "It didn't make sense, but everything inside me said you were safe. And you were. You were my safe place. Not trusting you in the end was a mistake."

Apparently, talking about the past and everything they'd had before was going to twist his guts up on a regular basis. His hand on her waist gripped a little tighter. "I'm the one who messed it up."

Thea shook her head. "Not at all. It was always meant to fail, but I just made it quicker." She sat up straighter and stretched her arms above her head. "Would it bother you if I took a shower? It takes me forever with my injured ankle, and I'm getting tired."

Brett eased her feet from his lap to the floor and stood, offering her both hands. She swayed a little when she rose, and he steadied her with a hand on each arm. When she found her balance and looked up at him, he wasn't ready to let go.

She was standing so close, and his breaths came in deep swells. He knew the feel of her lips on his, and it was more than a dream. It was a memory preserved in amber.

Leaning down to kiss her would be as natural as breathing. Nothing in the world existed except her. Nothing else mattered.

That was how he knew with all certainty that she was the one. Thea had always been the goal–the future he'd always wanted. It didn't exist without her beside him.

He didn't dare move. One step toward her would give him all he'd ever wanted. One step away would crush him.

Then, he felt it–her hands on his waist, moving up his sides, leaving a trail of fire in their wake.

No, loving her wasn't as natural as breathing.

He loved Thea more than the basic needs of his body because the air in his lungs had disappeared.

He took a half step toward her, and her hands wrapped from his sides to his chest–the only thing keeping their bodies from being flush against each other. His hand slid up her arm and over her shoulder, trailing a slow path up the sides of her neck until his fingertips found their way into the hair at the base of her neck.

His forehead rested against hers, and his nose brushed against her cheek as he dipped toward her lips. The breath that had vacated his lungs came back in a rush as she tilted her head back, lining up her lips with his.

The rumble of an engine outside stopped him, and his eyes flew open, perfectly in line with hers.

"Act like she isn't here," Brett said. She was so close that his lips brushed against her as he spoke.

"She'll be walking through the door in seconds. She always runs from the truck to the cabin," Thea whispered.

"I don't care. She can wait outside."

"She can't wait outside," Thea whisper-screamed.

Brett's grip on her hair tightened, and his voice was low and gravelly. "Why are we not kissing right now? She's still outside."

A small gasp let him know she was just as affected as he was.

Good.

Every second he wasn't kissing her was torture.

"Because we've been trying to decide what to do now that Hadley is home."

Hadley's steps were quick on the wooden porch just before the door flung open. "Someone turned it on frostbite out there. Whew!"

Thea's hands slid from his chest. Apparently, she'd been gripping his shirt because the wrinkles were front and center when she stepped away from him.

Hadley flopped her hood back and shook her hair out. Totally oblivious to the wreckage of the major kiss that was so close to happening.

He couldn't feel his fingers anymore.

Hadley was most definitely not getting a Christmas present from him this year.

"What's up?" Hadley asked.

"I was just about to take a shower," Thea said.

Right. Just what he needed–thoughts of Thea in

the shower. He needed to sit in timeout until further notice.

Brett flopped onto the couch, pressing his face into one of Hadley's decorative pillows. "I'll be here. Guarding the door," he muffled into the pillow.

"Good. I'll get a shower after you," Hadley said before disappearing into her room.

CHAPTER 17
THEA

Thea sat in the stables with her foot propped on a bucket. She'd been moving around without the crutches more and more, but there were times when the ankle still ached.

Star swooped down to nudge her cheek against Thea's.

"I know, girl. You're next."

Brett led Vanilla, a gorgeous palomino, around the indoor arena. Every few feet, he leaned in to whisper to the horse, and, despite the cold, Thea's heart melted like a popsicle on a summer day.

"He's good to you, isn't he?" Thea asked Star.

The horse anxiously stepped to the left, then back again.

"He's good to me too. Let me tell you, that man is a..."

He's a keeper, but Thea hadn't had the luxury of

keeping things that were too good for her. There was a point in time when she'd thought Brett was her ticket to freedom–her chance to have happiness after a lifetime of hate. Looking back, she truly believed God had sent him when she needed him most.

Now, was He sending Brett to her again for a reason she didn't understand yet? Or was He just hoping she wouldn't mess it up this time the way she had all those years ago?

Would he extend the forgiveness she desperately prayed for?

Brett said something to Vanilla before turning his attention to Thea. Even from across the arena, the intensity of his stare sent a wave of heat up her chest and neck. There was a silent plea in every look, begging her to trust him and let him in again.

And she wanted to. Oh, how she wanted to.

She got the feeling he wanted to try again, but things would turn out the same way this time as they had before. How could it be any other way? They were doomed, or they were doomed. No way around it.

Violent delights had violent ends, didn't they?

Brett finished his session with Vanilla and came to take Star for her turn. The younger horse eagerly followed Brett, and Thea chuckled low. Brett had a friendliness about him that even the horses could feel. They trusted him in the same way Thea had.

The same way she still did.

Would her regrets ever catch a break? Brett was opening up to her again, but she couldn't shake her guilt.

Paul came in with Thane, and the big dog set his sights on Thea. She welcomed him with open arms, and he nuzzled his face against her neck.

"Hey, snuggle bug. I missed you." She hadn't seen the wolf dog in a few days, and the reunion was well overdue. He lay down between her and the bucket supporting her foot, and she gave him all of her attention. "Does Paul know you're an attention hog? Does he talk to you more than people? I've never heard him say more than ten words at a time."

Paul walked up and cleared his throat. "I'll be in the storage shed if you need me."

"We're fine here. I'll take good care of him," Thea promised.

With a slight tip of his hat, Paul went about his business. Thea sat in Thane's quiet company for at least half an hour. Brett and Jess moved here and there throughout the barn, seemingly working together without communicating much. Jess pretended Thea didn't exist in the corner all afternoon, and their silent push and pull was enough to tie Thea's muscles in knots.

As badly as she wanted to pretend she didn't care what Brett's sister thought, her mind didn't get the memo. Thea *did* care, and there didn't seem to be anything she could do to mend the relationship.

Jess was right to feel the way she did. Thea caused problems for Brett whenever she was around.

Paul eventually came back and collected Thane from Thea's feet. With a wave, her friend was gone, leaving Thea in the quiet barn as twilight descended on the ranch. Brett and Jess had disappeared, and Thea's knee was stiff from sitting with her foot propped on a bucket all afternoon.

She stood, stretched her neck from side to side, and started looking for Brett. She'd been caught up in saying her good-byes to Thane and lost track of him.

Limping her way around the barn, voices came from Brett's office. Well, he called it an office. Thea thought it was more of a closet, but did he really need one when Jess handled all the paperwork?

"I'm over your attitude," Brett said. "Take it or leave it, Thea isn't going anywhere."

Thea sucked in a breath and held it. Could she quietly sneak away without attracting their attention?

"She'll be out of here in a heartbeat, as soon as she figures out she doesn't need you anymore."

"What would it matter to you if she did?"

"Um, you might not remember all your pining

when she left, but I do. Don't get attached this time."

"Too late," Brett said.

Thea had only heard that sharpness in his voice once before–when he'd confessed his hatred for his family and all they stood for. But Jess had always been that exception for him. Now, Thea was driving a wedge between him and the only family he cared about.

"You're making a big mistake," Jess said.

"Then it's my mistake to make, but you're not changing my mind. Get over it."

"Just wait until she screws you over again."

"My decision, Jess." Brett huffed. "I'll see you later."

His footsteps were quick and heavy just before he flung open the office door. The furrow in his brow was new, and he didn't smile when he noticed her.

His chest rose and fell in deep swells. "Let's get out of here."

Thea's throat burned. She'd ruined any chance of trust between them, and Jess was right about all of it.

He stepped around her, intent to keep up his stomping pace, but he turned around and paused, waiting for her.

"Are you okay?" she asked.

"Can we go somewhere quiet?"

Thea nodded.

He pulled off his hat and brushed a hand through his hair. "You want to grab dinner and eat at your place?"

"Sure."

He scooped her into his arms and resumed his quick pace. She didn't mind being close to him. Not at all. What she did mind was the awkwardness between them after she overheard his conversation with Jess.

He set her on her feet beside the truck and opened the passenger door for her. He didn't rush her as she climbed in.

After taking his place behind the wheel, he sighed. "Sorry about that."

"I'm sorry too," she said.

He parked in front of the dining hall and held up a finger. "I'll be right back. Wait here."

Her thoughts wandered in the darkness. She'd known leaving would hurt him. It hurt her too. But how could she make up for what she'd done? She left him at a time when half the town thought he was a murderer.

It wasn't long before he returned with a large brown paper bag. It was stuffed to the brim with to-go plates. He got in and stashed it in the backseat. "I didn't know what you wanted, so I got some of everything."

"Thanks." Thea picked at a fingernail she could barely see by the light of the moon. "Are you okay?"

"I'm fine. Jess won't be if she doesn't lay off. I'm assuming you heard some of that."

"I did. I was looking for you."

"It's fine. She'll get over it or keep stressing about it, but I'm through hearing about it."

When he parked at her cabin, he turned off the engine and asked, "Can I carry you inside?"

"Why do you like carrying me?" she asked with a laugh.

"Because I like caring for you. It makes me happy when you're happy."

Thea's shoulders slumped. "You're so sweet," she whispered.

"I've always felt that way about you. And you're good to me too, so it goes both ways."

"I haven't done anything for you since I've been here," she said.

"You don't have to do anything for me. I just like hanging out with you. And I like carrying you." He shrugged. "It is what it is."

Thea chuckled. "Okay, Prince Charming. You can carry me inside, and I will thoroughly enjoy every second of it."

Brett perked up as he opened the door and pulled out the food. "I'll be right back."

He closed the door and jogged inside, putting away the food before coming back to get her.

She wrapped her arms around his neck as he pulled her snugly against his chest. Nuzzling her face against his warm neck, she held on and relaxed into his embrace.

Inside, he kicked the door closed behind him and carried her to the kitchen. He set her gently in one of the chairs around the table and pulled another over for her to prop her foot on. "What do you want to drink?"

"Water is fine. I'll get the food sorted." She dug into the bag and started checking the boxes. He really had gotten some of everything.

He put a glass of water in front of her and another next to his seat. "I'm going to make a fire. Start without me."

Thea grabbed for his arm. "Wait. Can you say the blessing first?"

Brett sat in a chair beside her. "Sure."

"Thanks."

He bowed his head. "Lord, thank You for bringing us through another day. Thank You for everything you provide–the food, the shelter, and the safety. Please help me to be the man You need me to be. Amen."

Thea kept her attention on the food as she grinned. She'd been caught off guard the first time she heard Brett pray because neither of them had grown up with Christ in their homes.

Now, she sometimes craved Brett's thoughtful and gentle prayers. She had no idea hearing him give thanks to the Lord would be so attractive, but it pulled her heart closer to him every time.

Brett tended the fire while Thea divided the food onto plates, giving Brett extra helpings of the foods she knew he liked most. When he came back to the kitchen, he dug into the spread.

"So, Ava didn't need you this afternoon?" he asked.

"Nope. She was having a meeting with the food supplier before catching up on some emails. She was feeling good today, so she wanted to work."

"Good. I have to say, after seeing her suffer for six months, I'm extra appreciative of women who go through all that for their families."

Thea pushed to swallow the bite of grilled chicken she'd been chewing. If she'd stayed by Brett's side, would they have had kids of their own by now? "I hate that she's having such a hard time."

"Me too. It makes me wonder why my mom kept having kids. It's hard work, and she didn't care about us at all," Brett said.

"I'm sorry. I know that's confusing. I always knew my mom loved me, and she protected me from a lot. I'll always be grateful for that."

Brett smiled. "I always liked your mom."

"I think she would have liked you a lot more if the circumstances had been different. She was one of the few people I told about us, and it scared her."

"I get that. She cares about you."

Thea pushed her hair back and took a deep breath. “Do you have to go back to work?”

Brett finished chewing the last bite on his plate. “Not until later. I’ll go wrap things up at the barn when I leave to get into my jammies.”

“I like your jammies,” Thea said.

Seeing him relaxed in the evenings was the perfect way to end the day. Plus, the T-shirts hugged his chest and arms in all the right ways.

Brett took her plate and stood. “You ready to hang out on the couch, or do you have other plans?”

“No other plans. The couch sounds nice.”

Brett leaned down beside her, propping one hand on the table and the other on the back of her chair. He was so close–close enough that she could straighten up and press her lips to his. The air in the room thickened as she inhaled.

“Can I carry you?” he asked in a deep whisper. The words left a trail of fire in their wake as the vibration raced down her spine.

“It’s just a few feet away.”

“I still want to. If you’ll let me.”

Why did he have to be so sweet? Why did she want him so badly? Why was he the one she couldn’t get over?

When she hesitated, Brett inched back. “If you want to say no, it won’t hurt my feelings.”

“I want to say yes,” she whispered.

“Then say yes,” he said with a wink.

"Yes." The word rolled over her tongue like tea with honey, welcome and soothing.

Brett slid his arms around her and lifted her as if she weighed as much as a pillow.

"I'm going to be spoiled," Thea said.

"Mission accomplished. Now, I should just take care of you forever."

Thea rested her head on his shoulder. Being taken care of by Brett for the rest of her life would be a dream come true.

This was a dream come true.

Brett sat on the couch, keeping her in his arms. He pulled a pillow over to prop her foot on, and she snuggled against his chest. He hadn't even bothered to turn on the lights, and the dim glow from the fireplace cast shadows over the room. With his arms around her, she could almost forget the rest of the world existed.

Except it did exist, and so many parts of that dark world had stolen happiness from them.

With one arm wrapped around her back, he pulled her closer to him. The fingers of his other hand threaded with hers, dancing together in the firelight.

"I'm sorry," Thea whispered.

"Why?"

It was easier to be honest under the cover of darkness. "I'm sorry for leaving you. Sorry for how you were accused. I'm so sorry for all of it. I wish I hadn't left."

A single tear dripped from the corner of her eye, and she wiped it against his chest. He still smelled like the horses, and oddly, the familiar scent comforted her.

"Don't be. You would have been miserable here. We couldn't have been together in public then. Maybe ever. And you deserve more than that. And you've already said you were sorry a dozen times. Let's put it in the past."

"I didn't want fanfare or screaming from the mountaintops. I just wanted you."

Brett pulled her closer and threaded his fingers tighter with hers. "I missed you," he whispered against her hair.

"I missed you too." The words threatened to bring on tears.

"I know leaving was best for you, and that's all I've ever wanted–what was best for you. I couldn't have gone with you. The investigation was ongoing, and it was good that you got away from that. From all this."

"I'm sorry," she sobbed, gripping his shirt as if something might pull her away from him at any moment. "I'm so sorry."

He rocked her gently in his arms. "Shh. It's okay."

"It's not."

"It is. I'm over it. Well, I'm not over you. I won't ever be. But I promise I'm not mad at you. My pride was a little bruised, but I can live with that."

Thea wiped her eyes and lifted her head. "You're too good for me. For all this. You've been blamed for things you didn't do your whole life. You're so much better than your family, and you never get enough credit."

Brett's fingertips brushed against her cheek, smearing more of the wetness. "I don't want credit. I just want you."

The telltale rumble of Hadley's car grew louder outside, and Brett's grin widened.

"We really need to learn to get to the kissing part earlier in the evening."

Thea laughed and wiped her face again. "You'd think we'd learn."

"I'm definitely learning. I hope to keep learning about you for a long time." He lifted the hand that still clasped his and kissed it. "I need to wrap up a few things at the barn and change clothes. I'll be back soon."

Hadley burst in the door, shaking and shivering. "I don't like the cold!"

"We've noticed," Thea said.

Hadley brushed her hair over her shoulder. "It doesn't get this cold in Tennessee. Not even close. I don't know if I'll survive my first winter here."

"You can do it. You're tough," Brett said as he

wrapped his arms around Thea and stood. He turned and laid her back on the couch. “I’ll be back. Take care of my girl while I’m gone.”

Hadley’s brows lifted. “Your girl, huh?”

“My girl.” Brett winked at Thea, sending her heart into a marathon.

“Maybe I should start calling before I barge in,” Hadley said.

Brett snapped his fingers and pointed at her. “A heads up would be greatly appreciated.”

Hadley laughed and hung her coat on the hook. “You got it. See you later, bodyguard.”

Brett closed the door behind him, and Thea fell back onto the couch and let out a dreamy sigh.

“How cute are the two of you?” Hadley said as she stepped up to the couch with her arms crossed. “Seriously, it’s like romance movie cute.”

Thea grabbed a pillow and pressed it over her face. “He’s so amazing.”

“I wouldn’t go that far,” Hadley joked. “But really, it’s adorable. I’m happy for y’all.”

Throwing the pillow to the other side of the couch, Thea sighed. “I don’t know if there is an us, but I desperately wish there was.”

“It sure looked like it to me,” Hadley said as she sat on the coffee table in front of Thea.

Thea sat up and scooted down the couch so Hadley could sit beside her. “We’ve been told who we are our whole lives. He’s a Patton, and I’m a

Howard. We couldn't be ourselves. We couldn't love each other. We couldn't be friends with each other because *they* had already decided we couldn't. I just want to be me." She clutched the front of her shirt. "I just want to be free."

Hadley moved to the couch. "So you had that in Alabama?"

Thea tilted her head from side to side. "Sort of."

"And you came back?"

"For my mom."

Hadley clicked her tongue. "Not many people would have done that."

"But Brett would. He's like me. We love more than we could ever hate. He understands what it means to find someone you love who loves you back. No matter the cost."

"I see how much he cares about you. His heart is good."

"I know that." Thea pushed her hands through her hair. "It doesn't change the situation."

"Doesn't it? Love covers a multitude of sins," Hadley said.

"I know he wants to be here on the ranch. I do too. But we can't exist in the same place as our families. We'd never get away from that battle. It's not like we can love our families into loving each other."

Hadley rested a hand on Thea's brace. "Maybe that's what it'll take. I'm not saying the hate isn't extreme. I know it is. But maybe you have to decide to be the opposite and stick to it. I want you to stay here, but I feel like Brett would follow you anywhere if that's what it took."

"I know, but I don't want him to have to give up this perfect job, what's left of his family, and friends like the ones he has here. Do you know how rare it is to find people you can trust like this?"

"Trust me. I know what we have here. It's special, but Brett would say you're special too." Hadley stood and stretched. "You want to get a shower first?"

"It might take me a while, so it's fine if you want to go first."

"I'll let you go first. I bet a certain cowboy would like to spend some more time with you tonight before bed." Hadley winked and smiled.

"Thanks for being so great. I appreciate everything you've done for me."

"Don't mention it. And remember, only light can drive out the darkness."

Thea's lips stretched into a forced grin. It would take a whole lot of light to kill the darkness knocking on their door.

CHAPTER 18
BRETT

Brett stretched his arms over his head. Sleeping on the couch was killing his back, but he'd never let Thea know it. An extra long and extra hot shower would loosen up the kinks in his shoulders.

He rolled onto his back and covered his eyes with one arm. It was Sunday. He needed to wake up and round up the crew if his morning surprise for Thea was going to happen. Vera would have breakfast packed up. He had to pick Mr. Chambers up at the main house. Colt and Remi were taking the kids to church, so they were out.

The door to Thea's room opened, and Brett sat up. What was she doing up so early? How had he not heard her rustling?

She jerked back when he sat up. He made a point to be up and at 'em before the sun came up, so they hadn't exactly crossed paths in the early mornings.

Until now.

"Oh," Thea said. She brushed a hand over her hair. It was pulled back into a tight ponytail. "I thought you'd be gone by now."

He threw the covers off and stood, stretching his arms above his head. "I figured I could sleep in on a Sunday."

Thea's wide-eyed gaze didn't move, but her words were quick and short. "Right. You can. I mean, you know you can. I just..."

Brett squinted, taking a closer look at her. "What's wrong? You're acting different."

She was walking without the crutches now, but that wasn't the change he noticed now. She almost looked nervous.

She waved her hand in the air, and her smile was definitely fake. It wasn't anything like the sweet smile she gave him when she laughed at his crazy jokes. "I'm not acting weird. Nothing is weird."

Then she looked at the floor, covering her eyes with a hand.

Brett looked down, then at his shirt draped over the back of the couch. At least he was wearing gym shorts. "I'm not naked, Thea."

She didn't look up or uncover her eyes. "I know. It's just that I haven't seen your hot cowboy muscles before, and wow."

Brett threw his head back and laughed. This wasn't the way he expected their Sunday morning to start, but boy was it a nice surprise. "I'm glad you like what you see."

Thea lifted her gaze and uncovered her eyes. The cute scowl was anything but menacing. "Stop it. You know you're good looking. Quit flaunting your sexiness."

He crossed his arms over his chest and smirked. "You're right. I'll just turn off the sexy."

"Good," Thea said. His joke seemed to fuel her fire. "Please put those incredible chest muscles away."

Brett gave her a friendly salute as she set off toward the bathroom. "Yes, ma'am."

She closed the door a little too quickly. If Hadley wasn't up before, she would be now.

He grabbed his shirt off the back of the couch and pulled it on. Note to self: tease Thea with "cowboy muscles" as often as possible.

Hadley knew to stall Thea as much as possible this morning. With her sprained ankle almost healed, she was hard to keep up with. Her follow-up with the doctor had gone as well as could be expected. She could bear weight on her ankle, but she hadn't been released to fly.

Brett jogged to the truck and blazed a hot trail for his cabin. The unspoken conversation he needed to have with Thea was never far from his mind, but he had no problem running away from it or offering up distractions.

Not that his surprise for the morning was a distraction. He was actually hoping to gain some wisdom that hadn't shown up yet.

Barging into the cabin, he paused just inside the door. Linc stood in the kitchen holding a cup of coffee in one hand and his phone in the other. He didn't even look up from the screen.

"Earth to Linc."

Linc raised his head, looking completely bored. "Yeah."

"What are you doing?"

"Texting."

Brett closed the door and studied his roommate with narrowed eyes. "With who?"

"Whom," Linc retorted.

"Whom is not a name. Who are you texting? You never text me," Brett said, clutching the collar of his shirt.

Linc rolled his eyes and pocketed his phone. "None of your business."

Brett growled and pulled at his hair. Linc literally made him want to pull his hair out.

But it was such nice hair. He conditioned regularly. Maybe it would be better to pull Linc's hair out instead.

"Why are you the way you are?"

Linc shrugged, giving nothing away.

Brett tensed his jaw. Making friends was his specialty. Why was Linc such a hard one to crack?

"Got it. I'll just go pretend it doesn't hurt my feelings that you're texting someone. I'm going to start sending you memes again."

Linc raised his finger and pointed at Brett. "Don't."

Brett waved a hand above his head as he stalked toward the bathroom. "Meme ya later, alligator."

He showered, shaved, and dressed in his Sunday best in record time. Grabbing his Bible, he headed back out the door. The first stop was the dining hall where he picked up breakfast. Vera had pre-packaged everything from bacon to biscuits.

Next up was Mr. Chambers. The old man could get around on his own, but Brett liked making his boss's life easier whenever possible. With Bible in hand, Mr. Chambers stepped out onto the porch before Brett could make it out of the truck. They didn't speak more than a quick good morning on the way to Hadley and Thea's cabin. Hopefully, the man had some wisdom to impart later.

Mr. Chambers was light on his feet for the early Sunday hour, and they knocked at the cabin door right on time.

"Come in!" Hadley yelled from inside.

Brett opened the door but let his boss enter first. Was there time for another prayer? Hopefully, today would be a turning point for Brett and Thea. He was doing all he could to show her he was committed to her happiness, but she was still holding back.

Hadley sat at the small kitchen table with a newspaper spread out in front of her. Thea stood next to the coffee pot with a steaming cup in her hands. She looked back and forth between Hadley, Brett, and Mr. Chambers. When Hadley didn't explain, Thea's brow furrowed.

"Good morning. What's up?"

Mr. Chambers nodded his head once. "Morning, Miss Howard. I hope we're not imposing, but Brett thought you'd like to have an impromptu service this morning since you can't necessarily go out and about around here."

Thea's eyes widened. "Church?"

"Yep," Hadley said, hopping up from her seat. "Go get dressed."

Thea kept her gaze on Brett as she put her cup down and started for her bedroom.

When the door closed behind her, Hadley whispered, "I think she's in shock, but she's gonna love this. She told me she's been missing her home church."

Brett put the bags of food on the table. "Vera sent breakfast, and she's coming in a little bit with Stella."

Hadley looked at her phone. "Jameson and Ava are coming too. They're on their way."

Stella and Vera walked in just as Thea emerged from her bedroom. Stella's greeting was loud and true to her friendly nature, but Brett only had eyes for Thea. Wearing a white turtleneck sweater and a maroon skirt that hit the middle of her calves, she was a vision of modest beauty.

Thea tucked her elbows to her sides as she stepped out into the main room where their friends were making breakfast plates and hanging around chatting. The way her attention darted from one way to the other pricked a nerve of unease in Brett.

"You okay?" he asked.

"I'm fine. I just didn't expect this." She looked down at her feet. "Hadley picked up this outfit in town a few days ago, but I don't have shoes."

"I don't think you'll need them. We're not going outside."

She looked up at him with a nervous smile. "Thanks for whatever part you played in this. I was moping around about not getting to go to church."

Brett winked and pushed a strand of hair behind her ear. "I wouldn't want you to miss it. I'm sure Mr. Chambers has a good message for us today." He jerked a thumb over his shoulder. "Vera sent breakfast. Get something to eat before we start."

Thea eyed the spread of food laid out on the counter in the kitchen. "It smells amazing. I'm starving."

Jameson and Ava walked in just as Thea made her way to the kitchen. Brett wrapped Ava in a side hug and offered his hand to Jameson. "Thanks for coming."

"We wouldn't miss it," Ava said as she snuggled closer to Jameson.

"You feeling okay?"

"Much better today."

Brett gestured toward the kitchen. "Get something to eat. Vera sent all the good stuff."

He looked toward the kitchen where Thea stood with a plate in her hand. Stella was talking a mile a minute, but Thea's attention wasn't on the conversation. She kept her chin tucked as she pushed a piece of bacon from one side of her plate to the other.

Pasting on a smile that didn't drive out his worry, he joined them in the kitchen, hoping Thea was more excited about the surprise church service than she was letting on.

CHAPTER 19

THEA

Thea scanned the small cabin from her seat at the kitchen table, counting the friends who had taken the time out of their Sunday morning to give her the church community experience she otherwise couldn't have right now.

Everything was perfect. Breakfast was delivered hot, everyone had smiles on their faces, and Thea didn't even have to leave the house.

So, why was she so torn? She was getting everything she'd wanted–the community of Christ she'd been missing.

But that was the thing–she would always be missing it. If she wanted to go back to the four-walled building for a traditional gathering, she'd have to do it somewhere else. Her ankle was almost healed. She could walk, but she still couldn't go where she pleased without attracting the attention of her family or the Pattons.

The truth of the situation stung. She could mend things with Brett, but it would mean taking him away from this place if they wanted any semblance of a normal life.

Stella picked up a boat of white gravy. “Your biscuit is looking dry.”

That Thea could smile at. She held up a hand. “Thanks, but I’m not a fan of sausage.”

Stella’s eyes widened into a comical, dramatic expression. “Oh no. Don’t tell Vera you don’t like her sausage gravy.”

Thea made a motion of zipping her lips. “I wouldn’t dream of it.”

Brett stepped up beside Thea’s chair and bent down. “Everything good?”

“Perfect. Thank you so much for this.”

His mouth lifted on one side, showcasing that boyish grin that stole her breath every time. “You’re welcome. Let me know when you’re ready to start.”

Stella picked up her plate. “I’m ready.”

Thea did the same. “Me too. We’ll be there in a jiffy.”

The living room was packed. Hadley sat on a pillow by the fireplace. Stella, Vera, and Jameson pulled in chairs from the table. Thea, Ava, and Brett took the couch, and Mr. Chambers settled into the recliner with the worn leather Bible in his lap.

"When two or more of us gather together in His name, the Lord assures us He will be among us," Mr. Chambers said. "Let's pray."

Thea bowed her head, and it was easy to welcome the serenity of the moment. The cabin was quiet, the morning sun streaked through the windows, and her new friends were beside her—through her healing, through the chaos in her family past, and through her coming back to worship.

Mr. Chambers's message had to do with the force of love. Love for God, love for our friends, and love for those who wrong us. It was timely for her. Thea's life had been shadowed in hate, but she didn't have that inclination inside her. She wanted love more than anything. Love could solve all of her problems.

"How often do we consider right and wrong before we speak or act?" Mr. Chambers asked.

Not enough, that was for sure. Thea had made many mistakes in her life, but leaving Brett was one she couldn't shake. There had been a clear right and wrong, and she'd chosen wrong.

"It might not solve all of our problems, but each decision we make has a ripple effect. The Lord calls us to do everything with love in our hearts."

Thea glanced around the room. Everyone here had opened their homes and lives to her. They'd clearly welcomed her with love in their hearts.

But she hadn't received the same welcome at her

old home. How could strangers show her love when her own kin hadn't?

"Are we treating our neighbors with kindness? Not because they did something for us, but out of the goodness of our hearts?"

The room was quiet. Apparently, Thea wasn't the only one getting her toes stepped on this morning.

She hadn't treated everyone with kindness. She still looked at her family and Brett's as the enemy. She was no better than them because that hatred they loved so much had set up a home in her own heart.

"Would our world be different if we always chose love and kindness?" Mr. Chambers asked. "I know we're human and bound to falter, but what if we dedicated our hearts and minds to righteousness? Would we trust each other more? Would we call more people our friends? Would we have fewer enemies?"

Fewer enemies. Thea wanted that, but it didn't seem possible.

She hadn't asked for this. She hadn't done anything wrong. Her face heated as the injustice rose up her neck. She didn't deserve this. She hadn't started the fight.

"Take the animals, for instance. If you have a herd of cattle that you've moved far enough away from others, over time, they'll forget the ranchers they used to know. You're no longer their caretaker and friend, you're a potential threat, and they'll treat you as such.

"The same goes if we drift too far away from God. We forget that we used to know Him. We don't have the same connection as before. Your relationship moves from friends to acquaintances to strangers."

Thea thought back over the things she'd done that might have impacted her family. She had love in her heart. In fact, she had too much of it and no outlet. She was torn between the urge to seek revenge for the life they'd stolen from her and screaming for the peace that she'd been praying for over the years.

Which would make her happy? Revenge or peace?

Which would make God happy? He could forgive, forget, and move on, but was she capable of those monumental acts?

Would it even do her any good?

Mr. Chambers went on. "God's love isn't like any other kind of love. It's not conditional. It's unfailing. He doesn't only love us when we're perfect. He loves us when we're beaten down and broken in the same way He loves us when we're celebrating and joyous. His love is unending and unconditional. We might not be able to practice it to perfection, but every time we choose goodness and love, we're choosing to further His kingdom."

Maybe this message didn't apply to her as much as she thought. She hadn't been given a chance to choose goodness and love. Hate had been thrust upon her from the start.

Thea squirmed in her seat. Making things right within her family wasn't possible. She didn't have that kind of control. Her best option was to leave and forget the war that would continue to rage in Blackwater.

When Mr. Chambers closed with a prayer, Thea couldn't quiet the unease in her heart. What was she waiting for here? An end to the feud seemed too much to ask, and she was no closer to seeing her mom.

Everyone hung around and chatted for a bit, and Thea wanted to commandeer a horse from the stables and ride off into the mountains. She couldn't go for a drive. She couldn't go into town. She couldn't do anything. She couldn't call her mom, and she certainly couldn't have a peaceful life with Brett.

She wanted everything she couldn't have. It was selfish–all of it. But she couldn't stop the wanting.

When only Brett and Hadley were left, Hadley slipped on her coat and grabbed her purse. "I need to go check on mom. Will you be okay for a few hours?"

"Of course. I don't have any plans today," Thea said, but the stillness of the cabin would certainly drive her mad.

"Great. Call me if you need me." Hadley waved and skipped out into the cold afternoon.

Brett stood from the couch and let his hands flop down to his sides. "Well, what do you want to do?"

The extent of the question kicked her square in the chest. Of all the things she wanted, the freedom to answer that question honestly was at the top of the list.

"Thea?" Brett's brow creased. "You okay?"

She nodded, unsure if her voice would break if she tried to speak.

Brett wrapped his arms around her, cradling her close. She rested her head against his chest and fought the tears.

This was what she wanted. Safety. But it was too much to ask.

This man could do it. She knew that truth in her bones. But he'd be putting himself in the line of fire. He'd be sacrificing his own happiness, and she would be a burden, whether he realized that now or not.

"Thank you for arranging the service this morning. I needed it," she whispered.

"We can keep doing this. Everyone was happy to come."

Thea raised her head and pushed her hair back.

"No, we *can't* keep doing this. They deserve to be able to go to church. They're not the ones trapped here."

The arm wrapped around her stiffened. "Trapped?"

"I can't go anywhere. I can't leave."

"You can leave," Brett said quickly. "You're not a prisoner. I can't believe you think that."

Thea threw her hands out at her sides. "It'll always be like this. I'll always be looking over my shoulder here. I can't have a normal life, and that's why I can't stay here. That's why things would never work between us."

Brett stepped away from her and pinched the bridge of his nose. When he spoke, each word was laced with carefully controlled anger. "I'm sorry... Things would never work between us?"

Everything was spiraling. Her worries, doubts, and fears tangled together into a massive storm that was wrecking everything in its wake. "We can't do this. I–"

"I get it. You're not interested in me. Message received," Brett's words tumbled together as they bit at her. "But you're still not a prisoner here. You can leave at any time. I'll be glad to drive you to the airport. I would even drive you all the way to Alabama. Trust me, I won't keep you against your will."

"That's not what I'm saying." He'd never pushed

her. She'd always had a choice. It wasn't his fault that her choices were slim and included a mountain of baggage.

Brett stalked toward the door before rounding on her. "I'm sorry you thought I was holding you back, but I won't apologize for looking out for you. I'm going to be the first in line to tell you that you're worth protecting, whether your family sees it or not. You deserve more than this, you're right about that. But if I can't give you what you want, don't let me stop you."

Thea's eyes burned. Of all the people to be caught in the crossfire of this war, Brett deserved it the least. He'd always been there for her. Besides her mom, he was the only one she could count on.

"It's not you. I'm..."

Scared? Terrified? Afraid of losing someone else who didn't deserve the danger she carried with her?

Brett grabbed his coat and opened the door. "Call me if you need a ride out of town."

"Brett, I–"

The closing of the door cut her off. She made her way across the room with only a slight limp and threw open the door. Brett was already in his truck and seemed intent on running as fast as he could.

He'd be better off without her. She didn't have the strength to end things with him on her own, but maybe letting him walk away was the best option, even if it broke her heart.

CHAPTER 20
THEA

"Miss Thea! Cover your eyes!" Abby shouted.

Always shouting. The little girl didn't have an inside voice, though, and the constant excitement kept everyone on their toes. Apparently, Abby had the run of the house on Tuesday nights at Stella and Vera's. This was Thea's first attendance, and Abby was the perfect hostess.

Thea did as she was told. "Okay, okay. They're covered."

The pitter-patter of skipping feet on her right side had Thea's lips stretching into the first real smile in days.

"Open them," Abby said.

Thea removed her hands and gasped at the small crochet piece Abby held. "What's that?"

"I did it! Miss Stella taught me."

Thea took the square and laid it over her hand. It

barely hung over the sides, but it was an accomplishment. Especially since Thea's attempt earlier had looked oddly like a blue rat's nest.

"I'm so impressed." It wasn't perfect, but it was incredibly neat to have been made by a four-year-old.

"I tried real hard and listened real good," Abby said. "Do you want some more tea, Miss Thea?"

Picking up the plastic teacup on the end table beside her, she peered at the drop of juice in the bottom. "Yes, I would love that."

Abby took the teacup and skipped to the kitchen. Thea brushed her thumbs over the pink square in her hands. At least she wasn't bringing Abby down with her foul mood.

"Have you talked to him?" Hadley asked.

Thane stood from where he'd been lounging at her feet and rested his head on Thea's knees. She set Abby's masterpiece on the armrest and gave the perceptive dog her attention.

"Not much. What he's said to me has been cordial, but he still doesn't want to talk. I tried to talk to him last night, but I barely got through the introductory 'I'm sorry' before he cut me off. Then I left him a note this morning, asking if we could talk, but he didn't give me an answer."

"Brett won't brood for long. He'll get over it," Remi said. She was halfway into a gray-and-green baby blanket and didn't look up from her work.

"I don't want him to get over it. I want to apologize," Thea said.

"Did you mean what you said?" Hadley asked.

"Some of it. But not in the way he took it. I'm so grateful for everything he's done for me. And all of you too. I just hate tangling people up in this mess. He's been living here for five years without a problem. I show up and suddenly he's in the line of fire again."

"He said he doesn't mind it," Hadley said. "I'm sure he'd do anything for you."

"I know. That's what I'm afraid of. He *would* do anything, even at great cost to himself."

"Gotta let him make that decision on his own, babe. Been there, done that, got the ring to prove it," Remi said.

Thea studied the yarn in her hands. Remi learned her lesson and got a husband and kids to show for it. It was different for Thea. There was a war going on–a civil war. Her heart was torn between love and duty.

A sharp pain pricked her heart. Love. She loved Brett, and it wasn't a quiet love. It was a fierce, loud love that beat against the walls of her chest, begging to be set free.

Thane whined and scooted his nose a little more into her lap. "I'm okay, buddy," she whispered.

Vera let the quilt square she was working on fall into her lap and rubbed a hand over Thea's back. "I know expressing how you feel can be hard sometimes. Give him time, and maybe he'll calm down enough to talk."

Thea kept her head down and nodded.

As much as she'd dreaded the Tuesday night ladies gathering, she needed friends beside her. The women of the ranch had welcomed her with open arms, and they hadn't judged her and looked down their noses when she'd told them about the talk with Brett that had gotten her the silent treatment. Instead, they'd been encouraging and kind.

Thea had friends back in Alabama but not so many as this. The world needed more women like this who were dedicated to building each other up instead of tearing them down.

If the thought of leaving these friends made her want to dig her heels into this dirt and fight to keep it, how much stronger would Brett's loyalty be? Claiming her love for him would rip this place and these people away from them.

They would have to lose everything to have each other. Was it a price she was willing to pay?

"Brett is too good to me. I don't deserve his kindness," Thea said lowly.

"That's a load of bull hockey," Stella said. "We all deserve love, honey. Especially you."

"I want that. I do."

"You already have it," Vera said. Her response was temperate compared to her friend's outburst.

"I'm not just talking about Brett. The Lord loves you too. No matter what. And if you lean on Him and trust Him, He'll lead you where you're supposed to be."

"Okay! Here's your tea, Miss Thea," Abby said as she slowly walked into the room. She carried a teacup full of juice out in front of her with both hands.

"Thank you, sweetheart." Thea took the cup and sipped it, giving Abby a delighted expression. "It's delicious."

Abby bowed. "Anyone else want tea?"

"I think we need to wrap things up," Remi said.

"Already?" Abby whined.

"It's almost bedtime."

"Can't I stay with Miss Stella and Miss Vera again?"

Remi started tidying up her materials. "Maybe some other time."

Hadley stood and stretched her arms over her head and yawned. "It's my bedtime too."

Thea handed Abby's crochet work back to her. "Thank you for showing me what you made."

"You can keep it. I'll make another one now that I know how."

"Thank you." Thea held the gift close to her heart.

After everyone said their good-byes and made it out to the porch, Paul pulled up in his old truck.

Thane rubbed against Thea's legs and wound his way next to a few others before jumping into the passenger seat of his owner's truck.

Thea slid into Hadley's car and sighed.

"Don't stress about it," Hadley said.

Brett would be at the cabin when they arrived. There was a good chance he'd already be asleep or at least pretending to be. He'd done a good job of being unavailable whenever she was around.

"I'm trying not to." Recalling Hadley's whispers when she arrived late to Stella and Vera's house, she gasped. "Oh! Tell me how it went today."

Hadley's smile widened as she backed the car up. "It went great. I told Gage what you wanted him to know, and no one suspected a thing."

Thea relaxed. "Did he have any news about Mom?"

"He said her oncologist told her there is a clinic that specializes in her type of cancer, but any treatment they might be able to provide would be experimental."

She'd been trying to prepare herself for the possibility of good news and bad, but this was a mix of the two. Should she be thrilled or disappointed? "Can she get in to see them?"

"It's a long shot, but they're trying."

"Did Gage ask about me?"

"He did. I told him your ankle was healed and that the doctor seemed pleased with your lung recovery. I told him you flew back to Alabama yesterday."

They had all agreed that letting Gage believe she was out of Blackwater was the best option, but doubts kept tapping on her shoulder. Would he be a help to her and Brett if he knew she was still here? Or would it be all too easy for the information to find its way into the wrong hands? "Thanks for that."

Hadley wiggled a little in her seat as she drove. "You didn't tell me your brother was so...sweet."

Thank goodness the darkness hid the surprise on her face. "He is?"

"Yeah. I brought him lunch, just like you said, and he seemed super appreciative." Hadley paused and looked over at Thea, even though the darkness left them blind. "He said he would let me know about any updates with your mom, and he asked me to give him an update on you every once in a while. It was sweet. He cares about you, but he can't show it around your family. They would push him out of the inner circle, and he wouldn't know if they're planning to do something to you. He just wants to protect you."

"I hope you're right." If Gage truly cared about her, then she wasn't as alone as she thought. "Thanks for doing that."

"It was no problem. I'm glad you got an update on your mom."

Brett's truck was parked at the cabin when they arrived. Thea's hope swung back and forth like a pendulum. Did she hope he was awake so they could have a chance to talk, or did she hope he was asleep so she wouldn't have to see the disappointment in his eyes?

"Don't stress. Just be cool," Hadley said.

"I have no idea how to be cool. I'm a nervous wreck." Thea shook out her sweaty hands and rubbed them on her jeans.

"You got this," Hadley said as she hopped out of the car.

Inside, Thea scanned the cabin for Brett. She took her shoes and coat off before wandering into the living room. He lay sprawled on the couch on his stomach, with one hand under a pillow and the other hanging off the side.

She took the opportunity to study him. His dark hair was messy and thicker than it had been when they were younger. The blanket was pulled up over half of his back, but his bare shoulders were wider than the couch.

Thea knelt beside him. His face was so peaceful in sleep. She could almost remember the light-hearted, funny boy he'd once been. Any frown he'd worn lately had been her fault. Brett was inherently kind. His heart had been pure back then, and he'd grown sweeter with age.

No matter what length of time had passed, he

was still the same man with so much to prove. He was determined to be different from the rest of them, and he'd convinced her wholeheartedly.

Her fingers itched to brush through his hair, to touch him, to tell him how much she cared, to assure him that she knew his heart. "I'm sorry," she whispered.

She bit her lips and looked up at Hadley, who had paused with her hand on the bedroom door-knob. Hadley gave a small wave and mouthed, "Good night," before quietly excusing herself.

Thea turned back to Brett. How long would she keep hurting him? She wanted everything he wanted, and there was so much at stake. He'd forgiven her before, but would he forgive her this time?

She stood and tiptoed to her bedroom and closed the door behind her. Sinking onto the bed and stretching out on her stomach, she let the warm comforter cradle her. With her face against the pillow, she let the silent tears fall as she prayed.

"Please let him forgive me, Lord. I can't believe I hurt him again." She brushed her face against the fabric, drying her tears. "And I love these people. I wish I could stay," she whispered into the empty room.

CHAPTER 21
BRETT

Coffee. Where was the coffee?

Brett blinked through the heaviness in his eyelids. The sun hadn't even decided to peek through the windows yet.

But there was coffee. Somewhere.

He pulled his phone from underneath his pillow and checked the time. Two more minutes, and his alarm would have done the job for him.

Stretching out the aches in his elbows, he sniffed again.

Right. Coffee.

He stumbled to the bathroom and locked himself inside. He splashed a handful of water on his face, dried off, and brushed his teeth. He'd promised not to move his stuff in, but needing his toothbrush before and after sleep required one necessity.

Placing his blue toothbrush beside Thea's green one and Hadley's purple one, he ran a hand through his messy hair and went in search of the morning brew.

When he opened the bathroom door, Thea stood just outside holding a steaming cup. Her hair hung loose over her shoulders, and her eyes were tired.

How did she look so gut-wrenchingly beautiful this early in the morning?

She held the cup out to him, and he took it.

"A peace offering."

What did either of them know about peace? They'd been fighting for it for so long that it seemed like an impossible feat.

Brett accepted the coffee, and Thea kept her head down. It killed him to see her upset.

But nothing he could do would make her happy. He'd tried and failed.

"I was hoping we could talk. Please?" she asked.

He'd found excuses to avoid her let-me-down-slowly speech, but it seemed he couldn't run away from this one.

He nodded toward the living room and followed her. She took the couch, and he chose the recliner. He didn't want to be sitting close to her when she stuck a fork in his pride.

He sipped the coffee while she squirmed. Whatever she had planned for him was bound to hurt.

"I want to start at the beginning, but first, I need to tell you how sorry I am."

Great. The it's-not-you-it's-me talk.

Thea picked at her fingers in her lap. "I'm so sorry for making you feel like I didn't want everything you've given me here. I wanted all of this and more." She scoffed. "I've been pretty selfish."

Brett took another sip of coffee. Hopefully, it would cool down soon so he could chug it. He needed something stronger for this conversation.

"The beginning. After my dad died, I told my mom and Gage about us. You and me." She pushed a hand through her hair. "They weren't happy, to say the least."

"I never expected their blessing," Brett said, flat and numb like his heart.

"I told Gage you didn't do it, and we had to help you. He freaked out. He wanted me away from all this, and I get it. Two murders in as many weeks meant no one was safe."

"I agree with him on the one part. You needed to be away from here."

Thea sighed. "I agreed to go, but he said if you were innocent like you claimed to be, then he'd let me know when it was safe to come back. Actually, I wanted him to give you the option–run away with me or try for a life in Blackwater, together."

So, she'd actually considered coming back? She'd held onto their plans to run away together? She might have thought it was a stupid idea, but he'd latched onto the plan like a lifeline back then.

"Then, after the trial, Gage told me what he'd heard. I wouldn't believe him. I don't think I ever did. But he was so sure he'd heard you admit to killing our dad." She brushed a hand over her mouth. "I'm sorry."

Her voice cracked on the last word. Sorry was the word of the year. They'd both made a lot of mistakes.

So why was he holding hers over her head? He didn't want to. Forgiving her was his natural inclination, and he couldn't sit here like he didn't care while she was in tears.

"He sent me money. Gage. At least I assumed it was Gage. I tried to contact him once, and he told me not to call again. My younger brother, Max, had overheard our conversation the night I'd told Gage and Mom about our relationship. Max had told my uncles, and Gage said they considered me disowned. Gage asked me not to come back, reminded me that there wasn't anything here for me except a murderer who claimed to love me, and blocked my number."

Brett hung his head and took a few deep breaths.

"He said I knew too much. All the illegal things they did every day and got away with. I knew it all. I was a traitor. I had sided with you, and for all they knew, I would tell the Pattons all their secrets. If I ever came back, they wouldn't risk letting me tell it all."

Brett's head shot up. "Then why did you come back? Good grief, Thea, they were waiting for this chance."

"Because I–"

"Had to see your mom. I know." He put the coffee down and stood. Pacing around the room, he tried to hold onto the anger. Anger at her for leaving, for coming back and getting herself into this mess, for rejecting him again.

But the anger didn't hold. As much as he wanted to be mad at her, he couldn't. Not when he understood what she'd gone through and lost. Not when he knew his part in all of it. The secrecy, the leaving, Gage's reaction when he'd shown up at his door demanding to know where Thea had gone.

It all made sense. Even her rejection now was rational. She didn't love him the way he loved her, and she never would.

He had to pick himself up and go on. Without her.

Even the thought made him want to fall into bed and give up. What was he even doing if that light at the end of the tunnel didn't exist?

"Brett."

Her soft voice stilled what was left of his rage, and he turned to her.

She slowly walked toward him and picked up his

hand in hers. The softness of her skin on his made him want to hang on as if he needed the full eight seconds to even get a score.

"Brett, I don't want to push you away, and I'm sorry if that was what you thought. I want you. More than you'll ever know."

He looked up at her then, and the truth was written in her eyes. He'd been too stubborn to see it before.

"Please give me another chance," she begged. A single tear slid down her cheek as her chin quivered. "I love you."

Brett froze. What did she say?

"I love you, and I've always loved you. I want a life with you, no matter what that means."

Brett stared at her, unable to process what he'd just heard.

"Brett?" Her eyes squinted as if waiting for a harsh blow. "Please say something."

Words wouldn't be enough. He took a step forward, wrapped an arm around her waist, and pulled her in. Sliding a hand up her neck and into her hair, he took his time, savoring the memory of what she'd said.

"You love me?" he asked.

She looked up at him and nodded. "Yeah."

He dipped his head until his lips were an inch from hers. "Say it again."

"I love you."

That was all he needed. He pressed his lips to hers and gripped her waist, pulling her closer until she wrapped her arms around him.

He'd waited years, dreaming of this–Thea back in his arms–and it was all worth the wait.

Thea was worth the wait.

CHAPTER 22
THEA

Thea gripped the back of Brett's shirt, hanging on for dear life. Any moment, the short, shallow breaths would make her lose her mind completely.

Her lips danced with his, moving effortlessly in a fury of desire.

This was where she was meant to be. Brett was her home, and she'd gladly fight beside him against whatever battle came to their door.

Brett slowed the kiss, but she pushed back. It couldn't end yet. They were just getting started.

He pulled back just enough to smile against her lips. "I loved you first."

She laughed. Actually laughed through the tears that hadn't yet dried on her face.

Then he kissed her again.

Injured lung, don't fail me now!

He took his time, and she savored every second of his kiss. It was slow and adoring, torturous and assuring.

It was everything she'd ever wanted and more.

Finally, Brett pulled back, smiling like a kid who'd just snuck a cookie from the cookie jar. "I'm calling in sick today."

Thea rested her forehead against his chest and laughed. "Easy, cowboy. We have all the time in the world starting right after your shift ends today."

He looked into her eyes, and his smile eased the slightest bit. "Are you sure?" he asked.

"I've never been more sure of anything in my life."

He pressed his lips together, trying to hold back his grin. "I hit your brother."

Thea rolled her eyes. "I'm sure he deserved a pat on the jaw for something." She brushed a hand over Brett's jaw, getting used to the stubble that hadn't been there the last time they'd kissed. "I'm sorry I left you."

He wrapped her in a hug, and she rested her head on his chest. "I know all of that was hard for you. I hate that it happened."

"I didn't want to go," she whispered.

"If I had been a more selfless man, I would have asked you to go, at least until things died down here."

"Gage said if you were any kind of man at all you would have told me to go."

"Well, he was right. Now I feel bad for hitting him." He rubbed a hand over her back. "I'm sorry you had to go through all of that."

"Me? You were the one facing a murder charge."

"But I would have been happy knowing you were safe."

"I'm sorry I couldn't give you the life you deserved. The longer I stayed away, the harder it was to keep going without you."

She lifted her head and looked up at him with dry eyes now. "I was deep in depression when the ladies at Misty's church found out about me. They helped me through it. That's how I found the Lord. He sent me the sweetest, most selfless people when I needed to know about Him."

Tugging on his shirt, she smiled. "Then, when I ended up back here, and I needed to be reminded who I was and what I should have been fighting for, He sent me you."

Brett cupped her face in his hands. "Cupcake, I won't ever let you go again."

The smile nearly split her face. "I like it when you call me Cupcake."

"Seriously, watching you eat a strawberry cupcake with hearts in your eyes is the highlight of my life."

She leaned her head back and brushed her hands through her hair. Brett watched her with a look that held nothing short of desire.

He held her chin and tilted her head up to face him. “You’re so special. They never saw it–the light you bring. Every time you walk into a room, my world lights up.”

She pressed her lips together. Thinking about how little her family cared for her was always a sore spot, but it paled in the wake of Brett’s love.

“They don’t know you like I do,” he whispered, still brushing his thumb over her chin. “It’s selfish of me, but I hope they never see the parts of you I fall more in love with every day.”

Thea lifted onto her toes to press a soft kiss to his lips. “Where do we go from here?”

“Alabama. The east coast. Mexico. I don’t really care, as long as we’re together.”

“That’s not what I meant. I mean, what do we do next? You can’t leave Wolf Creek.”

Brett shook his head. “It’s just a place. It’s just a job. It’s just a small town like any small town.”

Thea opened her mouth to protest, but Brett stopped her with a finger on her lips.

“It’s not my home. You are my home, and I’ll follow you anywhere.”

When his finger slid from her lips, she took a second before speaking. “No. I don’t want to lose this either. I love it here. I want you, and I want this place. I want our friends. I want it all."

She stepped back and stood her ground, finally sure of what she wanted. "I'm not leaving, and neither are you. They've taken too much from us. I won't let them take anything else."

Brett grinned at her and nodded once. "Then we'll stay."

Thea's bravado deflated. "How though?"

Brett's comforting arms were around her again. "I know how."

"What? You do? Care to let me in on the secret?"

"We have to mend fences. Mr. Chambers told me what I needed to do a long time ago, and I've been resisting."

His gaze swept over her face, taking in every inch as he mapped out their plan for the future. "But now, I have to. If you want a life here. If you want a home where you feel safe. If you want a future here, with me, then I have to do it. If we don't, no one else will."

"What do we do?" she asked, unsure if she wanted to know the answer.

He gave her a playful grin. "You think Ava could spare you for the day?"

"Why?" She was bursting to know what he had in mind.

"First." He whispered in her ear until her heart beat wildly against the walls of her chest.

She looked up at him and gasped. “You’re crazy.”

“You’re not the first to tell me that,” he said.

Thea wrapped her arms around him and kissed him hard. “Let’s do it.”

CHAPTER 23
THEA

Thea finished the last of her lunch with a contented sigh. “This is amazing.”

Everly sat across from Thea at one of the long tables in the dining hall. “Her chicken and rice is the perfect comfort food. I added it to the offerings menu for weddings this year, and three couples have already requested it for their receptions.”

“I don’t blame them, but now I need a nap,” Thea said.

“You need a ride home?” Everly asked.

The wedding planner at the ranch had become another fast friend to Thea, even though her workload was massive due to the upcoming wedding season.

“That’s sweet of you, but I actually have a doctor’s appointment soon.” Thea looked at her watch. "Hadley is taking me. She's supposed to meet me here."

Everly locked the tablet she'd been tapping on all through lunch and stored it in her bag. "Don't forget about tonight."

Thea smiled. "How could I forget?"

After hearing about the church service Brett had put together at the ranch on Sunday, Everly had arranged for the adult Wednesday night class to meet at her house so Thea could attend.

It would be her first trip off the ranch that wasn't a quick follow-up doctor visit, and she was more than ready to hang out with her old friends and meet a few new ones. Everly had been sure to tell everyone to be secretive about Thea's whereabouts.

"Thanks for having lunch with me too," Thea said as she stood with her empty plate.

"Don't mention it. I had a blast. Hopefully, we'll be seeing more of each other." Everly winked and lifted the strap of her bag onto her shoulder.

With Brett and Thea's decision to stay at the ranch out in the open, everyone had been quick to include her. She'd called her boss in Alabama, and the three-hour phone call was emotionally draining, but Misty had been so understanding.

And supportive. Misty knew a lot about Thea's past, and her old boss was happy to know Thea was making a new life in Wyoming.

Hopefully, this visit with the doctor would end with permission to fly, and she and Brett could take a quick trip to Alabama to gather the rest of her stuff. She didn't have much worth worrying over, but she wanted to say a proper good-bye to her friends and the horses.

She'd also come clean to Gage through Hadley and let him in on everything she was planning with Brett. Her brother hadn't exactly been thrilled, but he promised to help with anything they needed.

Thea followed Everly to the trash bin, and they tossed their plates in just as Vera stepped out of the kitchen.

"That chicken and rice was amazing. Can you teach me how to make it?" Thea asked.

Vera grinned and wiped her hands on her apron. "Of course. I'll put it on the menu for the week after next, and you can help me prep it."

Thea rounded the trash bin to wrap her arms around the sweet woman. Vera's heart was as pure as fresh snow, and she'd turned into a quiet shoulder to cry on when Thea missed her mother.

Vera might not have had any children of her own, but she had a nurturing heart, and Thea gladly let herself be pulled under the older woman's wing.

Everly waved as she left. "See you later. Five-thirty, Thea."

"Wouldn't miss it," Thea said as she checked her

watch again. “Speaking of missing something, where is Hadley? We need to get on the road.”

Rhythmic, thundering booms came from outside, making both Thea and Vera turn.

The dining hall door flew open, and Abby ran in, followed quickly by Hadley.

Vera rested a hand on her chest. “Good grief, I thought there was a herd of buffalo outside.”

Hadley doubled over, resting her hands on her knees. “This isn’t over,” she panted.

“Yes, it is. I win,” Abby said. “Winner, winner, chicken dinner,” she sang.

Hadley raised her head, revealing a red face. “If anyone is making a chicken dinner, it’s that angel right there.” She pointed to Vera.

Thea clapped her hands together. “Speaking of chicken dinner, Vera is going to show me how to make chicken and rice sometime soon. Would you like to join?”

Abby raised her hand high. “Yes, yes.”

Thea winked at Abby. “I’ll call you when it’s time.”

“You’ll have to call my momma. I don’t have my own phone yet.”

“Okay, I’ll do that.”

Hadley propped her hands on her hips as she approached. “You be good for Miss Vera. I’ll be back soon.”

Abby gave a quick acknowledgment as she darted off.

Vera flashed one of her sweet grins and turned toward the kitchen. "She's always good when she helps me."

"Tell her my threat still stands," Hadley said with an authoritative finger in the air. "I will hang her up by her toes if she gets outta line."

Vera disappeared into the kitchen shaking her head and chuckling with Abby close behind.

Thea tried to hide her own smile. "You know Vera wouldn't say one word about it if Abby was bad."

Hadley turned her attention back to Thea and rolled her eyes. "She has been in rare form today. Bossy Pants is pushing the limits. Trust me, Vera will have something to say if she keeps it up."

"Are you sure you're okay to drive me today? I'm sure I could ask Stella for a ride."

Hadley waved a hand in the air as she started toward the door. "No way. Vera likes hanging out with the kids as much as I do."

Letting the matter slide, Thea followed Hadley outside. "I forgot about how long winter lasts here."

Hadley bounced with each step she took down the porch steps. "I'm still getting used to the weather here. I feel like I've been praying for spring for months now."

"Hold your horses!"

Thea turned at the shout. Brett was running toward them from the stables.

"What is he doing here?" Thea asked. "He said he had a meeting with Mr. Chambers."

Brett had been the one to take her to all of her follow-up appointments so far, but after taking the day off yesterday, he had a lot to catch up on. Plus, he'd set up a very important meeting with his boss.

Thea had attended her own meeting with Jameson and Ava earlier. So far, things were falling into place, and there was a spark of hope that making a life here with Brett was actually within reach.

He met Thea at the front of the car and pressed a quick kiss to her forehead. "Just wanted to tell you I love you."

"You ran all the way from the stables to tell me that? I have a phone, you know." Thea wrapped her arms around his waist and savored the feel of having Brett in her arms.

Clouds of his warm breath swirled between them as he dipped to rest his forehead against hers. "I'd run a hundred miles for a kiss from you," he whispered.

"Aww, that's precious," Hadley crooned from the other side of the car.

"Any news?" Thea had resisted the urge to call and ask him, but she had to know.

"No news is good news, right?"

She prayed that was the case. "Did he seem like he was mad?"

One of the many steps in their plan to settle in Blackwater for good included an attempt to mend fences. Brett had visited her uncle Bruce's diesel repair shop this morning with a white flag of peace.

"Not really, but I have no idea how to read the guy. He looked like he wanted to rip my head off, but he also didn't try to whop me over the head with a wrench."

"You're right. That sounds like progress." Anything that didn't involve bloodshed was a good sign, but they had a long row to hoe if there was any chance of patching things up between their families.

Brett looked over his shoulder toward the main house. "I have to go. Mr. Chambers is probably waiting on me. But I saw Everly on her way out just now. She was headed to Sticky Sweets for a cake tasting or something, and she said she'd bring you back a cupcake."

Thea melted into a warm puddle of happiness. "Are you serious? She didn't even mention it at lunch. I would give my left pinky toe for a cupcake."

Brett pulled her close to his chest and made a show of petting her head. "Shh. Don't be selling off body parts. I promised to give you all the cupcakes you wanted, didn't I?"

She looked up at him as moisture clouded her

vision. What did she ever do to deserve him? "You did."

He sealed his lips to hers, and she drew in a long inhale, breathing in the happiness she still couldn't believe existed. Each brush of his mouth against hers was a promise, and she met his sincerity match for match.

She reluctantly pulled away and sighed. "I have to go."

"I know." The pad of his thumb brushed against her cold cheek. "Be careful."

"I will." The only time she'd left the ranch since the attack was to visit the doctor in Cody, and he'd gone with her every time. If his chat with Bruce worked, maybe she'd be able to go into town without looking over her shoulder.

His hand slid down her neck, over her shoulder, and all the way to her hand. He lifted it to his lips and kissed it. "Let me know what the doctor says."

"Hopefully, I'll get the go-ahead to fly."

After spending the early morning on the phone with Misty, her old job was wrapped up. Thea had signed the last of the paperwork to accept her new position at Wolf Creek. She'd continue to help Ava in the office until the doctor released her for physical work, then she would move to a full-time position at the barn with Brett and Jess.

Brett took a few steps backward, letting Thea's hand fall slowly from his. "I've never been to

Alabama. Maybe you can show me around your old town."

Pell City, Alabama was slightly bigger than Blackwater, and it had a completely different vibe. First off, the draw was the lake, bringing in bass fishermen and families who spent weekends goofing off in pontoon boats and kayaks.

Brett would love it.

She waved as he slowly backed toward the main house. "Sounds like a plan."

The plans they'd put into motion yesterday and today gave her at least a semblance of control over the mess in their lives. At least they weren't sitting around waiting for trouble to knock on their door.

Once she was in the car, Hadley didn't waste a second before jumping in.

"How did it go?"

Thea shrugged. "He said he thought it went well. Everyone walked away unscathed."

She hadn't hid her concern when Brett said he wanted to visit Bruce. Talking it out wasn't something the Howard and Pattons had ever subscribed to.

"Gage wasn't a fan of the idea," Thea added.

Hadley pulled out of the ranch and turned toward Cody. "He said Bruce has been strangely quiet today."

Thea propped her elbow on the passenger door and studied Hadley. "So, what else did Gage say?"

"That he hopes your plan works. He's really missed you."

"What about you?" Thea asked.

"What about me?"

"Does he miss you too?"

She'd done enough talking about the family feud over the past few weeks to last a lifetime. Whatever fragile relationship was forming between Hadley and Gage was a welcome subject change.

"No. Why?"

"Just wondering. When was the last time you saw him?"

Hadley tilted her head and squinted one eye. "This morning."

Thea sat up straighter and gaped.

A blush bloomed on Hadley's cheeks. "Stop it. It's nothing."

"Doesn't sound like nothing. Are things getting serious?"

Hadley scoffed. "It's been like a week. I'm not riding off into the sunset with him just yet."

"I don't know much about him anymore, but he wasn't like the rest of them when we were growing up."

"I believe that. He really cares about you. And your mom. He's doing everything he can to make sure you're safe, especially since you've decided to stay."

"I can't thank you enough for doing this. I know

it's dangerous getting mixed up with this, and I hope you know I appreciate everything you're doing."

Hadley reached over and patted Thea's arm. "I'd do anything for you. You and Brett deserve this happiness. We'll make sure it all gets sorted out."

Hadley stared out the windshield, but her grip on Thea's arm tightened.

Thea looked up just in time to see the pickup truck drifting into their lane. With ditches on both sides of the road, there was only one option if they wanted to avoid a head-on collision.

Hadley gripped the wheel with both hands and slammed on the brakes. "Hang on."

Thea held onto the door and placed her other hand on the dash, bracing for impact.

The boom of the crash was loud, and the car jerked. Thea pressed her eyes closed as her shoulders hit hard surfaces on both sides. She pinged from one side to the other until there was no way to tell which way was up.

They finally came to a stop, rocking Thea's whole body forward, then back against the seat. Smoke filled the car, and she gasped for air. The pain in her chest was sharp, stealing her breath.

"Thea. Thea. Are you okay?" Hadley's voice was low as if it pained her to speak.

"Yeah. You?"

"My arm," Hadley said, gripping her left arm close to the shoulder.

Thea scanned the mess in the car. "Where's my phone?"

A trickle of something hot slid down the side of her face. Blood.

"Mine is in the console." Hadley lazily pointed to the closed compartment between them.

The screech of metal beside Thea jerked her attention to the passenger door. The dented door rocked back and forth twice before it was pulled open.

Icy fear raced down her spine at the familiar face. "No. No!"

"Thea!"

Hadley's hoarse shout had Thea reaching for her friend. She grabbed onto Hadley's uninjured arm as Cain wrapped his arms around her middle and pulled her from the wrecked car as if she weighed no more than a bag of groceries.

Her slipping hold on Hadley was useless as Cain dragged her out. She landed one solid kick to his leg before he righted her enough to slap the back of his hand across her face.

Hadley screamed from the car, but the shouts sounded farther away through the ringing in Thea's ears.

When her vision cleared, she saw who else was waiting for her.

Bruce.

All of the air left her lungs as she registered her uncle's pleased grin.

Brett's plan hadn't worked. It had backfired in the worst way possible, and the sinking in her stomach assured her that her family wouldn't have mercy on her this time.

CHAPTER 24
BRETT

Brett stood from the rocking chair on Mr. Chambers's back porch and extended a hand to the older man. "Thanks for everything."

Mr. Chambers stood with his mug and shook Brett's hand. "Always a pleasure doing business with you."

Mr. Chambers winked, and the wrinkles around his eyes deepened.

This was anything but business, but if he was lucky, he'd be doing "business" with Mr. Chambers for many years to come.

"I need to get back to the stables. The vet will be here shortly to check on Thunder."

"Go on. I'll be here if you need me."

Mr. Chambers settled back into his rocking chair, and Brett jumped the porch stairs, heading for the barn in an easy jog.

Thea wouldn't be back for hours, and he wasn't sure he could wait that long to tell her. Though, it would make for an awesome surprise. And seeing her face when she heard the news would be worth the wait.

He jogged into the stables and almost smacked right into his sister. Jess jerked back and raised her fist for a punch before she registered who he was.

"For heaven's sake, Brett."

"Sorry." The good news almost popped right out of his mouth. As much as he wanted to shout it to the world, he wanted Thea to be the first to hear it.

Brett propped his hands on his hips and took deep breaths to slow his heart rate. "Is the vet here yet?"

Jess pointed toward a stall. "Linc is with him."

"Any news?" he asked as they both headed for Thunder's stall.

"Not that I've heard," Jess said.

In the stall, Linc stood with his arms crossed over his chest, listening intently to the vet. Brett and Jess stopped right outside.

"I'll drop in tomorrow morning for another check," the vet said on his way out.

Linc shook the vet's hand. "Thanks for comin'."

Brett and Jess said their farewells and waited for Linc's explanation.

"No tendons or ligaments are severed. It's

shallow enough that it should heal on its own, but we have to keep an eye on it."

"That's good news," Brett said.

Thunder was more trouble than he was worth half the time, but Linc had developed some kind of unspoken understanding with the beast.

Brett's phone rang, and he pulled it out of his back pocket. "Sorry, it's Hadley," he said as he answered it.

"Hey. Everything–"

"They took Thea!" Hadley said.

The blood in Brett's veins went cold. "What? Who?"

Hadley was crying and gasping for air. "We wrecked. A truck ran us off the road. We're in a ditch on Pickens Road, and someone just pulled her out of the car and..."

Hadley's sobs took over.

"And what?" Brett shouted as his hand balled into a fist.

Linc and Jess stared at him, but he could barely make out their faces. His vision was blurry on the edges.

Not Thea.

"Someone pulled her out of the car."

"Who was it?"

He didn't need to hear her say the name. He knew. At least, he knew the last name.

"She said Cain. Brett, I'm trapped in the car. I don't know where he took her."

Brett's feet were moving, gaining speed with each step. "Just one guy?"

"She said Bruce too, but I didn't see anyone else."

"Where are you on Pickens? Are you hurt? Is she hurt? Did you call the police?"

Hadley cried harder. "Just past Kennedy Road. I don't think I'm hurt, but I'm stuck. The door won't open. I... I..."

Brett had made his way across the barn. The door was only a few feet away. "Breathe, Hadley."

"I don't know if she was hurt. I called you first."

"Sit tight. I'll send help. You call the police, and I'll call Asa. Maybe he can get a head start."

"Okay," Hadley said. Her voice shook too much on that one word.

"Which way did they go when they took her?"

Hadley gasped for a few breaths. "He came from behind the car, and I didn't see them drive by, so, um, maybe toward town? I don't know."

"Just sit tight. Help is on the way."

Hadley was still new in town, but that was enough information to let him know where they were taking her.

"I'm sorry," she said with a sniff.

It wasn't Hadley's fault they'd wrecked or that Thea had been taken.

If anyone was to blame, it was Brett. He'd confronted Bruce thinking it was the right thing to do. He'd sent Thea off the ranch without him. He didn't protect her the way he'd promised.

"It's not your fault. Make the call, okay?"

He ended the call as he stepped out of the barn.

"Brett!" Jess shouted close behind him.

"Hadley and Thea were in a wreck. Someone took Thea. Hadley is calling 911, and I'm letting Asa know what's going on."

Jess darted up beside him as he reached the truck. "Where are you going?"

"To find Thea. Call Jameson and tell him to go help Hadley."

Brett turned to Linc. "I need you with me."

Without hesitation, Linc started around the truck.

Jess grabbed for Linc's arm, but he slid away from her.

"Wait. Stop. You can't go. It's a trap," she said quickly as she reached for Brett.

He pulled back. Jess had every reason to worry, but this wasn't the time to hesitate. Thea needed him. "Well, they're gonna get me, but I'll make sure they regret it."

"Brett, don't do this," Jess said. There were real tears in her eyes–something he'd never seen before. "How many bullets are you going to take for her?"

He reached for the door and opened it. "Every last one."

"Even the ones coming from her smoking gun?" she asked, high-pitched and strained.

He slid into the truck and gave his sister one last chance. "Get beside me, or get behind me, sis."

Her attention darted to Linc in the passenger seat, as reality set in.

"Call Jameson," Brett said as he closed the door and started the truck.

"Where are we going?" Linc asked, steady and controlled like Walker, Texas Ranger just before landing a roundhouse kick.

"Bruce's garage." Brett slammed the side of his fist on the steering wheel. "I shouldn't have trusted him."

"I'll take care of him. You get her outta there."

Brett pulled his phone from his pocket and tried to control the panic rising in his gut. "Thanks for coming."

"No problem." Linc looked in the back seat. "You have something for me?"

Brett found Asa's contact and made the call. "Pistol, shotgun, or switchblade. Take your pick."

Asa answered on the second ring. "Hey."

"Hadley and Thea were in a wreck on Pickens Road just past Kennedy Road. Hadley is probably injured, but someone took Thea. Hadley is reporting the accident now, but I'm hoping you can get some backup sent to Bruce Howard's garage."

"You know it was Bruce who took her?" Asa asked.

"Bruce and Cain."

"What were they driving? I'll put out a bolo."

"No idea. Hadley said a truck ran them off the road. I'm assuming that was them, but she didn't say what it looked like."

"Hold on."

Brett could hear the call for dispatch in the background, but it took everything in his power to listen.

"They said it was an old red Chevy. I'll get some roadblocks set up. We'll find her."

"She's at Bruce's garage. I know it," Brett said.

"How do you know?"

"I went there this morning. I was trying to mend fences, but I guess this is his way of shoving it back in my face."

"That's not enough to go on," Asa said.

"Listen, Thea and I have been preparing for them to try something. I know about all the places they could take her, but my first guess is the garage."

They wouldn't take Thea to Tommy's place, not with her mom living there. Sharon would try to put a stop to what they were doing if she knew about it.

Bruce and Cain. Of all the Howards Brett didn't want anywhere near Thea, they were at the top of the list. They were two sides of the same coin, and they only had eyes for blood and revenge.

"I'll send officers that way. Don't engage until we arrive. Do you hear me?"

"I hear you, but I also politely disregard that order."

"Brett, I'm serious–"

He disconnected the call before hearing more of Asa's warnings.

Linc rummaged in the center console and pulled out a knife. He pressed the button on the side, and the five-inch blade shot out. "I'll take this one."

"Listen, the Howards are dangerous and don't give a rip about hurting or killing someone, but I do, so–"

"Don't drop a bunch of bodies. Got it," Linc said. He kept looking in the console until he pulled out another knife. "Oh, look. There's one for you too."

Brett took a deep breath. "We're here to save Thea. Do whatever you have to do if push comes to shove."

"Are you telling me to use force or not?" Linc asked.

"I'm telling you to use judgment!" Brett said.

Linc looked around. "What's judgment?"

Brett let out a short laugh. "I knew you were funny."

"Don't get used to it."

Brett picked up his phone and made another

call. Calling Gage was a risk, but if he was really on Brett and Thea's side, he could be the difference between life and death.

"What?" Gage answered.

"Where is she?" Brett asked.

There was silence on the other end of the call.

"Gage?"

A few more seconds of silence, and Gage whispered, "They're bringing her to the garage. It's on Finley Road."

"I know where it is," Brett said.

Gage hadn't been there earlier when Brett had stopped by to have the big chat with Bruce. Did Gage even know about it?

"They'll be here any minute. Tommy is here with me. Bruce and Cain are with her. They'll probably post Tommy outside when they get here."

"Anyone else we need to know about?" Brett asked.

"Not yet. I'll try my best to keep you posted, but they'll know what's up if I'm on my phone."

"The police are on their way too."

"Wait, weren't you with her?" Gage asked.

"How long have you known about this plan?"

"Five minutes. Answer the question."

Great. Brett might not have friendly feelings for Gage, but he didn't want to be the one to pass along the news. "Hadley was with her."

"Is she okay?" Gage didn't even try to hide the panic in his voice.

That was genuine concern. No doubt about it. If Gage could care about a woman he'd known for a week, how much more did he care about his sister?

"Yes, she seemed okay when I talked to her."

"Are you sure?"

"Yes, I'm sure. She was upset about the wreck and Thea, but she said she was okay."

Gage was silent for a moment.

"Buddy, they took Thea. Remember what they did to her? I promise Hadley has help on the way, but Thea is much worse off right now. Focus."

"I'll take care of Thea, but if you're headed this way, you better have a lot of backup."

Brett glanced at Linc. "I have one guy, but I'm pretty sure he counts as three."

Gage sighed. "Is that all? I thought you said you had friends."

"The police are on the way too. Just tell me how to get in."

CHAPTER 25
THEA

Thea focused on keeping her breaths even as the zip ties bit into the thin skin of her wrists. Each inhale ended in a sharp pain in her side.

What if she'd reinjured her lung? The possibility of medical care was slim, and Cain and Bruce didn't seem to care if she was injured. They'd done this to her.

The strap of fabric stretched across her mouth and tied behind her head was a minor discomfort compared to the stabbing in her side.

Focus. Paying attention was the only thing she could do, and whatever chance she had of getting out of this might depend on spotting a small life saver.

It hadn't taken long to figure out where they were going. Bruce's garage had been a pile of junk when she was younger, but she hadn't seen the place in years. Still, she knew these roads and trees like the back of her hand.

With her eyes open, she prayed–begged for help.

Lord, help me. I don't know what kind of help I need, but please help.

And Hadley. Please let her be okay.

Cain had dragged Thea out of the car before she'd had a chance to find out if her friend was injured. Now, the uncertainty was enough to break her. Was she well enough to call for help? What if she was pinned in and couldn't reach her phone?

Once again, Thea found herself without that lifeline. It had been in the car, but that was no help to her now.

The truck slowed and turned into the parking lot of Howard Small Diesel Engine Repair. Somehow, the place looked fifty years older instead of five. The dark metal of the building stood out like night against the bright light of day. The two bay doors were open, and one man was bent over, looking under the hood of a truck.

Thea pulled against the restraints on her hands, but she was only successful in forcing the plastic deeper into her wrists. When they let her out, maybe she could make enough noise to attract attention.

Bruce parked the truck behind the building, and both men got out. Cain opened the back door and grabbed her arm. He pulled, sending her falling onto her side across the seat.

"Get up." His sneer burned with impatience.

Without waiting for her to right herself, he grabbed her by both arms and pulled her out of the truck. Her feet hit the gravel so hard, a jolt of pain shot up her legs.

Cain didn't give her a chance to get on her feet before he dragged her toward the door. She worked to get her footing, but the pulling in her side prevented even a half breath.

They brought her through a back door and down a short hallway to what she knew was the waiting room. She'd never seen anyone use it when she was younger, and it had mostly been a storage room.

A row of three metal chairs were bolted to the floor in front of a TV mounted on the wall. Parts, tires, and boxes filled the corners of the room.

Cain flopped her around like she was a ragdoll until she was haphazardly seated in the middle chair. With her hands behind her, she couldn't readjust to sit up straight.

He grabbed one of her legs before she could pull away from him and tied it to the chair leg. She knew what was coming next and kicked her other leg. She aimed for his face, but he caught her ankle and jerked it down. Once he had a grip on her, there was no fighting free.

With her ankles tied to the chair, half of the fire inside her died. She kept pulling against the straps on her hands, but she was doing more harm than good.

The pain in her chest was worse, and each breath was labored. She'd just started to feel like herself again in more ways than one. Her body had been healing, and her heart was on the mend too. She'd started to believe she and Brett could make things work here.

All that healing was erased now.

She tried to swallow around the cloth in her mouth, but it was useless.

The door opened, and Gage stepped into view.

Cain stood in front of her with his arms crossed over his chest and nodded.

Gage didn't look happy to see her.

Dread filled her like lead. She'd wanted to believe he cared about her, but the hate in his eyes made her question everything she thought she knew.

No, she had to hope he was just playing along. Everything in the last few weeks, as well as the last five years, told her he cared.

But would he help her now? How far would his loyalty go?

"Police were dispatched to the wreck," Gage said. "They should be out of the way for now."

Cain checked his phone. "Where is Tommy?"

Gage positioned himself right in front of Thea.

She looked up at him, and twin tears raced down her cheeks.

Cain was on the phone, but Gage had his full attention on her. With his arms crossed over his broad chest and the dark look in his eyes, anyone would cower before him.

He was bigger than the man who had haunted her dreams. Thea had spent so many nights pushing back nightmares where her brother had chosen the rest of the family over her. Those were the worst–the ones where she was completely alone.

The scowl stayed firmly in place as he mouthed, "Brett is coming."

A rush of air half-filled her injured lungs.

Brett was coming, and that was both good and bad.

Thea shook her head. The movement was small enough not to attract Cain's attention.

He reached behind her head and tugged the cloth loose. She let the soaked rag fall from her mouth and tried to swallow. Everything hurt.

When she looked up at him, she whispered, "They'll kill you."

Gage's mask fell slightly, exposing the man she knew. "I'd rather die than do this to you. Hang in there, and trust us."

Us. Who was she supposed to trust? Gage and Brett?

The door opened again, and Gage's attention

jerked up. Emerson took one step into the room and stopped. Thea locked eyes with Emerson.

"Help! Get–"

"Get out!" Cain shouted above Thea's plea, pointing toward the door behind Emerson. "Forget what you saw, and don't come back."

Emerson's wide-eyed fear sparked hope in Thea. Would her cousin help, or would she save her own skin?

Then, pity replaced the fear, and Thea knew the answer. Emerson had her loyalties, and she would protect herself first and foremost.

As Emerson stepped backward toward the door, Thea couldn't find it in her heart to blame her. How could she ask anyone to risk their life against the Howards for her sake?

Emerson closed the door, locking out all hope of Thea's cries for help being heard by anyone.

Cain cursed and pointed toward the door. "Go shut her up."

Gage gave Thea one last sinister look, and she hoped it was all for show.

"Don't hurt her. Please," she begged as Gage headed for the door.

Left alone with Cain, panic kindled in her chest again. His malicious grin told her he would enjoy every second of her pain.

He'd taken one step toward her when the door opened again.

Bruce Howard hadn't changed much since she last saw him. He was a contrast to Tommy in many ways. Where Tommy was tall and round in the middle, Bruce was shorter and stocky all over. His skin was tan, despite the past winter months. His sandy-blond hair was cut close and blended with his skin over his face and head.

Bruce stopped in front of her and smiled, genuinely pleased to see her.

He pushed his shoulders back with pride. "We've been lookin' for you."

"Why?" Her word was sure, despite the shake in her arms and legs.

"It's one thing to get away with murder. It's another to walk back into my territory after killing my brother."

"Brett didn't kill my dad," Thea said, though the words were hot in her throat.

Bruce leaned down, resting his hands on the chair on both sides of her, and she pressed her back against the hard metal.

"He's a Patton," Bruce said calmly, keeping his brown eyes on her. "Did you ever think about that when you took his side? Did you care that he killed your dad?"

"He didn't–"

"My brother!" Bruce shouted.

Thea jerked and stilled. Her entire body shook, despite her attempts to calm her fears.

"He's a Patton," Bruce said again, lower and more measured.

"And I was a Howard," Thea said. Heat pressed up her chest and closed around her throat. "I can stand on the line and see both sides just fine. But you? You're too stuck in your hate."

The back of Bruce's hand hit the side of her face with a quick sting, knocking the rest of the air from her lungs. Flashes danced on the floor at the edges of her vision.

"This is war, sweetheart."

Hot anger allowed her to lift her head to face Bruce, and a freeing laugh danced in the back of her throat. "Nothing is fair in love and war. Isn't that ironic? You had a family, but you failed all of them. One by one, you lost them. There are only a few of you left!"

Bruce stared back at her, forgoing any attempt to hide his rage.

Thea huffed. "You've sacrificed them for this vendetta–your misplaced revenge. When will it end?"

"You better watch your mouth, little girl," Bruce seethed.

"There isn't an end. It consumes you."

Bruce grabbed her chin, and a traitorous gasp escaped.

"You're going to get me what I want," he said low.

"I never did anything to you. Neither did Brett."

"Anyone who would take up with a Patton is no friend of mine, sweetheart."

A loud bang at the door lifted Bruce's attention, and Thea let out a scream. She turned, but a second bang had her lifting her shoulder to protect what she could of her face as the door flew open, half-hanging on the hinges.

Bruce's rough grip on her chin fell away, and she looked up.

Brett stood in the doorway, staring at Bruce Howard with fire in his eyes.

Oh, no. If Brett had campaigned for peace before, that ship had sailed.

Brett set his sights on Thea's uncle and crossed the room in a few quick steps. The shock must have been hanging on because Bruce didn't protect himself as Brett's fist made contact with his face, landing the older man on his back.

Cain charged at Brett, but he'd been expecting that attack. Brett's elbow made quick contact with Cain's nose, sending his head jerking back.

With Cain cradling his cracked face and Bruce groaning on the ground, Brett pulled out his knife and cut Thea's ankles free.

"Brett, are you okay?"

"I was gonna ask you the same thing."

Bruce pushed up onto his hands, and Brett used

his boot to shove the man's shoulder, landing him back on the floor.

Brett braced himself and leaned over Thea's uncle.

"Touch my wife again, and you'll need a new hand."

CHAPTER 26
BRETT

Seeing Thea tied to a chair was both worse and better than the scenes Brett's imagination had been conjuring. He hadn't known what to expect, but the fact that his wife had been at Bruce's mercy was unacceptable.

His wife.

His *wife*.

She'd sworn it before the judge and Everly as a witness less than twenty-four hours ago, and they had big plans to share the news with everyone at a party the coming weekend.

There was no way on earth Bruce Howard was ruining that party. Brett had waited too long for this moment, and he intended to love Thea for many years to come.

One glance at Thea told him she was alive, and that was a balm to his burning soul.

Bruce, however, had a death wish.

The guy was humming with rage. The hatred in Bruce's eyes was palpable, but it didn't touch Brett's resolve.

"Cain!" Bruce barked.

Cain was shaking off the stars in his eyes as dark blood ran over his mouth, streaking down his gray thermal shirt. After a few blinks, Cain reached for the waistband of his pants.

So, it was going to go down like this. Any hope Brett had of walking out of here without bloodshed was already out the window. Still, he'd hoped to keep the body count to zero.

And Brett was certain he and Thea weren't going to be the ones meeting the coroner tonight.

This was the moment Brett prayed he'd put his trust in the right people.

He reached for his own weapon just as the familiar click of a pistol hammer pierced the room.

But it wasn't Cain's.

Cain's attention jerked toward the door, and Brett glanced that way, prepared to divide his attention between two threats if necessary.

Gage stood in the broken doorway, his gun pointed at Cain. "Drop it."

Cain cursed and raised his gun.

Gage shot first, and the impact jerked Cain's shoulder, twisting him around on his way to the floor.

Thea screamed as the shot echoed in the small room, but her scream was too low and strained. She'd still been healing from the last time they hurt her. What damage had they done now?

He had to hope the police would bring medics with them. Thea needed to be checked out as soon as they got out of this mess.

Brett reached for her, keeping an eye on Bruce who stared back at him, waiting for a chance to strike.

"Thea, tell me you're okay?"

"I'm okay."

He reached behind her for her bound hands and cut them free. Crouching in front of her, he rested his hands on both sides of her face, searching for any sign of injury. "Are you sure you're okay?"

Brett had a second to glance at Bruce, who was making his way to his feet. Cain screamed and writhed on the floor, holding his bleeding shoulder.

Once Thea was free, he positioned himself in front of her while she stood and shook out her hands. He spoke low over his shoulder, all while keeping an eye on Bruce. "Stay behind me. Linc is holding Tommy outside, and the police are on their way."

"Let them come!" Spit flew from Bruce's mouth as he sneered. "You're trespassing."

The sinister smile on Bruce's face should have brought on some fear, but Brett would never regret coming for Thea. Bringing her here had been a trap, but he'd walk through a field of landmines if necessary.

Nothing would keep him from saving Thea. Nothing.

"I gave you a chance," Brett said, hoping to keep more weapons from coming out long enough for the police to arrive. "I offered you a ceasefire. You were stupid not to take it."

Bruce shook his head and opened his mouth to plead his case for hate.

"If you think we win by killing each other, you're wrong."

Bruce pointed at Gage. "I knew you were a traitor."

There was a scrape of metal, and Linc stepped over the broken door with his pistol pointed at Bruce.

Emerson Howard was behind him, glancing between Linc and her dad. The tension in her shoulders said she'd made a decision and still wasn't sure it was the right one.

Bruce's jaw moved back and forth like he was chewing something sour, and the crease between his brows grew deeper as he pointed at Linc and Emerson. "And you, too. You were a Patton from the start."

Linc faltered for a second, clearly confused.

"What?" Emerson asked with narrowed eyes.

"You," Bruce said, jabbing his finger clearly at her. "Your stupid mom couldn't stay away from the Pattons. You're just as much a Patton as he is."

Bruce's finger swung to Brett.

Oh, no. No, no, no.

Brett pressed back against Thea, trying his best to hide her from Bruce, but she wasn't the only one in danger. Emerson had switched sides, and she had a new, shiny target on her back.

"That's not true!" Emerson shouted.

"She couldn't stay away from Oscar! You were a Patton from the start."

Brett fumbled through his memories, trying to disprove the claim, but it wouldn't have been a surprise if his dad had run around on his mom. The guy didn't have two morals to rub together. There had also been rumors of cheating spouses, but he hadn't considered his dad.

But Brett needed more than a few seconds to reconcile a secret sister, especially when it was Emerson Howard.

Thea's grip on Brett's shoulder tightened. "Linc–"

It was a small cry for help. Not for herself, but for Emerson.

Linc had already moved in front of Emerson, protecting her from Bruce's wrath.

And Bruce was getting ready to strike. His shoulders were tense, and his whole face was blood-red.

Emerson pushed around Linc, who stuck out his arm, trying to keep her behind him. "What are you talking about? I'm your daughter. I'm a Howard."

Bruce laughed. "Not enough of one."

"Let Thea and Emerson go," Brett said. "They didn't do any of this."

Instead of responding to Brett, Bruce let out a high-pitched whistle before turning to Gage with a grin.

"I have backup, and you're out of time."

Gage kept his gun pointed at Bruce, but his face paled.

A man Brett didn't recognize appeared in the doorway wielding a shotgun.

A shotgun? Really? This guy could take out any one of them with one pinch of his finger.

Then the man smiled, and the piece clicked into place. Brett hadn't laid eyes on Max Howard since he was a kid, but he'd remember that evil look anywhere.

How had Thea and Max come from the same blood?

Apparently, the same way Brett and Emerson had.

Another sister. Jess was going to flip when she found out.

Thea gripped his shoulder harder, clearly not happy to see Max any more than the rest of them.

Max swung the shotgun like it was a toy, aiming at Gage. "Hey, bro."

Gage stood impossibly still as he held his younger brother's stare. "What are you doing here?"

"Good behavior," Max said, showing all of his drug-eaten teeth.

Brett took a steady step back, pushing Thea away from her unhinged brother's weapon.

It didn't matter much because Max had his sights set on Gage, who held his pistol steady–aimed at Max.

"You'd kill your own brother?" Max asked with a pout. His tone dripped with fake sadness.

"No," Gage said, "I'm not like you."

"Where is Tommy?" Bruce asked.

Linc piped up, "He's outside. He'll need a Band-aid when you get a chance."

Max turned to Linc as if he'd just noticed him. He slowly swung the barrel of the shotgun toward Linc, looking all too eager to test out the short range on the buckshot.

Brett couldn't stand by while Linc got blown to smithereens. He dove for Max's back, latching an arm around his neck and using the other to pin his arms down.

Bruce dove right after Brett, more than ready to get his hands in the fight.

There was a fury of fists and elbows as Brett hung onto Max–who seemed to be the biggest threat. Bruce threw his weight around, while Max fought back like a cornered animal.

A powerful blow hit the side of Brett's face, bringing on a quick darkness, but he held tight to Max, hoping Gage had been able to get his hands on the shotgun.

Seconds later, the bulk of the weight was pulled off Brett as the sirens grew louder in the distance.

Finally! The police had certainly taken the scenic route. They could have been dead five times over by now.

Linc wrapped his arms around Bruce's stout body and lifted him just enough to body slam the older man onto his side.

Bruce groaned as he hit the ground, but Linc kept a tight grip on Bruce's arms as he twisted them behind him.

Brett adjusted his arms around Max, holding him down as best he could. The guy was completely frantic, and Brett wrestled him to the ground, pinning him with his weight.

The pounding in Brett's head throbbed harder as the sirens grew louder.

"Gage, put the gun down before the police get in here," Brett said.

Gage sighed and laid the gun in the corner as the police identified themselves somewhere outside.

With Bruce and Max restrained and Cain

groaning on the floor, Brett jerked his head up to check on Thea.

She was huddled into a corner, wrapped up with Emerson. Thea pressed her hand over her mouth and kept her gaze locked with his.

He'd get her out of this if it was the last thing he did in his life. He just had to hang onto Max for a little longer.

There was a loud bang from somewhere out in the garage.

Could they move a little faster? The garage might be doing business as usual, but Brett couldn't keep crazy Max held down forever.

A herd of SWAT officers dressed in black appeared in the broken doorway with guns raised.

Great. He was going to have to let go of Max.

"Drop your weapons and put your hands in the air!"

Brett didn't exactly have a weapon in his hands, but a pistol was on his belt. He couldn't just lift his hands to get to it. His arms were tangled with Max's.

"Now!"

Brett pulled back, resting onto his knees, and Max immediately lunged for one of the SWAT officers with his hands, reaching for the guy's throat.

The officer was quick, and a bullet hit Max before he could get his hands on the officer.

Thea and Emerson let out twin screams behind Brett as Max fell to the ground like a tree.

Seconds later, two other officers had their hands on Max, holding him to the ground and shouting orders.

Another local officer stood over Brett.

"Hands up. Don't move," Dawson ordered.

Brett did as he was ordered and took the opportunity to check on Thea. Two officers stood with her and Emerson. Thea leaned against the wall and held one hand to her chest as an officer radioed for medical assistance.

Asa barged in looking for Brett. "I thought I told you to wait for me."

"You were running late, and I made an executive decision."

"We can't just barge in when there have been reports of gunfire! We had to coordinate the SWAT team and the hostage negotiator."

Brett kept his hands in the air and jerked his head toward Thea. "Can I go to her?"

Asa let his head roll back and sighed. "Fine. Just don't do anything stupid."

Brett was on his feet at Thea's side in seconds. Blood streaked down her face from a gash on her head. "Are you okay?"

"Chest hurts," she said low.

Looking over his shoulder he asked, "Where are the paramedics?"

"On their way," one of the officers responded.

He cradled Thea's face in his hands and pressed his forehead to hers. "Hang in there, baby."

Thea gripped his arm, urging him to open his eyes.

"I love you," she whispered.

His own chest ached, as if his heart could be both broken and full at the same time. He pressed a quick kiss to her lips and whispered back, "I loved you first."

CHAPTER 27
THEA

One of the police officers led Thea from the small room to the small gravel parking lot outside. The officer's quick walk did nothing to calm Thea's fears about the pain in her chest.

Emergency response vehicles were parked everywhere around the building, and police and SWAT personnel moved in and out of the building.

Thea knew the feeling in her chest. Her broken ribs were further damaged, or her lung had been punctured again. Either way, the road ahead promised a bumpy ride.

The bright mid-day sun made the events of the last hour feel like a bad dream. The whole day was surreal. The hope that had filled her to the brim all morning before leaving the ranch was lightyears away now as she tried to calm her breathing.

But Brett was still at her side, holding her shaking hand in his.

He'd come for her. So had her brother and Linc. Even Emerson had come to her aid, despite the danger that waited.

Red and blue lights flashed from all directions outside the old building. They'd called in the whole team. Police stood all around the garage in various uniforms.

Two paramedics in red met her as she followed the officer to the ambulance. They pulled a gurney from the back and directed her to sit on the side.

"What are your injuries?" a man asked as he slipped gloves over his hands.

Thea pressed a hand to her side and tried to inhale.

"She had some broken ribs and a punctured lung from the attack," Brett said.

The male paramedic nodded. "Miss Howard, let me get your vitals, and we'll get on our way to Cody."

"It's Mrs. Patton now," Brett said.

The name tugged Thea's lips into a smile, despite the pain in her chest. The excitement of the quick wedding yesterday hadn't left yet. Now that this was over, they had so much to celebrate.

The man looked up at Brett with a grin. "Congratulations. I'm glad to hear it. I hope this wasn't your wedding present."

"How... How did you know my name?" Thea asked, nearly breathless.

"Unfortunately, I saw you in a similar condition a few weeks ago."

Brett squeezed her hand. "Thea, this is Matt. He took good care of you before. I'm sure he'll do it again."

Matt slipped on his gloves and said over his shoulder, "We need the longboard."

"I was wearing my seatbelt. In the car."

"Tell me about the wreck," Matt said as he gently prodded around the wound on her head.

"A truck drifted into our lane, and Hadley swerved to miss it. We ended up in the ditch."

"So your vehicle was the only one involved?" Matt asked.

"Yes." The more she talked and calmed down, the easier it was to breathe. Hopefully, that was a good sign. Maybe her broken ribs had just been aggravated. At least she could breathe.

Brett stood from where he'd been crouched beside her, and she looked up at him. His attention was drawn to the open bay of the building.

Gage stepped out flanked by two police officers and two SWAT officers. His hands were cuffed together behind his back.

"What's happening? What are they doing?" The panic was back, stronger than ever.

Brett rubbed a hand up and down her arm,

failing to rein in her fear. "I don't know. He shot Cain," Brett whispered.

Everything that had happened today jumbled together in her mind. Gage *had* shot Cain. She hadn't forgotten. The gunfire had drawn a terrified scream from her, and while she'd seen Cain writhing on the floor, she'd been too worried about Brett, Gage, Linc, and Emerson to pay him any more attention.

"Is he—"

"He's alive," Brett said.

Thea reached for Brett's shirt and gripped it hard. Gage had defended her. Cain would have shot first if given the chance. "But what are they doing?"

Gage's chin lifted, and their eyes met. If he was afraid of being escorted out in handcuffs, he didn't show it.

No. He'd protected her. He'd defended himself.

He couldn't take the fall for this. It wasn't his fault. He hadn't intended to hurt anyone.

"Thea!"

She turned at the call. Hadley ran over the gravel lot with Ridge and Cheyenne close behind her. She had a bandage covering the upper part of her left arm.

A police officer stopped Hadley, but she pointed and shouted, "That's my friend!"

The officer lowered his arm, and Hadley darted

past him. Locking eyes with Thea, she dodged a paramedic and kept running.

"Thea! Are you okay?" Dark makeup streaked down her cheeks, and the bandage on the side of her forehead had a small spot where the blood had soaked through.

"I'm okay. Are you okay?" Thea asked as she reached for her friend.

"I'm fine. Just a bump on the head and a scratch on my arm. Where is Gage? Is he okay?"

Hadley looked up then and spotted Gage where the officers led him out. A guttural sound burst from her, and she clamped her hands over her mouth. Running toward him, she dodged everyone in her way.

Gage pulled slightly against the officers who had a hold on his arms, trying to get closer to her. "Hadley."

Thea's heart broke. Would they really take her brother?

Hadley lunged for Gage and wrapped her arms around his neck. "I'm so glad you're okay," Hadley sobbed against him.

"Are you okay? I didn't know what was happening until it was too late, and I didn't know you were in the car."

"I'm fine," Hadley said again. "What are they doing?"

Gage pressed closer to her and rested his cheek

against her hair. "I'm okay. It's fine. They said we have to talk."

Hadley reared back. "This isn't fine!" She grabbed his arms and tried to shake him. "What happened?"

Gage glanced over to Thea. He'd done this for her. He could lose everything.

"He shot Cain, but he was defending himself," Brett said low. "They probably need to question him."

Hadley turned to one side and then the other. "This isn't right. He was only trying to help his sister!"

Thea pressed a hand over her mouth and squeezed her eyes shut. She couldn't watch them take her brother. Not in front of Hadley.

"Please!" Hadley begged.

Gage leaned to the side, trying to catch her attention. "Hadley, it's okay. I'll be fine."

"Ma'am, please step aside," one of the officers said. "We just need to question him right now."

"Okay," Hadley said in a shaky voice as she backed up a step.

Matt pointed to the flat board they placed on the gurney. "Mrs. Patton, do you think you can move to this board?

She rubbed her hands over her cheeks to wipe away the tears, but they kept coming. "Yes, I can do it."

Once she was on the gurney, Brett was beside her, clamping her hand in his. “I’ll be right here. I won’t leave you.”

“Won’t you have to stay?” The police were still getting statements and making reports.

“Asa said he’ll come with us, and I can give a statement when we get there. I already told him most of what happened.”

“What about Linc? Is he okay?”

Brett looked back over his shoulder. “I think so.”

Asa walked up, and Brett pulled him to the side. “Is Linc okay?”

“He’s fine. They’re finishing up his statement, and he’ll be free to go.”

More paramedics and officers poured from the building. Cain was strapped to a gurney and covered in blood.

Thea rested her head back and stared up at the bright sky. “I can’t look.”

“He’ll be fine. I think he lost a lot of blood. Gage hit his shoulder,” Brett said.

“What about Gage? Is he okay?” Thea’s entire body shook now, and she couldn’t release the tension to stop it.

“I’ll keep in contact with him. I’m sure they’ll let him go once they hear what happened,” Brett said.

Asa finished talking to another officer and walked over. “They’ll release him, but they’ll probably want him to come to the department for an interview with the detective. He said he has a lot of information on the Howards he's willing to share."

Thea swallowed hard. Would the things Gage knew be enough to put them all away, or would it just make things worse?

"I heard Cain was arrested a few years ago on multiple charges. I can't believe he's walking the streets now," Brett said.

Asa scoffed. "That one can worm his way out of anything. I'm hoping we can get Gage and Emerson attorneys so they can help us. Tommy is pretty clean on this one, and Cain at least had some involvement with the wreck, but Max and Bruce racked up a list today for sure."

"It's better than nothing," Brett said.

The police officers escorted Gage to a police car, and Hadley cried on her sister's shoulder near the open garage door.

"Is he going to be okay?" Thea asked Asa.

"He'll be fine. I'll keep you updated about him."

Thea jostled on the gurney as they loaded her into the back of the ambulance. Brett and Matt stepped inside, and within minutes, they were on their way to the hospital.

Matt started an IV and kept checking Thea's vitals. Brett had a tight hold on her hand, and she drew strength from him.

"I take it there isn't a truce?" she asked.

Brett looked down at their linked hands. "We'll

get through this. I promise, I'll make sure you're safe."

"But when will it end?"

"It ends with us," Brett promised. "We'll overcome this. Let's wait to see what the charges are going to be."

Thea blinked back tears. "Okay."

He was right. She was worrying before knowing all the details. Maybe Gage and Emerson could come up with enough to lock up the men in her family.

No, they weren't her family anymore.

Brett was her family–the family she'd chosen–along with Hadley, Linc, and every other person who had shown up for her lately.

The ride to the hospital was long and painful, but Brett talked enough to distract her. He took a few phone calls, letting their friends know how things were going.

By the time she'd braved the many tests and was wheeled back into a room, the sun was setting outside the high hospital window.

Brett stood from the chair when the nurse brought her in. "How'd she do?"

"Passed the test," the young nurse said.

"What's the verdict?" Brett asked.

"I don't know. We'll see when the doctor comes by," Thea said.

The nurse locked the bed in place and clicked on

the computer for a few minutes before promising to be back shortly.

Brett was at her side, clasping her hand in his just as she reached for him. "Are you okay?"

"I'm okay. What about you? The side of your face is swelling."

Brett winked. "You should see the other guy."

Thea sucked in a quick breath as the urge to laugh stung in her chest.

Brett squeezed her hand. "I'm sorry. Do you need to rest?"

"I'm too worried to rest. Have you heard from Gage?"

"Asa said they're interviewing him, and he has a long list of things they could add to Bruce, Tommy, and Cain's charges. Knowing the places as well as he does will help too. They're working on warrants to go in and get evidence."

"Really?" Thea laid her head back as relief washed over her. "That's good news."

"There's more," Brett said with a smile.

"What?"

"Gage told them Bruce killed my dad. They weren't able to pin it down to him before, but there isn't a statute of limitations on murder. He could go away for a long time."

Thea's eyes widened, and she was afraid to breathe. "Really?"

"Really, really," Brett repeated.

There was a soft knock on the door, and Thea looked at Brett.

"I'll see who it is," he said as he stood.

He opened the door and paused. There were dozens of people it could be. Was it a friend or an enemy?

Brett looked back at her, and for once, she couldn't read his face. He was smiling, but there was a hint of uncertainty that kept her on edge.

He stepped back and opened the door, allowing Thea's mom to walk in.

CHAPTER 28
BRETT

Brett stepped back, letting Sharon Howard into the hospital room. Holding his breath, he looked at Thea.

Her eyes widened, and she gripped the railing on the bed. “Mom?”

Sharon looked much older than the last time he saw her, and she moved slower. He pushed those details to the side. She was here, and that was a huge win for all of them.

Deep wrinkles gathered near Sharon’s eyes as she smiled at her daughter. “Thea.”

Thea struggled to sit up, and Brett sprang into action. “Wait, let me help you.” He held the button to lift the head of the bed, but Thea was already up and reaching for her mom.

Thea and Sharon hastily wrapped their arms around each other.

"Careful. Thea has some broken ribs," Brett said.

"I don't care," Thea whispered as tears fell over her cheeks onto her mother's shoulder.

Brett moved back, letting Thea and her mom have their long-overdue reunion.

Emerson stepped just inside the door, wrapping her arms around her middle.

He'd almost forgotten about Emerson's problem. Or was it *his* Emerson problem? They had some things to work out together and on their own.

"You brought her here?" Brett asked.

Emerson pulled her shoulders in closer. "Yeah. They arrested Tommy, and one of the police officers said they would be coming back soon with the ATF and a warrant. I went with them to tell Aunt Sharon that her house would basically be a free-for-all in a few hours."

"What does this mean? You think it'll stick?" Brett asked. With Tommy out of the way, could Thea and her mom have a normal relationship?

"I talked to the detective tonight. I told them everything I knew about Tommy, Bruce, and Cain. They said they had plenty to go on, and they didn't think we'd have to worry anymore. Max is stable, but he's being guarded by an officer. He'll go straight to jail when he's released."

Would Thea be upset about her brother? Max had always been a ticking time bomb, and he'd gone completely off the rails tonight.

Brett released a long sigh. "Thanks for doing that. I know it was scary for you, but you did the right thing."

Emerson shrugged and continued watching Thea and Sharon. "I know. Thea didn't deserve what they did to her."

Brett bumped his arm against Emerson's. "You didn't deserve it either."

Emerson looked up at him. "What?"

"You didn't deserve to be abused by Bruce all this time. None of it was your fault."

Emerson's tired expression turned to the floor, and she bit the inside of her cheek for a few seconds. "I didn't know he wasn't my dad."

"I'm sure it never occurred to you. It definitely didn't occur to me," Brett said.

Emerson took a deep breath. "What does this mean?"

"It means we're siblings. Like it or not." He gave her a little smile. "We don't have a dad, and we can't depend on most of our family, but we have each other."

Shaking her head, Emerson kept looking at the floor. "I don't understand any of this. I thought he was my dad."

Brett bumped the toe of his boot against her foot. "Hey."

She looked up, fighting back tears and probably a dozen other emotions.

"It doesn't matter who your parents are. It matters who *you* are."

Emerson shook her head. "I don't know who I am anymore."

"You can start over. Starting today. You can be whoever you want to be, and it doesn't have to have anything to do with your family. You chose to help Thea, and that's a good start in my book."

Emerson brushed the back of her hand over her eyes and lifted her chin to Thea and Sharon. "Those two deserve to be together."

"I couldn't agree more. If Tommy is out of the picture, you think she'll want to stay by herself?"

"Now that she can be with Thea, I can't imagine we'll get those two apart," Emerson said.

Brett smiled. "I think I can make that happen."

He and Thea had talked about moving in together now that they were married, but he hadn't had a chance to tell her the news about their new cabin on the ranch, and the urge to belt it out was almost overwhelming.

"I guess I need to find a new place. My house is in Dad's name. I mean, it's in Bruce's name. He won't be so inclined to let me live there now that I ratted on him."

"You know Thea and I aren't going to leave you homeless. We'll figure something out. But it's probably a good idea to get your things packed up."

Thea and her mom had separated only enough

to talk, and the smiles on their faces were worth every hard moment they'd faced in the last few weeks. Keeping those two women together had moved high up on his priority list.

Sharon turned around and locked eyes with Brett. "I can't thank you enough for saving her."

Brett held up a hand. "No thanks needed. I would do anything for Thea."

Sharon reached out a hand to him. "I'm glad the two of you have worked things out. I knew she loved you back then, and I'm glad you were still here when she needed help."

"I'll always be here," Brett said as he took Sharon's hand.

"And she just told me the two of you got married yesterday."

Brett nodded. "Yes, ma'am."

His own mother had been a complete failure, but now he had a new one–one he hadn't expected. Uniting their families had been a product of their love, and it came with pros and cons. Having Sharon as a mother-in-law was a blessing.

"Good. You two deserve all the happiness in the world. I wish you many good years together." Sharon wiped her cheek with her other hand. "I had no idea any of this was going on. Gage told me Thea left and she was safe, but that was all I'd heard."

"That's what we told Gage at first," Thea said. "We didn't know if we could trust him or not."

“Gage would do anything for you, sweetie,” Sharon said.

“I know that now. Have you heard from him?” Thea asked.

Brett gave Sharon’s hand another squeeze before letting it go to check his phone. “I’ll ask Asa how it’s going with the detective.”

“I had my interview with the detective first, so his started as soon as mine ended. He might still be at the station,” Emerson said.

Brett fired off a quick text and got an answer immediately.

Asa: Almost finished. Is Thea okay?

Brett: She’s good. Thanks for everything.

“He said Gage is almost finished with the detective. I’ll send someone to pick him up.”

Emerson pushed off the wall where she’d been resting. “Someone named Hadley was there when I left. She said she was with Gage.”

“Oh, yeah,” Brett said. “I hope she’s calmed down now that she knows Gage isn’t being arrested.”

“Me too,” Thea said as she released a breath and the tension in her shoulders.

There was a knock on the door, and Jess peeked in. “Hey.”

Brett waved her in. “She’s okay. Come in.”

Jess stepped inside, and Linc followed close behind her.

Brett extended a hand to Linc. "You okay, man?"

"Still standing," Linc said as he shook Brett's hand.

Jess fiddled with her fingers as she stopped right inside the room.

Thea straightened. "Hey."

Jess waved a hand. "Hey. I just wanted to see if you're okay."

"I'm okay." She turned to Sharon and rested a hand on her arm. "This is my mom."

Jess nodded. "It's nice to meet you. I'm Jess, Brett's sister."

"It's nice to meet you too," Sharon said with a genuine smile.

"I just heard these two got married," Jess said, giving Brett a side glance. "Thanks for the invite."

Sharon's smile grew impossibly wide. "I just heard too."

Jess looked at the ground, then back up at Thea. "I'm sorry. I wasn't fair to you. I get that none of it was your fault, but I was scared that Brett would get pulled back into the whole family feud mess, and I took it out on you."

Thea lifted one shoulder. "It's okay. I always understood your concern. I would have felt the same way."

"But probably wouldn't have been as mean about it," Brett added.

Jess jabbed an elbow into Brett's side, but he'd

been expecting it. If Jess could say what was on her mind, he could too.

"I can't believe I had to hear about your wedding from Linc," Jess said.

"We wanted it to be a surprise for everyone," Brett said. "Did he also tell you that we have a sister?"

Jess's and Linc's eyes widened at the same time, and she whirled around. "What? Why didn't you tell me?"

Linc held up his hands in surrender. "It slipped my mind."

"No, he didn't want to hear you yelling about it all the way over here," Brett said.

Jess whipped back around to face him, and her blonde hair fanned out around her. Despite her girly, innocent looks, Jess's eyes held a thunderstorm no one could ignore.

"What are you talking about?"

Brett jerked his thumb at Emerson, who looked ready to blend into the gray walls.

"Her?" Jess said, high and squeaky. "No way."

"Yes, way," Brett said. "Apparently, good ol' dad got around with one of the Howards."

Jess huffed and threw her head back. "While that doesn't seem unlikely, I still can't believe it."

"Trust me, it wasn't the best news for me either," Emerson said, holding her head high.

Jess opened her mouth to say something, but Brett cut in first.

"Emerson helped Linc get in when we needed help, and she just finished an interview with the detective telling him all kinds of things about the Howards that might get them locked up for life. Be careful what you say next, sis."

Jess clamped her mouth shut and huffed out of her dainty nose. "Okay." She held up a finger. "But we'll talk about this later."

"I suspect we won't," Brett said, knowing his sister's inclination to ignore him when she didn't have anything nice to say to him.

"But here's some more good news," Brett said, smiling at his bride. "Mr. Chambers said we could move into one of the new cabins on the ranch." Brett held his hands out and smiled, hoping to lift Thea's spirits again.

Thea sucked in a breath and winced before placing a hand on her chest. "Really?"

"Really, really," Brett confirmed. "Sorry, Linc. This means I'll be leaving you."

Linc stood propped against the wall with his arms crossed over his chest. He rolled his eyes at Brett's announcement. "Whatever will I do on my own?"

"You're gonna miss me, and you know it," Brett said.

Linc scoffed. “If that’s what you need to tell yourself.”

Thea lifted a finger, coaxing Brett to her side. He leaned down so she could whisper in his ear, and he was already smiling as she began the question.

“Of course, your mom can live with us,” he whispered back before pressing a kiss to her temple. He’d been excited about starting a life with his wife on the ranch, but having her mom with them would multiply her happiness. There was no way on earth he could say no.

“Thank you. I love you.” Thea pulled him closer and sealed her lips with his.

And he didn’t want it to end. What was left of their families were getting along, and he had Thea by his side forever.

“I love you too.”

There was a quick knock at the door, and the nurse stepped in.

“Oh, the whole crew decided to show up, huh?”

Thea gave a little chuckle, reaching for her side. “I guess so.”

“I think we’d better go,” Emerson said. “I’ll check on you in the morning. Sharon, you coming?”

“I want to stay,” Sharon said.

Thea rested a hand on her mother’s arm as the nurse checked the blood pressure cuff on her other side. “Mom, you need to get some rest. I’ll be fine here.”

"I know. You've been doing well enough on your own for years, but I still don't want to leave you."

Thea pressed her mother's hand to her cheek. "We'll see each other again. If you call Gage, I bet he'd ask Hadley to let you stay at her place at the ranch tonight."

"That's true," Brett said. "Thea has been staying there, and she's a good friend. I'm sure she'd be happy to have you."

Sharon rubbed her thumb over Thea's hand. "I'll think about it. Thank you." She looked up at Thea. "I'll see you tomorrow."

"And all the other tomorrows too," Thea added.

"Bye. Thank you," Thea said to Emerson as she turned to leave.

"Yeah, thanks for everything today," Brett echoed.

Emerson gave a soft nod before winding her way out of the room with Sharon behind her.

"We're going to head out too," Jess said. "Are you staying tonight?"

"Yeah. I'll call you in the morning and let you know if they're keeping her longer."

The nurse piped up without looking away from the computer. "You'll probably be released in the morning. Your lung isn't punctured again, but the doctor wanted to keep an eye on you at least through the night."

"Just let me know when you need a ride," Jess said.

Brett caught her as she turned to leave and whispered close, "Hey, um, I think Emerson might want to get away from the place she's been living–"

Jess raised a stiff finger between them. "Don't push it."

Brett held up his hands. "Just think about it."

Without another word, Jess turned and walked out. His sister would come around in time. She always did.

"Thanks for all you did today, Linc," Thea said.

Linc nodded once. "You're welcome."

When the room was quiet, the nurse finished logging Thea's information and handed her a small plastic cup with a pill in it. "This is for pain."

"I'll take it," Thea said as she reached for the cup.

The nurse looked at her watch. "Someone should be here soon with dinner. I'll check on you again in a little while. Call if you need me."

"Thank you," Brett and Thea said in unison as the nurse left.

Thea rested her head back, and her eyes drifted closed. "I'm exhausted."

Brett pulled a chair close to the side of her bed and gently brushed a hand over her hair, careful not to touch the bandage on her head. "Rest. I'll be right here."

Her eyes opened, and she gave him a lazy smile. “Thank you.”

Lifting her hand in his, Brett threaded his fingers with hers. “I think all of this might be over now.”

“I can’t believe we’re married,” she whispered.

Brett was having a hard time believing it himself. “I’ve dreamed about this for a long time.”

She shifted from left to right and pressed her eyes closed against the pain. “I hate that this is the way we’re starting our marriage. You’ve been taking care of me for weeks, and now I’m injured again.”

Brett lifted her hand and pressed his lips to the soft skin on the back. “For better or worse. In sickness and in health. I’m here for all of it, Cupcake.”

Thea’s eyes drifted closed, and a small grin spread over her face. “I could eat ten cupcakes right now.”

“I’ll get you a dozen a day when we get home. I’ll take care of you and bring you cupcakes for the rest of our lives.”

EPILOGUE

THEA

Thea tapped her fingertip against the empty punch cup in her hand as Mrs. Scott listed her grandson's advanced testing scores. Apparently, Jacob's academics were worth a lot of recognition, and Betty was more than happy to brag about his achievements.

"And he's just a wonderful, level-headed boy. He couldn't be here today because he's doing a canned food drive with the Science Club."

The wedding reception was beautiful, and considering Everly put it together in four weeks with little help from Thea while she was healing, the whole event had Thea's jaw hanging.

She'd expected a few friends from the ranch, but there were close to a hundred people filling the reception hall right now. Her old boss even flew out from Alabama for the weekend.

Twinkle lights were strung through the rafters, white tablecloths covered the round tables, and cupcakes covered an entire tiered stand near the front of the room. The place was gorgeous.

Having her friends and family all in one place was the best part of the day, but the cupcakes were a close second. She'd already helped herself to two.

"It sounds like he's a great kid," Thea said. Really, she'd met Jacob at the feed and seed once, and he'd been nice enough to carry her bags to the car for her.

"He comes from the best."

"I agree. I don't know where I'd be today without Asa."

The officer had gone above and beyond for her and everyone else at the ranch, and he'd made sure Thea's mom was safe and protected as she packed up her things and moved out of the house she'd shared–or been trapped in–these last few years with Tommy.

It had been a decade since Betty Scott gave Thea her first job, but the woman jumped back into Thea's life as if they'd been right across the street from each other this whole time.

"I'm proud of my boys every day." Betty held up the hand holding a small plastic cup and pointed across the room. "Did you meet my daughter-in-law, Lyric?"

Thea spotted Asa and Lyric and gave a friendly

wave. They were two of the many people in Blackwater who had become fast friends. "I did. She's the sweetest."

"Asa and Jacob are so blessed to have her. I am too. I thank the good Lord for my family every day."

That was something Thea was still getting used to–thanking the Lord for her family. Family used to be a dark spot in her life, but now, she had more than she could have ever dreamed. "As do I."

"You have no idea how good it is to see you two together. You look happy."

Thea caught sight of Brett dancing with Abby. "I am happy."

Happy was an understatement.

Mrs. Scott pulled Thea in for another hug. "It's so good to see you again."

The song came to a close and Brett made his way toward her.

Their wedding reception was a casual party with their friends, but he'd worn his Sunday best. Despite her assurances that he could just wear his usual flannel, jeans, and boots, he'd insisted on wearing a charcoal-gray suit.

And she wanted to eat her words because Brett Patton could have stepped off the cover of a men's fashion magazine today.

"It's great to see you too."

"I'm going to say hello to Stella. I haven't chatted with her in a while."

Thea waved good-bye to her friend as Brett found his way to her side. He slid one arm around her waist, pulling her in to press a soft kiss on her temple.

"Are you having fun, Mrs. Patton?" he whispered.

"I can't believe all of these people are here for us," Thea said.

Brett scanned the room with a smile. "They all love you."

"They love *us*," she corrected. "You've been making friends since you were in diapers. I'm just getting the hang of it."

Brett looked one way, then the other, before whispering close to her ear, "Come with me."

A shudder ran down Thea's back at his warm breath on her ear. She'd follow him anywhere. "Okay."

Brett took her hand and led her through the crowd. It still blew her mind that all of these people were here to congratulate them on their marriage. They'd been officially married for a month, and the newlywed stage wasn't even close to wearing off.

She had a feeling it wouldn't fade much. Brett wasn't ashamed to flaunt her around town, letting everyone know he had the best wife in the state.

It was laughable, but his adoration kept Thea's cheeks pink around the clock.

When they reached the small hallway leading to

the offices, Brett looked over his shoulder before leading her into the alcove.

As soon as they were hidden behind the wall, Brett slid his hand into her hair and pressed his lips to hers.

She immediately melted into his arms. A firm hand pressed the small of her back, pulling her closer.

Her mouth moved against his, and she wrapped her arms around him. Her ribs were healed, but Brett's adoring kisses still left her breathless.

He pressed her back against the wall and his strong hand slid down the side of her neck. She tilted her chin up, and his kisses moved to her jaw, then her neck, leaving a tingling fire in its wake.

"You are so beautiful," he breathed against the sensitive skin of her neck.

He said something else, but she was gone–completely lost in his touch. "What?"

Brett lifted his head and pressed his forehead against hers. "I said I love you."

"I love you too," Thea said quickly. "Have I told you that today? If not, here's your reminder. I love you. I love you. I love you."

It felt good to say exactly what she felt. When her heart was full to bursting, she could turn to the man she loved and let it pour out. Loving Brett was easy and beautiful.

It was also fun when he still asked to carry her everywhere. She'd decided to take him up on those offers. She'd also been saying yes to the cupcakes a lot more lately, and she didn't have an ounce of regret.

Brett pushed a lock of her hair behind her ear and let his warm gaze run over her face. "I loved you first."

"Have you seen Brett and Thea?" Everly asked nearby. Apparently, she hadn't spotted them yet.

Brett pressed a fingertip against Thea's lips, and she stared into his hazel eyes. They were almost all green today. She noticed they were lighter when he was happy and playful.

"She'll find us," Thea whispered, brushing her lips against the rough skin of his finger.

"But I'm not ready to let you go yet," he said, pressing a kiss to the top of her cheek.

"But we have our whole lives together," she said, practically giddy to remind herself of the same thing.

"It's not long enough."

Brett pressed his lips to hers again, and the world caught fire. She was burning, blissful, and more alive than she'd ever been in her life.

"Psst. Dude, Everly is looking for you," Colt said as he peeked his head around the corner.

Brett and Thea laughed together.

"We'll be there soon," Thea said reluctantly.

Colt disappeared, leaving Thea to admire her husband.

Brett rubbed a hand gently over her side. "Are you feeling okay?"

"I'm great. I actually sneezed this morning, and it didn't hurt."

He'd been handling her with kid gloves since she reinjured her ribs, and he'd taken his caretaking very seriously. She'd basically been waited on hand and foot for weeks, and Brett showed no signs of giving up his service.

He pressed another kiss to her forehead. "Good."

Thea took his hand and tilted her head toward the reception hall. "Let's get back out there before Everly sets up a search party."

They found Everly quickly, and she greeted them with a giddy smile. "There you are. It's time for some photos."

Brett squeezed Thea's hand. She wasn't a fan of pictures, and Brett knew it. When she looked up at him, inwardly groaning, he gave her a playful wink. She'd bet money he would goof off in at least a few pictures. That should make things interesting.

Thea smiled until her cheeks were sore as Everly and the photographer positioned them for dozens of photos. Thankfully, the whole ordeal lasted about half an hour.

"Okay, you're free to go," Everly said.

Brett pressed a hand to the small of her back and leaned in close. “Do you want some punch?”

Of course, he was chugging the punch. He’d made a point to ask Everly to have extra. “I’m fine. I’ll have some later.”

“I’m going to get some. I’ll find you in a minute.” He kissed her forehead before heading off across the room.

Thea spotted the table where her mom, Emerson, Gage, Hadley, Ridge, and Cheyenne were sitting and made her way over.

Emerson stayed close to Thea’s mom since they both moved to the ranch. Thea’s mom moved in with them the week Tommy was arrested, and Emerson moved in with Hadley.

Having Emerson here eased Thea’s mind. She’d accepted a full-time position as a horse trainer for the ranch, and Emerson would be working with Vera in the kitchen as soon as the tourist season started, which was soon.

Everything at the ranch would change in the next month, but Thea welcomed the excitement. Tommy, Bruce, Cain, and Max had all been arrested and racked up more charges than Thea could count.

Bruce was to be tried for the murder of Oscar Patton, and even though Brett and Jess didn’t have any good memories of their dad, it was good to have some closure.

Cheyenne waved Thea over to the empty seat

beside her. "I can't believe how beautiful this is. I hope mine is half this nice next week."

Thea laughed. "Yours will be a wedding *and* a reception, and Everly has had months to plan it. I'm sure it'll be even better than this."

"I'm so excited. I'm not sure I could have waited much longer."

Ridge lifted his punch cup. "I'll drink to that."

"I heard you got the go-ahead to ride this week," Hadley said.

"I did! Just in time too. The guests will start arriving before we know it."

Thea was used to working with horses, but she'd never been a part of a ranch where the horses were a big part of the day-to-day activities. She'd trained for shows, but these horses went on multi-day trail rides and were part of the weekly rodeo. It would be a change but a welcome one.

"Can we come watch?" Hadley asked, pointing to Gage, Emerson, Thea's mom, and herself.

"I'd love that!"

Hadley had taken both Emerson and Thea's mom under her wing and included them in anything she could at the ranch.

Emerson still didn't seem to fit in anywhere, but it wasn't because Hadley wasn't trying hard enough. Without her place in the Howard family, Emerson hadn't figured out where she belonged. Hopefully, she'd thrive under Vera's mentorship.

Gage was spending more and more time at the ranch, and Thea wouldn't dare complain. He helped out with her mother, and he stuck to Hadley's side like glue. After growing up under the Howard family thumb and having to watch his back for so many years, he needed a place where he could rest.

Hadley was a great woman to have beside him. If Thea had ever met someone who would lay down her life for her friends, it was Hadley.

Thea studied her mom. They'd found a doctor who recommended chemotherapy and radiation treatment, but it required driving to Cody three to five times a week. Between Brett, Hadley, Emerson, Gage, and Thea, they made sure she got the help she needed to hopefully fight the cancer.

They didn't know whether or not the treatment was working yet, but her mom had been willing to give it a try, despite the harsh side effects.

Now, dark circles shadowed beneath her eyes, and she slumped a little too much in her seat.

Thea stood and looked for Brett. "We'll get started with the toasts so you can get a nap before you come to the barn," she told her mom.

She spotted Brett with Everly and Blake, and she headed toward them.

"Hey, Mom's looking tired. Can we do the toasts so she can get some rest?"

"Sure," Everly said as she directed them toward

the main table. She quieted the room and took a microphone from her coordinating partner, Linda.

"Thank you all for coming to celebrate our friends Brett and Thea. They wanted this to be a special afternoon with their closest family and friends, and you see how that turned out."

Everyone gave a collective light chuckle, but the sound vibrated through the room. How blessed were they to consider a hundred folks their closest family and friends?

"We have some people who want to share a few words about the happy couple. Please welcome Thea's mother, Sharon Howard."

The room applauded as Hadley helped Thea's mom to stand.

"Hello everyone. I know you're all happy to be here, but you can't possibly be as happy as I am."

Thea's mom looked her way, and her smile didn't look tired at all. In fact, it was bright and hopeful.

"Thea has had a heart of gold since she was born. It is a miracle that she has kept that kindness strong through everything she's had to endure."

Her mom lifted her chin higher. "I know so much of that is a credit to this man beside her. When I first heard that Thea had fallen for him, I was scared. The history between our families was dark, and they had a troublesome road ahead of them."

As Thea's mom paused to swallow hard, the mood in the room shifted. Almost as if everyone took a collective moment of silence to mourn the bloodshed that'd stemmed from the long-standing feud.

"But I had no idea how strong they would be together," she went on, and her warm smile banished the temporary bout of solemness. "Brett stood beside my Thea, even when times were tough. Even when it was a danger to his safety. He never left her."

Her mom reached for Brett, and he took the frail hand in his.

"And I love that Brett and Thea have put their faith and trust in the Lord. I've been coming to know Christ myself in the last few weeks, and I can say He gives comfort and strength when all seems lost. There was a hole in my life I didn't know how to fill, and these two have led me to know Jesus, and my heart has never been so happy."

The room erupted into cheers as Thea bit her lips between her teeth. She'd noticed a difference in her mother lately, and it was all because of the Lord. Coming to terms with her diagnosis wasn't as hopeless with God on their side.

Thea's mom lifted her glass. "To Brett and Thea. May you always keep the Lord between you, and may your years together be blessed beyond measure. I love you both."

Everyone stood and cheered as Thea's mom handed the microphone to Mr. Chambers.

The older man had proven himself more than just a boss to Thea. He'd welcomed her into his home and his ranch and treated her like family.

Mr. Chambers studied the mic in his hands, looking at both ends to make sure it was right side up before clearing his throat.

"I don't have much to say about these things. The Lord knows who we'll end up with, and I don't think any of us have much of a say in the matter. But I think these two have fought for each other plenty, and that's a true mark of loyalty."

Mr. Chambers looked down and worked his jaw from side to side. If he kept the mic much longer, Thea was going to ruin her makeup.

"I've seen a lot of love in my day, and these two got it right." He looked at Brett and gave him a stern nod. "I'm proud of you, son."

Thea gripped Brett's arm and held her breath. She would not cry. She would not cry.

But hearing Mr. Chambers claim Brett like he was his own was more than Thea's fragile heart could take.

"And I have a wedding gift for you. Well, Brett already knows about it, but he wanted it to be a surprise for his bride."

Thea jerked her attention to Brett. She hadn't

expected a gift from Mr. Chambers. He'd done so much for them already.

"There's a little spot on the western side of the ranch. It's not far off the road, and it backs up to one of the horse pastures. I figure it'll be a nice place to build a home one day, and I suspect you'll both enjoy watching the horses graze from your back porch."

"What?" Thea breathed. She looked back and forth between Mr. Chambers and Brett.

Then, the tears came. She covered her face and let them fall into her hands. They both loved this place, and now it would be their home forever.

Brett's calming hand rubbed over her back, but she couldn't stay in her seat. Thea stood and wrapped Mr. Chambers in the biggest bear hug.

"Thank you," she whispered.

"It's my pleasure, Thea. Welcome to the family."

She released Mr. Chambers and turned to find Brett waiting for her with a smile brighter than a belt buckle.

"You knew about this."

"I did. Surprise, Cupcake."

Thea wrapped her arms around his neck and looked up into his eyes.

This was who she was meant to be. She'd happily taken Brett's name because he'd broken the curse on their families. "I love you."

"I loved you first."

She kissed him in front of everyone, earning them a round of cheers.

This love was worth waiting for, but they didn't have to wait anymore. She was ready for their love to grow into a family–a new one they'd make on their own.

BONUS EPILOGUE

LINC

Linc stepped into the ranch garage and stretched his neck to one side, then the other. It felt good to be back in jeans after the reception. He was happy for Brett and Thea, but two hours in a suit was his limit.

He fit in at a fancy party about as much as a bucking bronc fit in at a China shop.

Not even a little.

He rolled up his sleeves and grabbed the wrench. He'd change the oil in a few of the ranch vehicles and feel like himself again.

He jacked up the old Ford F-150 and found the oil pan. He laid back on the creeper before sliding under the truck.

He'd barely lifted his wrench when soft footsteps drew his attention to the side.

Unfortunately, he knew those shoes. They were

the ones Jess had worn to the reception, and he'd spent a little too much time looking at her legs.

Why'd she have to look so good in a dress? Better yet, why'd she have to be gorgeous on a good day without even trying.

It was a cruel joke–one he hadn't gotten over.

"Can I help?" Jess asked.

Linc closed his eyes, but it did nothing to block out the image of Jess's red lips forming those words.

Lipstick should be outlawed, especially when it came to Jess. Her blonde hair, red lips, and green dress today had been a lethal combination.

"Probably don't want to mess up that outfit."

Really, he hoped she listened to reason because he wanted to see her in that dress again someday.

She crossed her legs at the ankles. "Can I get a ride home when you get finished?"

"Sure."

"Thanks." She sighed. "I hate standing around. Are you sure I can't do something to help?"

"Let me get this oil draining, and we'll go. In the meantime, you can just stand there and look pretty."

Jess gave a sarcastic laugh. "That's rich."

"Think of it as helping with minimal effort or expense."

"That's the definition of not helping at all," Jess said.

Linc lifted the wrench, unscrewed the oil filter, and positioned the pan to catch the old oil.

Jess cleared her throat. "What do guys like on a date?"

"Wha–" Linc raised his head, banging it on the frame rail.

"You okay under there?" she asked.

Stars sparkled at the edges of his vision. What was he doing here? Why was he under a truck?

Oh, that wasn't the strange part.

Jess asking him for dating advice was.

The only topics that were safe to talk about were horses and the ranch. He avoided everything else like the plague, hoping to spare himself from this conversation specifically.

He might not be boyfriend material, but he didn't want to hear about Jess's dating life.

"Fine." He rubbed the spot on the side of his head and slid out from beneath the truck.

There she was. Jess Patton, looking like the woman of his dreams in a dress that hugged all of her curves.

She reached out a hand, and he took it. He gave one little pull, and she came tumbling down from her pedestal atop the sparkly heeled shoes.

Jess landed on his chest, pushing him back onto the creeper.

She stared down at him, and her hair fell in a wall beside them.

"Oops," she said, shrugging one shoulder.

Linc didn't dare move. Even taking a breath was out of the question.

His arm was wrapped around her waist. How'd that get there?

This was a terrible joke. The last thing he needed was Jess on top of him–fueling the fire of his very unwelcome feelings for her.

Unwelcome.

That's definitely what they were. He didn't want to have it bad for Jess. They worked together every day, and he liked it enough the way it was.

That was the problem. He liked it too much. He liked her straight-forward attitude. He liked her work ethic and her dedication to her job. He liked her honesty.

And it definitely didn't help that she was too beautiful for her own good.

She stood, brushed off her knees, and extended a hand to him again.

Linc chuckled and waved her hand away. "I got it." He got to his feet and twirled the wrench in his hand.

Jess looked him up and down. "Are you okay?"

"You might weigh a hundred pounds. I think I'll live."

Her neck and face were blooming pink. "Sorry."

Jess never blushed, and certainly not around him. He got the impression she had absolutely no romantic interest in him, and that was a good enough reason to stomp out his wayward feelings whenever they chose to rise up.

Which was all the time. He really needed help.

"If you wanted to throw yourself at me, you could have waited about thirty more seconds and I would have caught you."

"For the record, I think you did catch me."

Linc bit his tongue and opted for the safer response. "Happy to do it, ma'am."

Jess rolled her eyes and crossed her arms in front of her chest. "Like I was saying, can you help me? I have a date tomorrow, and I'm lost as a goose."

"Do geese get lost? That seems unlikely."

She slapped his shoulder. "Focus, Linc. I need to know what guys want on a date."

Nope. He did not want to have this conversation. He turned to the toolbox and stored the wrench where he'd gotten it.

"Please? I don't know what I'm doing," Jess said, almost pleading.

How to answer? He knew what he would want on a date with Jess, but he couldn't speak for anyone else. If the guy had his head on straight, he'd see Jess was special and do everything to make her happy.

Then, he'd pray she said yes to a second date.

The thought of Jess giving any guy what he wanted on a date made him want to punch a brick wall.

"I think you should ask someone else," Linc said.

"I can't go to any of the girls here. They'll get all mushy and talk about how it's time to settle down and do the whole ring, babies, and minivan thing."

"What about your brother?"

Jess's shoulders sank. "I don't want anyone to know about it. I'm not even sure I want to date, so I don't want there to be expectations when this falls apart before it even gets started."

Linc rested his foot on the creeper and rubbed a hand over his cheek. How could he be helpful but not too helpful?

"What if he wants to kiss me?"

Linc jerked his attention to Jess, and his foot resting on the creeper went flying. His back hit the dirt so hard his teeth rattled.

"Are you okay?" Jess asked for the second time in as many minutes.

No, he wasn't okay. Jess was going to be the death of him, or at least the cause of internal bleeding.

"Yep." He'd probably dislocated a few ribs, but he'd live.

"Good. If you could compose yourself long enough to stay on your feet, I'll be waiting in the truck."

Linc inhaled as much as his rattled chest would allow and made the mistake of watching Jess leave the garage.

Jess was going on a date, and it wasn't with him.

OTHER BOOKS BY MANDI BLAKE

Unfailing Love Series

Complete Small-Town Romance Series

A Thousand Words

Just as I Am

Never Say Goodbye

Living Hope

Beautiful Storm

All the Stars

What if I Loved You

Blackwater Ranch Series

Complete Contemporary Western Romance Series

Remembering the Cowboy

Charmed by the Cowboy

Mistaking the Cowboy

Protected by the Cowboy

Keeping the Cowboy

Redeeming the Cowboy

Wolf Creek Ranch Series

Contemporary Western Romance Series

Truth is a Whisper

Almost Everything

The Only Exception

Better Together

The Other Side

Forever After All

Heroes of Freedom Ridge Series

Multi-Author Christmas Series

Rescued by the Hero

Guarded by the Hero

Hope for the Hero

Blushing Brides Series

Multi-Author Series

The Billionaire's Destined Bride

About the Author

Mandi Blake was born and raised in Alabama where she lives with her husband and daughter, but her southern heart loves to travel. Reading has been her favorite hobby for as long as she can remember, but writing is her passion. She loves a good happily ever after in her sweet Christian romance books and loves to see her characters' relationships grow closer to God and each other.

ACKNOWLEDGMENTS

I'm incredibly grateful that I get to write the books I love. It's truly a dream job, but I don't do it alone. There are so many people who leave their marks on these books, and I couldn't do it without them.

Some books are a breeze and others are tough. This one took everything out of me and made me want to rip my hair out regularly. It would be so easy to throw up my hands and quit, but I have hope that there's a reason I have to struggle sometimes.

It's the mark of an author to question everything. Every word, every sentence, every paragraph. I could overthink every letter until the story loses its meaning without the sweet ladies who keep me in line every step of the way.

Tanya Smith, Vicci Lucas, Natasha Wall, Laura De La Torre, Demi Abrahamson, Stephanie Taylor, Haley Powell, and Kera Butler are fantastic at guiding the story, and they make every book better. Jenna Eleam and Pam Humphrey are the best beta readers, and they catch things no one else does. I'm so grateful for their advice and encouragement.

I have a huge group of friends who cheer me on. Hannah Jo Abbott and Stephanie Martin are there for me daily, and their prayers are surely felt in every book. Jess Mastorakos, Kendra Haneline, and Elizabeth Maddrey help me navigate the scary world of publishing, and I don't know what I would do without them. If you don't have friends who lift you up, get some. It'll change your life.

Thanks to Amanda Walker for creating such beautiful covers, and to Brandi Aquino for catching all of my errors. These ladies make the inside and outside into a finished book, and they both do things I could never do on my own.

I like to use the phone-a-friend option whenever possible, and Dana Burttram is always kind enough to answer my questions about law enforcement procedure. I also owe a big thanks to Stephanie Taylor for keeping me on the right track when it comes to medical topics.

I'm blessed to have such amazing readers. You have no idea how you change my life just by reading a book. I love writing sweet romances that point toward the Lord, but it's your support and kindness that makes it all possible. I'm so grateful for you, and I love you dearly.

FOREVER AFTER ALL

WOLF CREEK RANCH BOOK 6

He's stranded with his best friend. Is it a chance for love, or will a threat from his past steal their happy ending?

Jess Patton is blunt, but there's one person who never bats an eye when she speaks her mind. When that same man rescues her from a bad blind date, her rapidly beating heart is impossible to ignore. Suddenly, she's second-guessing everything she knows about Lincoln North.

After everything he's seen and done, Linc knows he doesn't deserve a woman like Jess. Not only is she gorgeous, but she doesn't play games, and being around her is as easy as breathing. She's also the only woman who has ever made him wish he were a better man, so watching her try to find love with anyone but him might just be the death of him.

In a twist of fate Linc never saw coming, they wind up stranded together in a mountain cabin. As Jess starts to see Linc in a whole new light, he's tempted to believe he might have a shot at happiness with her.

But Linc's past is as dark as midnight, and it's waiting for him back at the ranch. Linc and Jess have more than a storm standing between them and their happily ever after. Will they weather it together, or will he be forced to push her away to keep her safe?

Made in the USA
Columbia, SC
31 July 2023